"What Happened To Make You So Afraid To Live?"

he asked, linking his arms loosely around her waist.

She gripped his forearms, feeling the muscles underneath the rich material of his jacket. "I've faced more than you'll ever have to, and I've come out a winner."

"It depends on your definition of winning. If cutting yourself off from human response is winning, then I guess you're a success."

"I have a daughter whom I love very much," she protested, renewing her efforts to get away. Still, the same strange magic was working its spell, fanning the embers that smoldered from their last encounter.

"You know what I'm saying." His head descended until his lips were just inches from her face. "What about this?"

TRACY SINCLAIR
has traveled extensively throughout the continental United States as well as Alaska, the Hawaiian Islands and Canada. She currently resides in San Francisco.

Dear Reader:

Romance readers have been enthusiastic about Silhouette Special Editions for years. And that's not by accident: Special Editions were the first of their kind and continue to feature realistic stories with heightened romantic tension.

The longer stories, sophisticated style, greater sensual detail and variety that made Special Editions popular are the same elements that will make you want to read book after book.

We hope that you enjoy this Special Edition today, and will enjoy many more.

The Editors at Silhouette Books

TRACY SINCLAIR
Pride's Folly

Silhouette Special Edition
Published by Silhouette Books New York
America's Publisher of Contemporary Romance

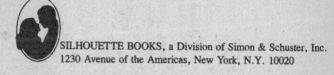
SILHOUETTE BOOKS, a Division of Simon & Schuster, Inc.
1230 Avenue of the Americas, New York, N.Y. 10020

Distributed by Pocket Books

ISBN: 0-671-53708-3

First Silhouette Books printing December, 1984

10 9 8 7 6 5 4 3 2 1

Map by Ray Lundgren

America's Publisher of Contemporary Romance

Printed in the U.S.A.

BC91

● *Greenfield*

LAKE MICHIGAN

N
W————E
S

Wilmette ●
Evanston ●

Des Plaines ●

Oak Park ●

Chicago ●

Cicero ●

CHICAGO AND
VICINITY

Places in <u>italics</u> are fictitious.

Chapter One

"Are we almost there, Mommy?"

Michele Carter's lovely face held compassion as she took her eyes off the road for a moment to glance at her daughter. Even without that telltale treble of anxiety, she would have known that Corey was feeling insecure. After her seventh birthday two months previously, Corey had decided that the term *Mommy* was only for babies. Michele had become Mom, except at times of great stress. This was obviously one of them.

"Just a few more miles." Michele paused imperceptibly before saying, "You're in for a real treat . . . wait till you see the house I rented for us." When no comment was forthcoming, she prodded, "Won't it be wonderful to have a room all to yourself?"

"I didn't mind sharing with you." Corey's mournful, velvety brown eyes surveyed her mother. "Don't you want to be with me anymore?"

"Of course I do, darling!" Michele squeezed the small

hands that were clasped tightly together. "We're still going to be together; your room is right next to mine. The house isn't *that* big." She laughed.

"It won't be the same," Corey maintained stubbornly, her eyes suspiciously moist. "I don't know why we had to come to Greenfield anyway."

Michele sighed. This was the second time in Corey's young life that she had been uprooted, although the move from Los Angeles to Chicago hadn't been nearly this traumatic. Corey was only five at the time, and they had stayed for a month with Fran, Michele's sister. Getting to know her lively young cousins had made the transition practically painless. Corey was delighted to be part of a family since she had never had one. That accounted for much of her reluctance at leaving Chicago—along with her natural trepidation about someplace new and totally un-known.

Michele tried to keep her own reservations out of her voice as she reassured her child. "I know you hate to leave Aunt Fran and Uncle Jerry and the boys, but we're only a couple of hours away. We'll visit each other often. Perhaps Joey and Mike will even spend their vacations here. They'd love having a yard to play in instead of just that dinky little park." When this didn't stop the small mouth from trembling, Michele added casually, "By then maybe we'll have a dog too."

That produced the desired transformation. Corey turned a radiant face to her mother. "Do you really mean it? Can I honestly have a real, live puppy?"

"I don't see why not, as long as you're the one who takes care of it."

"Oh, I will, Mommy, I *promise!* I'll take him for walks

and he can sleep on my bed, and I won't ever, ever forget to feed him.''

As the little girl launched into rhapsodic detail, Michele smiled wryly, wishing her own fears could be as easily diverted. Had she done the right thing in accepting this job? After many sleepless nights, Michele still wasn't sure.

Her reasons were valid enough. For one thing it paid a great deal more. That was important when you were raising a child alone, with no nest egg to fall back on. Michele had awakened in a cold sweat more than once after dreaming that she had lost her job. Although she made a good salary, there never seemed to be anything left over at the end of the month. Prices rose much faster than wages, and there was always an unforeseen expense.

Money wasn't the only factor, however. The increasing danger of city living was something she could no longer allow Corey to be subjected to. Michele's clear gray eyes clouded as she remembered the day the sitter hadn't shown up; nor had she bothered to call. Corey had been perched on the doorstep of the apartment building when Michele got home at six o'clock on a dark, blustery winter evening. Thinking of all the things that could happen to a little girl alone on a city street at night made a shudder ripple through Michele's slender body.

A long strand of pale, silky blond hair momentarily obscured her vision. She brushed it back impatiently, wishing that she could cut her hair short and wear it in the current feathery, feminine style. But research chemists weren't supposed to be trendy, she reminded herself dryly. Especially when they worked in a field men considered to be solely their own.

"Is that Greenfield, Mommy?" Corey interrupted her

somber thoughts, pointing to the small town visible in the distance.

Michele summoned up a cheerful smile. "Yes, isn't it pretty, honey?"

It was really a little jewel of a town, with a church spire instead of a skyscraper dominating the landscape, and mellow brick buildings surrounding a small park. Michele had been entranced with it when she came for her first interview. In a way, it reminded her of the little college town on the outskirts of Los Angeles where she had lived when she was married to Gary.

Her thoughts flew resentfully to the man who had interviewed her at the Blaylock Chemical Company offices. The man she would have to report to. Drake Hollister was enough to make any woman's pulse beat faster; Michele had to admit that. He was over six feet tall, with the broad-shouldered, lean-hipped build of an athlete. Thick, dark hair fell carelessly over a broad forehead, as though he were in the habit of running his long fingers through it. That air of impatience had been echoed by the look in his deep blue eyes as he had surveyed Michele, with none of the appreciation she was used to receiving from men. Instead, his generous mouth had been compressed in a straight line, making his high cheekbones seem more prominent.

Michele had responded to the scarcely veiled antagonism with instant dislike, raising her rounded chin pugnaciously. What right did he have to decide that she couldn't handle the job without even reviewing her qualifications—because that's obviously what he'd done. She'd answered his questions tersely, convinced that the interview was a waste of time.

He had started off with what had always been a stumbling

block in Michele's career. "How old are you, Miss Carter?"

"It's *Mrs*. Carter, and I'm twenty-eight."

His dark eyebrows had risen. "That's rather young."

"For a tortoise perhaps, but a hamster that age would be considered quite remarkable," she'd answered flippantly. What difference did it make since she wasn't going to get the job anyway?

His eyes had turned to blue ice. "I must congratulate you on your knowledge of the animal kingdom. Unfortunately, it isn't germane to the subject."

"I can't alter my age." Nor my sex, she'd added silently. Because he was clearly one of those macho men who didn't want to work with a woman.

He had scowled, glancing down at her résumé on the desk. "Greenfield is a small town, Mrs. Carter. It doesn't have the . . . uh . . . diversions that Chicago has to offer."

It must have *something*, Michele thought sardonically. A man like that didn't stay home nights watching television. She had looked at him squarely. "I'm not looking for a social life, Mr. Hollister. I applied for this position because it sounded interesting—and because I think I'm qualified," she had added pointedly.

It was something he couldn't very well have refuted. Although she had only been in the field four years, Michele was proud of her record. For the first two years she had worked on a grant from the government, the next two in private industry.

"You realize that as supervisor of the new products division, you'll have working under you men who are older and have more experience," he'd stated distastefully.

"It won't be any problem for me," she had assured him, stressing the last pronoun almost imperceptibly. "I assume that your own people aren't ready to step into the job or you wouldn't be looking outside the company."

He had leaned back in his chair, gazing at her through long lashes that were much too luxuriant for a man, yet which in no way detracted from his masculinity. "That's correct," he'd answered almost absently.

His eyes had wandered over her in a silent scrutiny, taking in the delicate bone structure of her lovely oval face, the fine texture of her smooth, flawless skin. Michele's shining blond hair was carefully restrained in a knot at the nape of her slender neck, and her suit was severely tailored. But when his gaze had drifted to her slim figure, she'd felt a rising warmth. It was a wholly male look.

For just an instant she'd wondered what those eyes would look like if they were warm with ardor, what that firm mouth would feel like on her own. Gritting her teeth at her own stupidity, Michele had blotted out the image. Even if she got the job—which she wouldn't—there could never be anything but enmity between herself and Drake Hollister. After being married to one male chauvinist, she certainly didn't want anything to do with another!

"Is there anything else you'd like to know?" she'd asked sharply, slightly unnerved by his close examination.

"Oh yes, Mrs. Carter," he'd answered softly. "There's quite a lot I want to know."

His questions were pointed and comprehensive, revealing his own knowledge of the field. He had been familiar with the government project she had worked on, and also several new research theories that were discussed only by insiders. Michele had been surprised, not expecting an administrator to possess such specialized information.

"Are you a scientist, Mr. Hollister?" she'd faltered.

He had smiled for the first time and the transformation was devastating. Even, white teeth had blazed in his tan face as he'd said, "No, but I make it a point to learn everything about whatever business I'm engaged in at the moment."

Michele had shown her surprise. "You haven't always been in research?"

He had shaken his head. "I'm a troubleshooter. I take basically sound but ailing companies, and put them back on the track."

"Then you won't be here permanently?"

The moment of goodwill had vanished. His face became autocratic once more as he'd said, "That's correct, Mrs. Carter. If you do happen to grace Blaylock with your presence, our association won't be indefinite."

"That sounds like a promise to yourself." Michele's anger had risen along with the feeling that she had taken enough from this man. "Is it something personal about me you don't like, Mr. Hollister—my perfume, my clothes? Or is it *all* women you dislike?"

"What makes you think I dislike women, Mrs. Carter?" he'd drawled, the male look back on his face.

Michele had steeled herself not to react. "Then I have to assume it *is* personal."

He'd made a disgusted sound deep in his throat. "That's the trouble with women—even the so-called scientific ones." Before she could lash out in response he'd gotten to his feet. "Thank you for coming in, Mrs. Carter. You'll be informed when we make our final decision."

Driving back to Chicago, Michele could barely contain her fury. Of all the arrogant, overbearing, patronizing men she had ever run across, Drake Hollister took first prize!

The whole excursion had been a complete waste of time. What aggravated Michele even further was the realization that she had never been in the running for the job. It was obvious that the Hollister man had been pressured into interviewing a woman—not *hiring* one, just talking to her. Today's sensitive political climate demanded that he go through the motions. Never mind that he had wasted her time—after all, what else did women have to do?

After fuming impotently all the way home, Michele had put the whole unpleasant incident out of her mind. It had come as a shock three weeks later when she was informed that she was hired. The disdainful Mr. Hollister wasn't omnipotent after all, Michele had discovered gleefully. He must be answerable to someone higher up, because it was a cinch that Michele wasn't *his* choice.

A buoyant sense of victory had lightened the drudgery of dismantling the apartment and packing up all their worldly goods, but now that she and Corey were actually in Greenfield, Michele began to have second thoughts. She had been hired as Blaylock's token woman. What kind of basis was that for securing a job? And how could she possibly work for Drake Hollister under the circumstances?

"I don't see any houses, Mommy." Corey's anxious voice broke in on Michele's introspection. "You told me we were going to live in a house with a yard."

"This is the downtown section," Michele explained. "The residential area is out a little way."

As they drove through pretty, treelined streets, she marveled at the lack of traffic and the courtesy of the occasional motorists. No taxi drivers blared impatient horns, no one shouted rude remarks. It was certainly different from big-city living. Even the air was different. In Chicago the August heat would have been oppressive; here it was leavened with a breeze redolent of wild flowers and newly cut grass.

"I have to go to the bathroom," Corey suddenly announced.

They were on a stretch of country road without a gas station in sight. Except for an occasional house set well back from the road, the only other sign of habitation was a group of concrete-block-and-glass buildings a short distance ahead.

"We'll be home in just a few minutes," Michele assured her, pressing a slim, sandaled foot down on the accelerator.

"I have to go *now!*"

"Try to wait," Michele begged.

"I can't."

They were approaching the cluster of modern buildings set in parklike grounds. The colorful flower beds and stone benches bordering the walks gave the place the look of a well-kept college campus. Only a discreet brass plaque over the door announced that this was the Blaylock Chemical Company.

"I'll bet they'd let us use their bathroom in there," Corey declared.

"Oh, honey, I really don't think we should."

Michele glanced down in despair at her own bare legs and brief white shorts. To make matters worse, she was wearing a T-shirt bearing the likeness of a big green frog under the legend, "You Have to Kiss a Lot of Frogs Before You Find a Prince." It had been a birthday gift from her adored nephew Mike. To please him, Michele had made a point of wearing it often. It had shrunk from many washings and now hugged her high, firm breasts much too tightly. How could she possibly walk into a place where she was going to work, dressed like this?

"Please, Mommy!" Corey's face wore a faintly desperate look.

With a sigh of resignation, Michele turned into the parking lot at the side of the building. She knew exactly where the ladies' room was, having stopped there to compose herself after the stormy interview with Drake Hollister. With any luck, they could slip in and out without being seen.

The devoutly wished-for good fortune was with them. The receptionist's desk was deserted for the moment and there was no one in the lobby. Michele whisked Corey into the bathroom with a sigh of relief.

After combing her windblown hair and securing it off her face with a circular barrette at the crown of her head, Michele decided to use the facilities too. There was no telling what condition the bathroom would be in at the rented house. Everything would probably have to be scrubbed thoroughly.

By the time she came out, the tiled room was empty. After hurriedly washing her hands, Michele made a dash for the door, but it was too late. Her worst fears were realized as she saw Corey talking to a tall, rangy man—a man Michele almost didn't recognize in this guise.

Drake Hollister was smiling easily, little laughter lines radiating out from his deep blue eyes. "That's quite all right. I hope you'll feel free to use our accommodations whenever you like."

Corey saw her mother. "You didn't have to worry, Mommy. I told the man why we're here and he didn't mind at all. He's nice."

Drake's face wore a look of astonishment as his eyes slid over Michele's slender, curved body and long, tanned legs, retracing the path to the shining mass of curls cascading down to the nape of her neck. Michele knew he was comparing this casual, tousled image to the cool, formal woman he had interviewed. When his eyes returned to her tilted breasts, reading the ridiculous legend, she felt herself flushing a bright, rosy pink.

"It *is* Mrs. Carter, isn't it?" he asked sardonically.

Michele raised her chin in the air, mindful of her grandmother's adage—a lady never apologizes for her attire. "That's correct, Mr. Hollister—as I'm sure you always are."

As soon as the tart words were out she regretted them. What was the point in provoking the man needlessly? But there was some kind of combustible chemistry between them. His assured, arrogant manner aroused all her combative instincts.

"On the contrary." His response to her comment was a mocking smile directed at her chest. "For instance, I never would have guessed your hobby. Does your husband know about your . . . research project?"

"Mommy doesn't have a husband," Corey volunteered, before Michele could answer. "But Aunt Fran is looking for one for her."

"Corey!" Michele gasped.

"Well, it's true. I heard her talking about it lots of times." The little girl felt her word was being challenged. "She said what you needed was a good man."

Drake's eyebrows climbed. "Did you run out of prospects in Chicago?" he asked Michele.

"I gave up the quest long ago," she answered furiously. "My sister is the one who believes there *is* such a thing."

"It sounds as though you don't have a very high opinion of men."

"I hold them in about the same regard as you do women," Michele replied shortly.

Drake chuckled. "You implied that at our first meeting, but I can assure you I'm not a misogynist."

Michele could well believe it. Drake Hollister looked like a man who had thoroughly enjoyed many women. The trouble was that he thought they belonged in only two places—the kitchen and the bedroom. If he had a wife, the poor soul had Michele's sympathy.

"I also like dogs and children," he said, giving Corey a completely natural smile.

"We're going to get a dog," Corey volunteered.

"That's nice. What kind?" Drake asked, as though he were really interested.

Corey looked faintly uncertain. "I don't know. I never had one before. We always lived in apartments except when my daddy was alive, and he was detergent to dogs."

"Allergic," Michele murmured, her lips twitching slightly at Drake's puzzled expression.

He smothered a grin, saying gravely to the little girl, "That's too bad about your father, but I'm sure you'll have a lot of fun playing with your new dog."

Corey's small mouth suddenly drooped. "I don't have anyone else to play with. We don't know anybody here."

Drake's voice was soft with sympathy. "I'm sure you're going to meet a lot of boys and girls in just a very short time."

"Do you have any little girls?" Corey asked hopefully.

He shook his head. "I'm afraid not."

Michele was surprised at the compassion she detected. It gave an unexpected dimension to this man who might be more complex than she had originally assumed.

Just then the elevator doors in back of them whispered open and a man got out. He was in his middle forties, with deep frown lines between his eyebrows, and thin lips that curved down at the corners. His disinterested gaze flicked over Michele and Corey before dismissing them as unimportant.

"I want to go over the results of our latest experiment, Drake, before that dame shows up on Monday," the man said, ignoring Michele.

Drake's face was enigmatic. "I'd like you to meet Mrs. Carter, George, the new head of your department." Turning to Michele, he said, "This is George Browder, one of your two assistants."

Browder looked at Michele, seeing her as though for the first time. He wore an expression of incredulity as he turned to Drake. "You're kidding!"

Michele controlled her rising anger at his insulting tone, extending her hand gracefully. "How very nice to know you, Mr. Browder. I've been looking forward to meeting you."

Actually, Michele *had* been curious about the two men who would be working under her. She had anticipated the meeting with reluctance, however, rather than the pleasure she was indicating. Now it seemed her apprehensions were justified.

George Browder evidently shared Drake's reservations, without possessing the younger man's innate good manners. His fingers barely brushed her own, the pinched mouth tightening into a compressed line instead of returning her pleasantry. Such overt hostility was a little overwhelming. Especially if she met with the same reception from her other assistant.

Michele had an irresistible urge to bundle Corey in the car and head back to Chicago. An inadvertent glance at Drake put the steel back in her spine. The comprehension in his darkly handsome face indicated that he knew exactly what was going through her mind—and was amused by it. Michele set her chin grimly. If he thought she was going to turn tail and run at the first sign of heavy weather, he was due for a surprise. They all were!

"I'm sure you gentlemen have a lot to do so we'll be on our way." Michele's voice was very firm as she added, "I'll be here bright and early on Monday morning."

Taking Corey's hand, she led her to the door, conscious of Drake's unfathomable blue gaze burning into her back like a laser beam.

The small white bungalow on Appletree Lane was trimmed with shutters that had originally been dark green, but were now badly in need of a coat of paint. The summer sun had faded them to a muddy, indeterminate color that gave the house a shabby look. The grass needed cutting too, and the flower beds were choked with weeds, adding to the air of neglect. In contrast to the neat homes on either side, the property looked definitely seedy.

Assuring herself that it was only because the yard had gone untended in the three weeks since she had rented the place, Michele fought down a rising feeling of depression.

"Well, here we are," she announced brightly. "Why don't you start taking in your toys while I tackle the cartons."

"Is this where we're going to live?" Corey's expression wasn't promising.

Ignoring the quiver in her daughter's voice, Michele

hurriedly grabbed a Raggedy Ann doll and stuffed it into Corey's arms. "Let's go inside and look around. I can't wait till you see your room."

The living room had the airless smell of a house that's been closed up for weeks. A fine film of dust covered the bare surfaces of the tables, and it was suffocatingly hot.

Michele's first act was to draw back the drapes and open the windows. Then she sent Corey out to the car to bring in all the small articles. Once the place was filled with their familiar things, maybe it wouldn't seem so dreary.

After all the cardboard cartons and suitcases were inside, Michele left Corey to hang up her clothes while she unloaded the kitchen equipment. Mixed in with the toaster and assorted pots was a lucky find—a small transistor radio. She immediately tuned it to a rock station. It wasn't her favorite kind of music, but it effectively dispelled the gloomy silence.

After the kitchen was organized, Michele dusted and put out some favorite knickknacks before going to unpack her own things. It was getting late by that time. Shadows were gathering as the light faded. She thought longingly of a shower, before shelving the idea reluctantly. Corey must be getting hungry.

When she went into the kitchen and snapped on the light, nothing happened. Michele sighed, thinking it was a minor annoyance, a burned-out light bulb that would have to be replaced as soon as dinner was underway. After she tried to turn on the stove, the unpleasant truth occurred to her—the utilities hadn't been turned on.

"I *phoned* them!" Michele muttered in frustration. "I gave them the exact date and told them the key would be at the rental agent's." Now they'd have to get back in the car, all hot and sweaty, and drive around looking for a restaurant. If that wasn't the absolute end!

"Did you call me, Mommy?" Corey appeared in the doorway.

Michele pinned a smile on her face. "I'll bet you're getting hungry, honey. How would you like to go out for a hamburger?"

"Couldn't you make dinner here? I want to watch my program on television."

Michele glanced at the blank eye of the small TV set on the kitchen table, wondering how to break the news to Corey that "The Brady Bunch" would have one less viewer tonight. It was apt to be the last straw. The doorbell postponed the moment of truth.

Michele was so grateful for the reprieve that she didn't even stop to wonder who it could be, since they didn't know anyone in town. Opening the door, she found an older woman with a basket over her arm.

"Hello, I'm Flora Hotchkiss, your next-door neighbor." The smile on her round face was warm and friendly. "I hope I haven't come at a bad time."

"Not at all." Michele opened the door wide. "Please come in."

Mrs. Hotchkiss shook her head. "I know you have a million things to do, getting settled and all." She extended the basket that was covered with a red and white checked cloth. "That's why I thought you might like a little dinner. I know how it is on moving day; it takes a while to locate things."

"How extraordinarily kind of you." Michele had a lump in her throat. This was the first welcoming gesture she had encountered since coming to Greenfield.

"Not at all. What are neighbors for?" Mrs. Hotchkiss shrugged off Michele's thanks, peering down at Corey, who had appeared at her mother's side. "Well, hello there, missy."

"This is Corey, and I'm Michele Carter. We're certainly happy to meet you," Michele said.

"It's going to be so nice having you here." Mrs. Hotchkiss beamed. "We haven't had a youngster in the neighborhood in a dog's age."

"There aren't any children around?" Michele cried in dismay.

The older woman misunderstood her distress. "Not since the Talbots moved away three years ago. But don't you worry. We all have grandchildren and we just love to hear the young ones playing."

"That's nice," Michele answered politely, wondering who Corey would have to play with.

"Well, I promised myself I'd only stay for a minute and here I am nattering away, keeping you from your chores." Mrs. Hotchkiss extended the basket once more. "There's a casserole in here; put it in a three-fifty oven for thirty minutes. I would have brought it over hot, but I didn't know exactly when you'd be ready to eat."

A look of dismay crossed Michele's face. "It was very thoughtful of you, but they haven't turned on our utilities the way they were supposed to. We don't have any gas or electricity."

Mrs. Hotchkiss made a disgusted sound. "Doesn't that beat all? Well, don't you worry, my dear, we'll get them out here first thing tomorrow morning. In the meantime you'll come over to my house for dinner."

"Do you have a television set?" Corey asked suddenly.

"You bet I do, a great big one." To Michele, Mrs. Hotchkiss said, "I'll go pop this in the oven and you come over whenever you're ready."

Sitting in her neighbor's pleasant kitchen an hour later, Michele felt a great deal more relaxed. Corey was ensconced in front of the television set in the living room, looking more cheerful than she had all day. She and Mrs. Hotchkiss had established an immediate rapport, with Corey requesting permission to call the older woman Aunt Flora.

As the two women sat over coffee at the round oak table, they quickly found themselves on a first-name basis also, exchanging bits of information about their lives. Among other things, Michele learned that Flora was a widow whose husband had also worked for Blaylock Chemical until his death a year previously.

"This is a company town," Flora explained. "You'll find that most of the people here work for the Blaylock family in one capacity or another."

"I didn't know it was a family-owned company."

"Oh my, yes. It might be a corporation, but the Blaylocks have the last say about everything." There was amusement in Flora's smile. "Especially *Mrs*. Blaylock."

"She works in the business?"

"Let's say she's the power behind the throne. The old man is dotty about her. Not that Simon Blaylock is exactly ancient." Flora's brow wrinkled in thought. "Let's see . . . he was sixty-one when he married her, and that was two years ago. She was an actress—Clarice Cummings was her stage name. Do you remember her?"

"It sounds vaguely familiar, but . . ."

"I guess that would be a little before your time. Clarice is in her fifties now, and she gave up her career when she married Simon. She's still a beautiful woman." Flora's grin was surprisingly youthful. "And I guess she's still a good actress. At any rate, she knows how to get everything she wants out of Simon. Twists him around her little finger."

"I wouldn't think a woman like that would be interested in chemicals and research," Michele said slowly.

"She probably isn't. It's the power and the people she likes, I reckon."

Michele was beginning to get the scenario. A beautiful woman married to a rich, older man, and stuck in a small town, away from the excitement she was used to. Add to that a much younger man, handsome, virile and unattached. Was Drake Hollister unattached? No matter—it probably wouldn't bother either of those glamorous, predatory people. Michele had wondered what a man like that was doing in this quiet, sleepy village. Now she knew.

"I suppose Mrs. Blaylock was the one who recruited Mr. Hollister to head up the company," Michele remarked, trying to keep the disapproval out of her voice.

Flora's answer surprised her. "No, he was already here."

That called for only a slight revision in the plot. Michele wondered cynically how long it had taken them to find each other, so to speak. "Does Mr. Hollister happen to have a wife?"

"No, never been married either that I know of." Flora chuckled. "Isn't it a shame? A gorgeous man like that going to waste?"

"I imagine he manages to keep busy," Michele remarked dryly.

"You can bet on it, my dear. He could have a different

girl every night if he chose." Flora hesitated, eyeing Michele obliquely. "That one is a real heartbreaker."

Michele recognized the tacit warning. "I suppose he might be to some women. He doesn't happen to be my type, however."

"Maybe it's just as well," Flora murmured.

Michele knew she ought to change the subject, but it was a stellar chance to find out something about the man who was going to control her destiny to a great extent. She needed all the ammunition she could get, Michele assured herself.

"Isn't it a little strange that he chooses to live in a small town like Greenfield?" she asked casually.

Flora shrugged. "Chicago is only a couple of hours away if he gets cabin fever. And sometimes he does go away for a weekend. But Drake Hollister isn't a man you can put a label on. I've seen him dressed up in formal clothes, looking like a picture out of one of those slick magazines. And then I've seen him in jeans and an old shirt, tinkering with that fancy car of his. I guess you could say he has the best of two worlds."

"It's a wonder he finds time to work," Michele commented lightly.

"Don't you believe it. When my Sam was alive he had nothing but praise for Drake. Said he knew everything that went on at the plant from the top floor to the basement."

Michele wasn't surprised, remembering Drake's comprehensive knowledge at their first interview. She devoutly hoped he wasn't going to stick his nose into her projects, though. Dealing with George Browder was going to be enough of a chore.

"Do you happen to know a man named Browder?" she asked Flora. "A thin man, kind of on the short side."

"George Browder?" The other woman made a face. "He's a pain in the posterior, if you'll pardon my plain speaking. Nothing but trouble on the hoof. Take my advice and stay away from that one."

Michele's heart sank. Knowing it was wishful thinking, she had been hoping that she'd merely caught him in an off moment. "I can't very well. He's going to be one of my assistants."

Flora raised her eyebrows. "I guess I shouldn't have been so outspoken."

"No, I appreciate all the help you can give me. Could you tell me something about him?"

"Well, let's see. George was born right here in Greenfield. He went away to college, but then he came back and married a local girl. Myra Brown she was then, a darling girl. They had two adorable little children, but nothing they ever did was right as far as George was concerned. He wasn't just strict, he was downright unreasonable."

Michele didn't want to hear the man's life history. She tried gently to nudge Flora back on the track. "What I really wanted to know was something about his position at Blaylock."

The other woman smiled. "I know you think I'm a garrulous old lady, but to understand George you have to know something about his background. He and his older brother are complete opposites. Donald is tall and handsome, a real charmer. To top it off, he's a brilliant research chemist. Donald Browder got his start at Blaylock too, but then he went on to bigger things. Last I heard, he was doing research in London for some worldwide company."

Michele was beginning to get the picture. "George resented his brother's success?"

"He resented his brother, *period*. I guess it was only

natural. Everything came so easily to Donald. In order to compensate, George became a perfectionist; it's what broke up his marriage.''

"He's divorced?"

Flora nodded. ''Myra might have stood it for herself, but she couldn't take the way he treated those two little tykes; like privates in his own personal army. Her parents had moved to Washington, and one day she just up and took the children to live with them.''

"That should have made him see the light."

"Not stiff-necked George. It was simply one more rejection in a long line—or that's the way he took it. He lives alone in a small apartment now, and spends his time trying to get even with the world.''

Michele was appalled. How was she going to deal with this bitter man?

Corey suddenly appeared in the doorway, rubbing her eyes. ''I don't think I want to watch television anymore.''

Looking at her watch, Michele was smitten by conscience. ''It's time you were in bed, honey.'' She turned to Flora. ''How can I ever thank you?''

"For what, a little casserole and some salad?'' The older woman brushed aside Michele's thanks, putting her arms around Corey. ''Do you like pancakes? Come over in the morning and I'll make breakfast.''

"I like Aunt Flora,'' Corey declared, as Michele was putting her to bed. ''Maybe I'm going to like it here after all.''

"We both are, sweetie,'' Michele assured her, not believing it for a minute.

After she had undressed by the flickering light of the candle Flora had contributed, Michele slid between the fresh sheets. Every muscle in her slender body was protesting, but sleep didn't come. What had she gotten them into? After winning the first skirmish, she had been so confident. Was Drake laughing at her even now? She could almost see his handsome, mocking face.

Forcing her tense body to relax, Michele made a vow. She would succeed at this job. No matter what Drake Hollister threw at her, she would field it—and she would survive!

Chapter Two

$\mathcal{E}$verything looked a lot brighter the next morning when sunshine chased away the gloomy shadows.

Flora brought hot coffee over for Michele, then took Corey back to her house for the promised pancakes after Michele declined. The older woman also volunteered to call the utility company as soon as the offices opened. Michele accepted gratefully, happy to leave the chore in her hands. She knew Flora wouldn't be fobbed off with any feeble excuses.

After they left Michele took a tingling cold shower, yelping involuntarily as the water pelted her supple body. It promised to be another hot, end-of-August day, so she selected a different pair of brief shorts, khaki-colored this time. A cream-colored, oversized shirt reached to the top of her thighs, making it appear that she had nothing on underneath. Michele didn't even notice that the effect was very sexy. Her only objective was to select something comfortable that she could work in easily.

After opening all the windows and the front and back doors to let in the sweetly scented morning air, Michele started to work.

With Corey taken care of, the rest of the unpacking was accomplished speedily. By eleven-thirty all of their personal belongings had been put away. Then it was time to start on the house. Michele decided to begin with the breakfast room curtains, which looked rather limp. The cheerful floral print should be quite attractive, though, after a trip through the washing machine.

The rickety stool she brought from the kitchen was tall enough, but when she yanked at the curtain rods it teetered alarmingly. Hearing footsteps at the front door, Michele called out to Corey, "Would you come here, honey? I need you to hold the stool."

A few seconds later two hands circled her slim waist as a deep male voice said, "Why don't you let me do that?"

It was so unexpected that Michele whirled around incautiously. The ancient stool skittered out from under her and she toppled into space, reaching out instinctively to save herself. Michele's arms clutched Drake about the neck as his arms wrapped around her slim body, gathering her close. With her feet dangling inches off the floor, she was pressed tightly against him, unavoidably feeling every hard, masculine muscle in that lithe body.

For one mind-spinning moment she remained pliant in his arms, the unaccustomed male embrace awakening feelings long buried. Michele's gray eyes darkened to pewter as she gazed into the rugged face just inches from her own. The scent of his after-shave filled her nostrils, spicy and subtly seductive. She was tinglingly aware of the length of his firm thighs, the hard breadth of his chest pressing against her breasts. Then reason returned and she struggled out of his arms, her cheeks the color of the cabbage roses in the garden outside.

Michele yanked at her hiked-up shirt, pulling it down and wishing it were longer. "Just what do you think you're doing?" she demanded.

He watched her self-conscious efforts with amusement. "Saving you from a nasty fall. Don't you know better than to stand on a three-legged stool?"

Michele treated him to a ferocious scowl. "I would have been fine if you hadn't sneaked up on me."

"I didn't sneak, I was invited. How could I refuse when you used such a charming endearment?"

"You know perfectly well I thought you were my daughter. What are you doing here anyway?"

He seemed to be enjoying her discomfiture. Drake's smile revealed perfect white teeth in a lean, tanned face "Are you always this hospitable?"

"I am to my *invited* guests," she answered pointedly.

His laughing blue eyes chilled. "My mistake, Mrs. Carter. I guess I've lived in a small town so long I've forgotten my big-city manners. Excuse the intrusion." He paused in the act of turning away. "One bit of advice, though. If you expect to be able to report for work on Monday, I'd suggest you find something sturdier than that stool to stand on."

His calm masculine assumption that she wasn't competent to take down a curtain infuriated Michele. "Don't get your hopes up, Mr. Hollister. I intend to be there with bells on," she assured him grimly.

"And a little something more I hope," he drawled. His comprehensive gaze traveled over her body, pausing at the pink peaks faintly visible under the gauzy shirt since

Michele hadn't bothered with a confining bra. "I'm not complaining, you understand, but I doubt if we'd get much work done."

Michele felt a warm tide sweeping through her. She had to stifle the urge to wrap her arms around her breasts. "I wish I could be as sure of your professionalism as I am of my own," she commented coldly.

"How can you doubt it?" he asked mockingly. "I hired *you* didn't I?"

Not because you wanted to! she felt like shouting. Taking a deep breath, Michele inquired sweetly, "Tell me, what did you usually do on Saturday mornings? Before I was here to provide you with entertainment."

His arched eyebrow took note of her veiled sarcasm. "A lot more rewarding things."

"I can just imagine," she remarked caustically.

"I doubt it. Ordinarily I'd be playing tennis or golf."

"Don't feel you have to forgo it for me."

"I didn't," Drake stated flatly. "I had an . . . errand to do this morning."

"Shouldn't you be attending to it then?" Michele realized that she was being rude. It was completely unlike her, but this man made her so *angry!*

This was the second time he had caught her at a disadvantage. At the office the day before, his well-tailored suit and immaculate linen had seemed to mock her disheveled state. Today he was doing the same thing.

Drake was a picture of understated elegance in an expensive-looking pair of fawn-colored slacks that rode low on his narrow hips and stretched tautly across his muscular thighs. His brown silk shirt looked equally costly, although it was worn casually unbuttoned almost to the waist. Michele tried not to look at the dark, curling hair on his broad chest. Didn't he ever wear scroungy jeans in his off hours like everyone else? she wondered angrily.

"Mommy, Mommy!" Corey's breathless voice preceded her. "This is my friend, Diane." A small, dark-haired girl trailed after Corey into the breakfast room.

Michele forgot the man beside her in the pleasure of seeing her daughter's face filled with animation the way it used to be. It was a relief that she had found someone to play with.

"Well, hello, Diane, it's so nice to meet you," Michele beamed.

"She's going to my school," Corey continued. "We're in the same grade."

"How nice!" Michele exclaimed. "Maybe you could ride to school together." It would go a long way toward easing the trauma of Corey's first day.

The child's answer dashed her hopes. "I don't think so. I live over in Rosewood Park; it's a couple of miles from here."

Michele was aghast. "You walked all that way alone?"

"Oh no, Mr. Hollister brought me."

Michele looked helplessly at the saturnine face of the man towering over her. "I don't understand."

"Why don't you youngsters go outside and play?" Drake cut in smoothly. "In a little while I'll take you both to the hamburger place for lunch."

"Can Mommy come too?" Corey asked.

"I think your mother lost her appetite in the last few minutes," he replied mockingly.

"She didn't have any breakfast," Corey said doubtfully. "You want to come with us, don't you, Mommy?"

Michele's head was filled with unanswered questions. "Do as Mr. Hollister said, dear. Maybe Diane would like to see your toys." When the two little girls had skipped off, Michele turned to Drake. "Did you make a special trip to bring Diane here today? Was that your errand?"

He shrugged. "I know how tough it is to move to a new town and not know anyone."

Michele was reminded of their conversation at her first interview. Drake had told her he was a troubleshooter who moved from place to place, but it was inconceivable that such a man would ever have trouble fitting in. How could he understand the trauma of a little girl faced with that same situation? Yet it was obvious that he did. Remembering her rudeness, Michele felt slightly smaller than a pygmy.

Her voice was husky as she said, "I think that's the nicest thing anyone ever did for me."

Drake wasn't in a forgiving mood. "You have a lot to learn about small towns, Mrs. Carter. It wouldn't be considered remarkable here."

Michele accepted the implied rebuke. "I'm still very grateful."

"I did it for Corey," he replied, so there wouldn't be any misunderstanding.

"I realize that," she answered quietly. "You're a very kind man."

Drake surveyed her sober face for a long moment. Then a mischievous grin showed gleaming white teeth. "Are you trying to confuse me? I've grown to expect brickbats from you, not bouquets."

Michele returned his smile ruefully. "You're not exactly defenseless."

He raised his eyebrows in mock surprise. "Is that the impression you got? Not so. I'm a real pussycat when you get to know me."

If this man was any kind of cat it was one of the big ones,

Michele reflected—a leopard perhaps, or a sleek black panther. There was a sense of leashed power in that lithe body, emphasizing its inherent danger. A tiny ripple ran up her spine unexpectedly.

Trying to ignore it, Michele said lightly, "I'm sorry I can't offer you a saucer of milk; there isn't any in the house."

"Are you trying to make me purr?"

"No, I . . . I'm just sorry I can't offer you anything." Michele was furious with herself. What had happened to the poise she prided herself on—and her immunity to the whole male species?

Drake chuckled softly. "That's a very provocative remark."

Michele felt a peculiar sensation in the pit of her stomach. Why did romantic novels always set their seduction scenes amid candlelight and low, schmaltzy music? Michele had never felt more aware of her own sexuality than she did right now, with bright sunlight streaming in the windows, and the mundane sound of someone's lawn mower whirring outside.

She was achingly conscious of the man standing over her, of his clean, crisp scent and the male body that was contoured to fit her own. Michele's breath caught in her throat. Dear God, what was she thinking!

"It certainly wasn't my intention to be provocative," she said stiffly, putting distance between them.

Drake inspected her flushed face with interest. "I'd be quite crushed if I didn't suspect the same feeling extended to the whole male gender."

Michele forced herself to look at him calmly. "I doubt that your sensibilities are that tender, but if it's any consolation to you, you're correct."

"How long have you been widowed?" he asked abruptly.

"Four years." The answer was startled out of her.

"A long time to grieve," he mused, his eyes narrowing. "Or was your marriage so unsatisfactory that it spoiled you for other men?"

"I consider that a very personal question!"

"You're right. I was completely out of line."

Michele knew that he wasn't really penitent, but he *had* done a lovely thing for Corey. He was also Michele's boss. She told herself not to lose sight of that fact.

"Under the circumstances, I think it would be better if we didn't engage in personalities," Michele said with dignity.

"What circumstances are those?" he teased.

"You know perfectly well," she stormed, ruffled in spite of her good intentions. "Since I'm your employee, I don't think we should be . . . well . . ."

"Involved?" he asked innocently.

"That's as good a word as any," she answered grimly.

"Can we have lunch now?" Diane appeared in the breakfast room, closely followed by Corey. "I'm starved."

"Me too," Corey chimed in.

"Sure thing." Drake looked at Michele. "How about it?"

"No, thank you."

"Please, Mommy," Corey pleaded.

"I don't think a hamburger would commit you to anything irrevocable," Drake commented mildly.

Michele realized that Corey wanted her to accompany them. Despite her new friend and her affinity for Drake, she was still an insecure little girl. Michele was torn in two directions. "I'm not dressed," she said helplessly.

"It's only the Hamburger Hut," Drake told her. "You can go like that."

"No, I . . . it will only take me a minute to change," Michele capitulated, concern for her child overriding her very real reservations.

In her own room she seized a pink and white flowered sundress from the closet, bypassing the jeans that were her normal uniform. The low, square neckline and wide straps set off her golden tan, and the tight-fitting bodice hugged her high, firm breasts. Michele was pleased with the quick glimpse she caught in the mirror, although she assured herself that she had chosen it merely because it was cool.

To save time, she brushed her hair and left it to hang loose in a shining curtain that skimmed her slim shoulders. After a swift application of pink lip gloss, she slipped into a pair of high-heeled white sandals. The whole operation took only the few minutes she had promised.

Drake's eyes were admiring when she reappeared. "I've known women who took hours without achieving that effect."

Michele forced down the rising pleasure his words brought. He used that practiced charm on every female, she reminded herself. "Real women don't spend hours on their appearance anymore," she replied primly.

"If we didn't have two hungry kids on our hands, I'd be fascinated to hear your definition of a real woman," he murmured.

Ignoring that, Michele turned to her daughter. "Run and close the back door, and be sure the—oh my!" She stopped abruptly. "I can't go anywhere. The man is coming to turn on our utilities."

"Leave the door unlocked," Drake advised. "Believe me, it will be safe."

"I couldn't do that." Michele shook her head decidedly.

"I see it's going to take a while for you to become accustomed to small-town living," he chuckled.

"Aunt Flora could let them in," Corey piped up.

Drake looked surprised. "You have relatives here?"

"Flora Hotchkiss is our next-door neighbor," Michele explained. "We just met her last night but she's been tremendously kind."

"She's a super lady," he agreed. "I've known Flora for years but I didn't know this is where she lived."

Corey tugged at Michele's hand. "Shall I go ask her?"

"I don't really think we should keep on imposing," Michele said reluctantly.

As she stood uncertainly on the doorstep, Flora came out of her own home, her plump figure encased in a brightly printed housecoat.

"Hello, Drake," she called. "I thought I recognized your voice."

"Hi, Flora." He went to meet her as she walked toward them, giving her a kiss on the cheek. "It's good to see you again. How's it going?"

"Can't complain." Her eyes sparkled impishly behind the round glasses. "Outside of the fact that I can't seem to find a good man to take Sam's place."

"He'd be a hard act to follow," Drake answered gently.

"You're so right." Flora banished the momentary sadness that clouded her pleasant face. "Did you come over to help Michele get settled in?"

With a mischievous sidelong glance he said, "She spurned my help, but I did manage to convince her to come out for lunch. The only trouble is that she just remembered the utilities man is coming."

"No problem," Flora said. "I'll let him in."

"It isn't fair to ask you to hang around for that," Michele protested. "Maybe you have somewhere to go."

Her neighbor chuckled. "Well, I *was* considering having lunch with the mayor, but all he ever talks about is himself."

"No really, Flora, I can't keep—"

With a gentle push, Flora said, "Run along and enjoy yourself. By the time you get back you'll have lights and hot water, or I'll blister the hides off that gas and electric company." A slight frown clouded her normally placid face as she watched Drake's arm casually circle Michele's shoulders, shepherding her toward the low-slung sports car at the curb. "See that she eats lunch," Flora called sharply. "She didn't have any breakfast."

Drake turned with a slow smile. "Don't worry about a thing. I'll take care of her."

"I think I just gave the fox the key to the hen house," Flora muttered, staring after them.

A short time later the two little girls were in seventh heaven. Drake had ordered hamburgers, french fries, colas and strawberry cheesecake. They were busily anointing everything but the dessert with catsup, giggling between themselves.

Michele watched the children with fond amusement. "You certainly know how to bring instant delight," she told Drake.

Something electric flared in his eyes as they rested on her soft mouth. "Giving pleasure is part of receiving it," he murmured.

The words were innocent enough, even laudable. It was his tone of voice that was suspect. Michele knew he wasn't talking about the little girls—it was a big one he was stalking.

"That sounds like something you read in a fortune cookie," she commented tartly.

His smile was slow and lazy. "I see you're going to need some convincing."

"Don't bother, I'll take your word for it."

"I'd consider it a privilege." His low voice dropped another note.

Michele felt a curl of excitement unfolding inside her. Damn the man anyway! He was undeniably sexy. But the knowledge that all that disturbing charm was automatic made her unaccountably angry. It was time to set the record straight.

"I'm not quite sure why you're doing this, Mr. Hollister, but it's not only unnecessary, it's disagreeable," Michele said crisply.

He regarded her with concealed amusement. "I wasn't aware that I was doing anything, but it's obvious that I've upset you."

"Confused is more like it," she answered coldly. "Our first interview was a mere formality. You made no secret of the fact that you weren't interested in me *or* my services. Suddenly I not only got the job, but I'm treated to the mating dance of the black-haired wily bird. I'd like to know why."

A curtain had descended behind Drake's eyes at her first words. When she finished speaking, his expression was bland. "You're a very beautiful woman. Surely I'm not the first man to notice it."

"You managed to overlook the fact when you interviewed me."

His well-shaped mouth thinned a trifle grimly. "I'm a different man at the laboratory—as you'll find out."

"I don't expect any special consideration."

Drake's smile didn't reach his eyes. "Then we should get along just fine."

"Not if you continue to resent having to hire me." Michele felt the time had come to bring it out into the open. "My credentials were first rate. What could you possibly have had against me except the fact that I'm a woman?"

He no longer tried to evade the issue. "I don't think we're going to profit by discussing it, but since you insist, I'll answer your question. I've placed women in positions of authority in the past, and it didn't work out."

"Did you ever think that perhaps your own judgment was faulty?" Michele cried. "Maybe they just weren't right for the job—regardless of their gender!" Unwittingly her voice had risen.

Corey looked doubtfully at her mother's impassioned face. "Mommy?"

Drake drew a handful of coins out of his pocket. "If you young ladies are finished with your lunch, I think that Pac Man machine over there would like to be fed."

Michele was ashamed of her outburst. "You're right, this isn't the time to discuss it."

The smile he had worn for the girls was gone. "Since you brought it up, however, I think it's something we should get settled. My experiences with women in business have been . . . flawed. That might have been what you detected at our interview."

Michele wanted to ask who had forced him to hire her then; it would help to know who her ally was. But rubbing salt into the wound wouldn't get her anywhere.

"Can I hope you'll at least keep an open mind?" she pleaded.

"I've never been accused of being unfair," he replied steadily.

Michele sighed. "I guess I'll have to settle for that."

"What more would you like? You've just stated that you don't expect special consideration," Drake remarked cynically.

He sounded as though he didn't believe her. "What I'd *like* is to understand you a little better!" Michele cried angrily. "If you really think I'm a disaster on its way to happen, why are you coming on to me today?"

He chuckled suddenly, a deep, rich sound of amusement that banished all the former coldness. "If you weren't such a suspicious young woman, the answer to that would be obvious."

"Forgive me for continuing to be suspicious. I just find it hard to believe that you're suddenly smitten by my charms when you found them so resistible the first time around."

"Now there's where you're wrong. I wondered for days about the color of those fabulous eyes." His long fingers curled around her chin, holding Michele's face for his inspection. "They're gray, aren't they? A stormy, pewter color when you're angry—which is practically the only way I've ever seen them." His hand stroked her cheek in a feathery light caress. "What color are they when you look at other men, Michele?"

She jerked her chin away, lowering long lashes to hide her awareness of this virile male who stirred her senses against all reason. "I don't have time for those games."

"You're very young to have put love behind you."

"I wasn't aware that we were talking about love," she said scornfully.

"Sex is part of love," he answered mildly.

"Spoken like a true male!"

"I don't intend to be diverted into a battle of the sexes. I want to know why you have such a low opinion of men."

"I could ask you the same thing in reverse."

"You know that isn't true. I'm exceedingly fond of women."

"I'm painfully aware of that! Do you know what a male chauvinist that makes you?" Michele cried.

"Only because you insist on forcing me into a mold. You're dead wrong if you think I'm only interested in women when they're in my bed. I have a great admiration for a lot of the women I've dealt with."

"The ones with adoring, supplicating manners, I suppose," Michele commented waspishly.

Drake seemed to find that very amusing. "Quite the contrary, as a matter of fact."

"Then what was the matter with me?" Michele demanded.

His laughter stilled. "That's the only valid point you've made. Perhaps I let my annoyance temper my impartiality," he said slowly.

Annoyance at *whom*? Michele wanted to shout. It was maddening to grope in the dark. How powerful was Drake? If he had no say in her hiring, how much would he have over firing her?

He covered her tightly clenched fist with his big, warm hand. "How about starting over as friends?"

She didn't trust him for a minute. That low, seductive voice was a trap in itself. "I think it would be better if we kept our relationship strictly business," she said carefully, removing her hand.

"You're making a mistake. I'm the most eligible bachelor in town," he informed her with a big grin.

"That's the last thing I'm looking for. I have a full-time job, and a daughter to raise."

"Does she remember her father?" Drake asked suddenly.

Corey never talked about him. Did she remember Gary? And if so, did those memories include the degrading arguments, the cold silences after the cutting remarks had found their target?

"She was only three when he died," Michele murmured, avoiding a direct answer.

"Was he ill long?" Drake asked gently.

"No, he died in a laboratory accident at the college where he worked."

"Your husband was a research scientist also?"

Michele shook her head. "He taught history. Gary was just visiting a fellow professor when there was an explosion."

"I'm sorry." Drake's voice was muted in sympathy. "It must have been very difficult for you to continue in your chosen field after that. Your husband would be very proud of you."

Michele had a hysterical impulse to laugh. If Drake only knew! When a puzzled frown brought his dark brows together, Michele knew her face must be expressing some of her inner turmoil.

She controlled herself quickly. "I think I'd better go round up the girls." As she started to slide out of the booth, Drake stopped her with a hand on her arm.

Michele braced herself for more questions, but surprisingly, he said, "Were you serious about getting Corey a dog?"

With a sigh of relief she answered, "Yes, it's hard to leave all the people and places you're accustomed to. I thought a pet would . . . fill the void."

His eyes searched the delicate contours of her lovely face. "And you, Michele? Will it do the same for you?" he asked softly. Before she could answer, Drake released her arm and sat back, his manner becoming briskly impersonal. "I thought if you agreed, we could stop by the animal shelter. They have a wide selection of dogs crying out for love."

Corey was ecstatic when the offer was presented to her. But when they reached the shelter, it promised to be a lengthy selection process.

Wire cages lined the narrow corridor on both sides, each filled with dogs of every description—big ones, little ones, recognizable breeds and mixtures that defied identification. The one thing they had in common was an overwhelming desire to get out. As the attendant led their little group down the aisle, each animal flung itself against the wire, presenting its case in an irresistible manner.

"You shouldn't have brought me here," Michele shouted to Drake over the din. "I want to take every one of them home."

"I know what you mean," he shouted back. "I have the same urge."

Michele glanced at the handsome man next to her, a man who disturbed her in more ways than one. Well, at least he told the truth about liking children and dogs, she reflected wryly. He can't be all bad.

After much mind changing, Corey chose a small white ball of fluff with shiny, black, shoe-button eyes. It had been leaping into the air trying to see over the bigger animals, demanding its share of attention. The endearing little scrap had undeniable spirit, although it looked like an animated mophead.

When it was placed in Corey's arms, the look on her face

made a lump rise in Michele's throat. Drake's arm went around Michele, pressing her head against his solid shoulder as though he understood her emotion.

"This is a milestone," he murmured, his warm breath stirring the soft hair at her temple. "Corey's first dog."

Michele realized it was also the first milestone she had ever shared with anyone. For just a moment she allowed herself the luxury of leaning against Drake's satisfyingly solid body, feeling his warmth envelop her. It had been a long, lonely road of milestones—Corey's first day at school, the first baby tooth she lost. Michele had been so busy being both father and mother that she hadn't even realized how it enhanced the pleasure to share those moments with someone.

As Drake's arm tightened around her, Michele swallowed hard. Wasn't it too bad that this was all an illusion? Drake was her employer, a man she would undoubtedly do battle with often in the coming weeks. He wasn't a part of their lives—he wasn't even a friend.

"I'm going to name my new dog after Mr. Hollister." Corey's excited voice dispelled Michele's poignant thoughts. "Would that be all right?" she appealed to both of them.

Drake lifted the squirming bundle out of her arms, inspecting it quizzically. "I'm very honored, but the question is, whether dog here would like it."

After a quick glance into his mischievous eyes, Michele made her own inspection. Attempting to smother her laughter, she said, "It might be a little confusing, honey. Maybe you should pick another name."

"How about Fluffy?" Diane suggested.

"Oh yes, that's even better," Corey quickly agreed.

After the formalities had been taken care of, the two

excited children and yapping dog were herded into the white Ferrari. Michele gave Drake a rueful smile. "You really are a good sport."

He raised a questioning eyebrow. "Why is that?"

"I don't imagine we're your typical passengers."

He acknowledged that with a grin. "You're right. I'm not usually lucky enough to squire four nubile females all at the same time."

"Fluffy is the lucky one. I'm sure this is her first ride in a Ferrari."

"I hope she considers it the honor you seem to, and acts accordingly," Drake responded dryly.

"You don't think she'd . . . misbehave?" Michele was horrified.

"Don't look so stricken—unless you're thinking I'd make you clean it up."

"Well, of course I—" Michele stopped as she realized he was teasing. She regarded him with interest. "Do you have a dog? You seem to like them so much."

"No, but I wish I could. It wouldn't be fair; I'm gone all day and too many of the nights."

Michele didn't need to be told that. Drake must have an active social life. What was it Flora said?—a different girl every night. That must account for some memorable evenings.

"I'll share yours with you."

"I beg your pardon?" Michele turned a startled face toward him.

"Your dog. I said I'd share her if I may."

"Oh . . . oh, of course." A warm tide of pink colored her fair skin as Drake looked at her bemusedly.

Fluffy blessedly chose that moment to escape from the overly enthusiastic demonstrations of love in the back seat.

Nimbly evading both little girls, she scrambled into Drake's lap.

"Fluffy, no!" Michele made a grab for her.

"It's all right." His long fingers gently scratched behind the small dog's floppy ear.

"She'll get hair all over your good clothes," Michele insisted, lifting her off his lap.

"That wouldn't be cataclysmic," he answered mildly.

When Fluffy had been banished to the back seat once more, Michele looked critically at Drake. "Don't you ever wear jeans on the weekend?"

"Very often," he nodded. "I would have today, but I have to stop by the Blaylocks' after I take Diane home."

"Jeans aren't acceptable even though it's your day off?" Michele asked coolly.

Drake chuckled. "They are with Simon, but Clarice—Mrs. Blaylock—is something else. She's a great gal, but she deplores the modern trend toward informality." His voice was a fond mimicry.

"And you go along with her," Michele remarked evenly.

Drake shrugged. "If it makes her happy, why not?"

What else do you do to make her happy? Michele wondered, knowing the answer. In her glow of gratitude she had forgotten exactly what kind of man Drake was. She certainly wasn't sitting in judgment on his morals. There was no reason why he should remain celibate—or any remote chance! It was his choice of bed partners Michele objected to.

No matter how fascinating Mrs. Blaylock was, the fact remained that she was years older than Drake—and more importantly, the wife of his boss. How much of their affair was passion on his side, and how much was ambition? Flora had indicated that Clarice Blaylock wielded a lot of power.

The whole idea was odious, besides being unnecessary. A man like Drake Hollister could make it to the top on his own business acumen, not his athletic ability in bed.

Unaware of her silent disapproval, Drake was saying, "You remind me of Clarice in many ways."

"I can't imagine why," Michele said with marked distaste.

His enigmatic eyes surveyed her set face. "You've met her?"

"No, I . . . Flora told me a little about her. She was an actress, wasn't she?" Before she married Mr. Blaylock for his money, Michele wanted to add.

"One of the best. She was also before her time in her thinking. Clarice would have been in the spearhead of the women's movement if it had come along when she was twenty years younger."

That was hard to believe. But had he classified Michele as a militant feminist? If so, it would account for Drake's verbal passes today. Perhaps his normal conquests were too easy. His masculine ego required the stimulation of a challenge.

Michele wrapped her arms around her suddenly shaken body. Now that she knew what the challenge was, she would be doubly on guard.

"Clarice is interested in meeting you," Drake was continuing. "You'll be hearing from her."

"I can hardly wait," Michele murmured.

A small frown creased his broad forehead, but before he could pursue the subject they pulled up in front of Michele's bungalow.

Fluffy escaped through the open car door, with the girls in screeching pursuit, and for the next few moments bedlam reigned. It was so noisy that Flora came out to see what all the commotion was about.

After Fluffy was captured, Drake placed her securely in Corey's arms. "I think you picked yourself a dog with a mind of her own." His laughing eyes flicked for just a moment to Michele before returning to the breathless child. "Take my advice and show her who's boss. It's the only way you're going to be able to live with her."

"Take Fluffy inside before she gets away again," Michele instructed. She turned to Drake, her eyes stormy. "Thank you for everything, Mr. Hollister—including the advice. I wonder if it would have been the same if we'd chosen a male dog."

"Everyone has to learn where the boundaries are, Mrs. Carter," he answered mockingly. "Those who don't are in for a rather painful experience."

After he had taken Diane and left, it was a great deal quieter.

"Your gas and electric are on," Flora announced.

"That's nice." The older woman's words didn't really register. Michele was still fuming at Drake.

Flora took a long look at Michele's taut body and tense expression. "Did you have a good time?" she asked tentatively.

"I didn't go for a good time, I merely went to have lunch." Suddenly Michele was ashamed of herself. She was taking out her temper on a woman who had shown her nothing but kindness. "Forgive me, Flora. I . . . I have a headache. I think it's the heat."

"It's fierce today," her neighbor agreed. "Why don't you go in and lie down for a while?"

"That's a good idea, maybe I will."

As Flora watched Michele's drooping figure disappear into the house, her usually smiling mouth turned down at the corners. It hadn't taken the fox long to put the chickens in an uproar. *Men!* she thought disgustedly. They were like satin sheets—alluring to look at, but too slick for real enjoyment.

Chapter Three

*I*t seemed strange to be back at work after the past two weeks of hectic activity, packing, moving and getting settled. Or maybe it was just the unfamiliar surroundings and unnatural quiet. This feeling of being an alien in a strange, hostile country would vanish once everyone came into work, Michele assured herself.

Corey had been up that morning almost as soon as it was light, filled with excitement over her first day at the new school. She was dressed and waiting long before it was time to leave. Her second thoughts came when the hour finally arrived.

"I won't know anyone there. Suppose nobody plays with me?"

"You know Diane," Michele reminded her comfortingly. "And you're going to meet a lot of other children just as nice."

It was enough to get Corey into the car. On the way, Michele went over the instructions one more time. "Remember now, the school bus will pick you up after class, and you're to go to Aunt Flora's when you get home."

Bless Flora Hotchkiss, Michele prayed fervently. May her place in heaven be assured! So far, Michele hadn't been able to locate a sitter to come in during the hours before she returned from work. When she asked Flora for suggestions, the older woman couldn't think of anyone immediately, but had offered her services until someone could be found. Michele had no other choice but she hoped it would be a very temporary arrangement.

Michele dropped her daughter off at school, her heart warming as Diane ran out of a knot of children to greet Corey and lead her back to the group. Wouldn't it be nice if she met with the same reception at Blaylock, Michele thought wistfully, not expecting it for an instant. Corey was the important one though; Michele was used to fighting her own battles. Unconsciously her slender shoulders straightened.

As she drove down a country lane, Michele sniffed appreciatively. The oppressive summer heat had broken with the advent of September. Fall was definitely in the air. Although it was still early, it seemed foolish to go back home. She might as well go to the lab and start getting acclimated.

Her office was a little, glassed-in cubicle adjacent to a large room fitted out with all the latest laboratory equipment. On her desk were several folders detailing the work in progress on new products. Michele glanced through them casually at first, quickly becoming deeply interested. Blaylock wasn't a giant corporation concerned only with making money. Some of these products would be a boon to humanity if they could be perfected.

An experiment designed to ease the pain of a crippling children's disease was of special interest. When she noticed a footnote referring to extensive research that had been completed, Michele went to a metal filing cabinet in the corner.

The information she was looking for was in the bottom drawer, filling several manila folders. Sitting on the floor with her back propped against the wall, she became completely engrossed in the subject.

At first the voices in the lab didn't penetrate her deep absorption. By the time they did, it was too late. George Browder was talking to a man who could only be Tim Fenwick, Michele's other assistant, and the conversation was definitely not for her ears.

"I wonder what time the great lady intends to honor us with her presence," George said with heavy sarcasm. "She evidently keeps bankers' hours."

"It's only a few minutes after nine," Tim answered mildly.

"You'd think she'd try to be on time the first day at least."

"The layout here is unfamiliar to her. Maybe she's having trouble locating the lab."

"Oh, great! We're supposed to work with a researcher who can't find her own office?"

"I didn't say—look, George, I know you wanted this promotion, but it isn't the woman's fault that you didn't get it. For some reason, the powers that be decided to go outside the company. If they hadn't picked her, it would have been someone else."

"Whose side are you on anyway?"

"I'm trying not to *take* sides."

"Well, you're going to have to, friend. It's either her or me. I'm going to get that broad if it's the last thing I do. And if you're not with me, you're against me."

Michele's anger was mitigated by her discomfort. Why hadn't she made her presence known as soon as she became aware of them? And how was she going to do it now without having it look as though she had been purposely eavesdropping? When she heard Drake's voice, Michele wanted to crawl inside the file cabinet.

"Mrs. Carter hasn't come in yet?" Drake inquired.

"You mean the new boss from the big city?" George's tone was insolent, but there was nothing in his actual words that Drake could take exception to.

Michele could almost see Drake's scowl, however. She hastily slammed the metal drawer closed to cut off further conversation. Rising to her feet from behind the concealing desk, she faced the three surprised men.

"Oh, there you are." Drake strode to her office door. "I see you've already met the others."

"No, I . . . I'm afraid I didn't hear them come in." It was a feeble excuse, yet the best she could come up with.

Michele smoothed her shining hair, trying to take comfort from the fact that it was severely coiled at the nape of her neck. At least she looked professional for a change. No one could fault her tailored beige suit, or the white blouse and little string tie.

It didn't seem to impress the two men who were regarding her with ominous expressions after their initial surprise. Michele could have predicted the ill-concealed enmity George was displaying; it was Tim's attitude that bothered her.

He was a tall, lanky young man in his early thirties,

although the shock of light brown hair that fell over his intelligent forehead gave him a rather boyish appearance. Michele had a feeling that Tim Fenwick was normally very pleasant—when his wide mouth wasn't compressed as it was now.

Her heart sank. From the little she overheard, Tim had been willing to reserve judgment. By her stupid hesitation, it appeared that she had turned him into an instant enemy. How could she convince him that she hadn't been spying?

Drake wore a slight frown as he looked at her flushed cheeks. "Well, come and meet Tim. I assume you remember George from the other day."

A quick glance at Drake showed that no gibe was intended. He had been telling the truth when he said he was a different man at work. In his elegantly cut business suit, Drake was coolly remote—neither friendly nor unfriendly. Well, that was the way she wanted it, Michele assured herself.

She acknowledged the introduction to Tim, putting warmth in her voice as she added, "I hope you'll bear with me until I learn the ropes around here." The proffered olive branch went ignored.

It was George who answered for his colleague, while the younger man stood by with a carefully blank expression. "Don't worry, we're both going to be on the lookout for you."

The double-edged statement was reinforced by the satisfaction on George's face. Tim was now his ally. Score one for the home team, Michele thought grimly.

Drake couldn't help being aware of the undercurrents, but he stayed strictly aloof. "If you'll come into your office, Mrs. Carter, there are a few things I'd like to discuss."

Michele followed, almost feeling a knife between her shoulder blades as the eyes of the two men rested on her back.

After briefing her on the current projects, and what the others were working on, Drake said, "It's your department, of course. You can change their assignments."

"That would seem to be counterproductive," she answered crisply. "I have no desire to interfere in their research; it's my own I'm concerned about. Is there anything that's top priority?"

"We're very keen to start manufacturing Chidactron, as soon as we're convinced there are no side effects, naturally." He reached for the folder she had been studying. "I think you'll find very comprehensive notes here and in the file cabinet."

"Yes, I . . . I was reading them when you came in."

Drake was clearly puzzled by her suddenly heightened color. "Is anything wrong, Michele?"

"No, certainly not!" she answered breathlessly. "I'm anxious to get started."

He hesitated a moment. "Well . . . if you need me for anything, my extension is 402."

Michele noticed that he didn't suggest she pop by his office. She wouldn't have anyway, but a small gesture of warmth from *anyone* would have been appreciated. Still, she was used to struggling against the odds—and so far she had beaten them.

Michele squared her shoulders. "Thank you, but I don't anticipate any trouble," she said formally.

For just a moment his austere facade cracked, although it wasn't necessarily an improvement. A sardonic eyebrow raised as Drake said softly, "You're a very optimistic young woman, Mrs. Carter."

After he left, Michele put on a starched white coat and took her notes to an empty table in the lab. No one spoke to her, the two men appearing to be engrossed in their individual experiments. She glanced helplessly around the big room, wondering where to find the equipment she needed. Under the circumstances, she didn't like to ask for assistance.

A long wall filled with drawers and cabinets seemed the most likely place. After opening and closing a dozen of them without locating what she wanted, Michele was beginning to feel frustrated. It was like trying to cook in someone else's kitchen, she thought disgustedly.

"The test tubes are in the closet on the left," Tim told her unexpectedly.

At first she was filled with hope, until it occurred to her that the noise was probably distracting him. "Thank you," she murmured.

Quiet settled on the room after that, but Michele no longer minded. She became completely absorbed in her work, forgetting all the problems and tensions. This was what she was trained for, what she had chosen to do with her life.

Hours later, the sound of muted, melodic chimes broke her concentration. Michele lifted her head questioningly, but no one enlightened her as to their source.

A few minutes later, George took off his lab coat. "Are you coming, Tim?" he asked, ostentatiously ignoring Michele.

"No, you go ahead." Tim was squinting into a microscope. "I want to finish this first."

Michele was beginning to get hungry. Where did people go for lunch, she wondered? The surrounding area was all open country. Well, she would just have to get in the car and find some place.

After a short time, Tim took off his lab coat and shrugged into his jacket. He passed her table silently, pausing at the door. "Those chimes meant the cafeteria is open."

"Oh, is that what they were? I wondered."

"Do you know where the cafeteria is?" The question was asked reluctantly.

"No, but I'm sure I can find it." She smiled. "I'll just follow my nose."

He hesitated for a long moment. "If you're ready for lunch, I'll show you the way."

Michele got up quickly. "I'm not only ready, I'm starving! My daughter got me up so early that breakfast seems as though it took place yesterday."

As they walked down the hall together, Tim looked at her with the first semblance of friendliness. "How old is your little girl?"

"An energetic seven." She had noticed a gold wedding band on his finger. "Do you have children?"

"Not yet."

There was something reserved about his manner. Had she gotten too personal? Maybe he and his wife didn't want children. Many couples didn't nowadays. That seemed to be the case because he changed the subject to the experiment he was working on.

They chatted amiably enough until they reached the cafeteria. It was filled with noisy groups, but George Browder was sitting alone at a table facing the door. His eyes narrowed with rage as he saw them come in together.

Michele knew this could be a sticky situation. There was probably no way she could overcome George's animosity, but it was something that was strictly between themselves. She didn't want to put Tim in the middle. The innate good manners Tim had shown might prompt him to ask her to join them for lunch—which George would certainly take as a betrayal by the other man.

Thinking swiftly, Michele stopped in the doorway. "Oh dear, I've forgotten my purse."

"No problem, I'll take care of the check," Tim offered.

"Thanks, but you go ahead. I . . . I have a phone call to make too." Hurrying out into the hall, she almost collided with Drake.

His hands reached out to steady her. "Finished lunch already?"

"No, I was just going back for my money."

He turned her toward the cafeteria once more. "Be my guest."

Michele hung back. "I'd really rather not."

"Why would that be?"

She raised her chin, mindful of his manner that morning. "I said I wasn't going to ask for special consideration and I meant it."

A smile twitched the corners of his firm mouth. "I scarcely think lunch in the cafeteria comes under that heading."

"Someone else might," she insisted stubbornly. "I don't want there to be any mistake concerning our relationship."

"I wasn't aware that we had one," he said dryly.

"We don't, and that's the way I'd like to keep it," she answered sharply.

"If you continue to look at me like an unwelcome bug in your salad, I think 'they,' whoever they are, will get the idea." His grip on her arm tightened. "Come on. If it will satisfy your sense of the proprieties, we'll talk business. You can tell me what headway you're making.''

Michele had no choice but to go along with him. Her soft mouth set mutinously as she pushed her tray down the counter, banging her cottage cheese and fruit plate down with unnecessary vigor.

''So that's how you keep your fantastic figure,'' Drake commented, reaching for a Waldorf salad to accompany his roast beef and mashed potatoes swimming in gravy. ''I wondered what your secret was.''

''The secret is aggravation,'' she snapped. ''Whenever I'm hungry, something happens to take my appetite away.'' Eyeing his loaded tray, she remarked acidly, ''I don't know how you can eat like that and keep *your* figure.''

''Thanks for the compliment,'' he mocked. ''I didn't think you noticed.''

She couldn't very well deny it. It would be a lie anyway. Michele was acutely conscious of the man next to her, of the male vitality that a sober business suit couldn't disguise. He vibrated with health and sexuality. Even his hands were masculine, the backs sprinkled with fine, dark hair.

''I was merely making an observation,'' she remarked coldly. ''Most men who work at a desk job have to watch their weight.''

''I get a lot of exercise outside the office.'' He grinned.

The knowledge that he was laughing at her goaded Michele unwisely. ''I wasn't aware that the indoor sort was that beneficial.''

''It depends on what problem needs remedying,'' he murmured. Eyeing her innocently, Drake added, ''Anyway, I don't think I specified the locale.''

Their arrival at the cashier's stand saved Michele from

the necessity of a reply. She braced herself for further innuendos when they sat down at a table, but Drake had evidently had his amusement. He asked about her work as he had promised.

"We're pinning great hopes on Chidactron. What's your thinking on the subject?"

Michele forgot all of her personal involvement with this exasperating man. "I think it's wonderful," she cried enthusiastically. "If it turns out to be what it seems, it will be a blessing."

"That's what we're all hoping. Clarice is especially interested."

The mention of Drake's paramour was like a bucket of cold water. "Yes, I suppose another fortune is never amiss," Michele commented acidly.

Drake's face set in stern lines. "I wish I had your omniscience, Michele. You're the only person I know who has complete faith in her own judgment."

He was clearly angered by any implied criticism of his ladylove. Well, that was too damn bad, Michele thought angrily, ignoring the tiny hurt the knowledge brought.

She lifted her head proudly. "What you find objectionable in my character is exactly what has enabled me to survive and provide for my daughter—without any help from anyone," she added pointedly.

Drake's stern expression softened somewhat. "I suppose that would account for it."

"I don't need explaining, Mr. Hollister. Anytime my work isn't up to expectations, you can fire me."

His face hardened once more. "You can count on it, Mrs. Carter."

When Michele started to get up, Drake stopped her. "Now that we've settled that point, there's no need for you to skip lunch. Sit down and let's try to find a subject we agree on."

Michele didn't want to make a scene so she did as he said. Her eyes were blazing, however, as she swallowed cottage cheese that tasted like sawdust. This was absolutely the last time she would subject herself to Drake Hollister's company.

"What do you think of Tim Fenwick?" he asked neutrally.

"He seems very pleasant," she replied distantly.

"More importantly, he's a damn good researcher. Tim needs experience, but when he gets it, I predict he's going places."

Michele kept her eyes on her plate. "I'll accept your word for it."

"That will be a first," Drake said, chuckling.

Her head jerked up, sparkling gray eyes spitting fire "Even when I agree with you, you're not satisfied! What can I do to please you?"

His gaze lingered on the delicate contours of her face. "Ask me that when I'm on my own time," he answered softly.

"Oh, I see! You mean you don't mind my abrasiveness outside the office."

"I'll have more time to smooth it out then," he replied calmly.

"There isn't that much time in the world!"

"Then I'll have to take a shortcut, won't I?" There was a veiled threat under his light words—or an unthinkable promise.

Michele felt the fine hairs on her arms rise. How could a man she disliked so much cause this strange flutter in her stomach? That made it all the more reprehensible. Sex without love was one of the urges of the lower animals. When her own marriage bed rose up to haunt her, Michele banished the thought resolutely.

Pushing her chair back, she stood up. "I'd better get back to my department before you give me a black mark for overstaying my lunch hour."

Drake looked at her steadily. "I told you I've never been accused of being unfair."

"Too bad your perfect record just came to an end," she snapped, turning around and marching out the door.

Michele went directly to Flora's house after work, hoping Corey's first day had been better than her own. When she heard her daughter's delighted laughter ringing out over Fluffy's excited barking, Michele's tense body started to relax. Her child's happiness was what really mattered.

Corey was not only happy, she was ecstatic. "Everybody was so nice to me, the teacher asked me to stand up in front of the whole class and tell all about Chicago, and Diane's mother asked me to sleep over this weekend. Can I, Mommy? Can I?" Corey finally stopped for breath.

"We'll talk about it at home, honey." Michele made a grab for the wildly wagging Fluffy. "Right now I think we'd better clear out of here and let Aunt Flora have a little peace and quiet."

"We're staying for dinner," Corey announced.

Flora overrode Michele's immediate protest. "What do you expect me to do with a whole great big pot roast? Besides, I didn't think you'd feel like cooking after your first day at work."

Michele shook her head helplessly. "How am I ever going to repay you?"

"Friends don't say things like that," Flora reproved her. "You look tired. Sit down and relax, put your feet up."

"Aunt Flora's going to take me with her to the foot doctor tomorrow," Corey was reminded.

"I've had the appointment for two weeks. If I cancel it, there's no telling when I'll get another," the older woman explained. "I hope it's all right with you."

Michele was deeply distressed. "Of course it's all right, but you shouldn't have to be bothered with Corey. I simply *have* to find someone to come in after school."

"That's the good news." Flora looked speculatively at Michele's drooping shoulders. "I was saving it to serve up with dessert, but I have a feeling you could use a little cheer about now. Did you have a hard day?"

"It was okay," Michele answered briefly. "What were you saying about good news?"

"I think I found someone to be here when Corey comes home."

"Who?" Michele demanded breathlessly. "Is it someone you know? Someone who can be trusted?"

"Absolutely. I've known Carole since she was born— Carole Spellman is her name. I don't know why I didn't think of her before. She goes to college over in Heraldsburg, just a few miles from here."

"But if she goes to school herself, she isn't free during the day."

"Her classes are over before Corey's; I checked with her." Flora restored hope to Michele's dejected face. "She's very interested. She can really use the money, and I think you'll like her. Carole always was a sweet little thing."

"If you can vouch for her, I'll *love* her," Michele cried extravagantly.

"Good, then that's all settled. We can eat."

After dinner Michele and Flora sat over coffee while Corey took Fluffy for a walk.

"Tell me about your day," Flora urged.

"It was all right." When that sounded faintly negative, Michele added, "Things are always a little confusing at first."

"I don't suppose George was any help," the other woman commented dryly.

"I didn't ask for any." George was a lost cause; Tim was the one Michele wanted to find out about. "You know everybody, Flora; what can you tell me about Tim Fenwick?"

"He's another hometown boy—so's his wife, Polly."

"Are all Blaylock's employees local people?"

"Pretty much. They're either from Greenfield or one of the little towns around here; except for you and Drake—and Clarice Blaylock, of course."

"Do you think they resent outsiders being brought in to fill managerial positions?"

Flora shrugged. "I guess some do, and some don't. I shouldn't think Tim would, if that's what you're driving at. He seems to take things pretty much in his stride—except when it comes to Polly. Tim worships that girl, and rightly so. Too bad they can't seem to have children."

Michele showed her surprise. "I gathered they didn't want any."

"Where did you get that idea? They've been trying for years. Polly's had several miscarriages but she won't give up. I heard just the other day that she's pregnant again. Maybe this time they'll be lucky, please Lord."

It just goes to show that you shouldn't jump to conclusions, Michele thought. She was to learn that lesson more than once in the days to come.

The next few days were uneventful. George's sullenness and veiled remarks were unpleasant, yet nothing Michele couldn't handle. Drake was no problem either, mainly because she didn't see him.

Michele went home for lunch those days, utilizing the time to straighten the house and organize things for dinner. It was always such a rush in the morning, and again at night. It seemed as though she was *always* in a rush. By the time the beds were made, the table set for dinner and a few other little chores accomplished, there was only time for a quick snack at the kitchen sink. Remembering Drake's remark about the way she kept her figure, Michele smiled grimly. A single, working mother, with no help, didn't have to worry about her weight.

When the phone rang in the middle of the afternoon, Michele wasn't prepared for the velvety voice that announced, "This is Clarice Blaylock."

"Oh . . . I . . . you must have been given the wrong extension."

"Not at all. This is Ms. Carter, isn't it?" When Michele confirmed the fact, the woman continued, "I've been wanting to call you. Drake—Mr. Hollister—has told me such a lot about you. I'm really quite intrigued."

Michele couldn't imagine an experienced man like Drake committing such a tactical error—except to make his ladylove jealous? The nerve of the man to try and use Michele in his power play! She wanted to assure the woman that she'd only be interested in Drake Hollister if he were stuffed!

"He must have exaggerated," Michele answered coolly, repressing her anger. "I'm really quite ordinary."

"I doubt that seriously. Research chemistry is rather an unusual field for a woman, isn't it?"

Michele wondered if Mrs. Blaylock suspected Drake of a less than professional reason in hiring her. "I think you'll find that I'm completely qualified," she replied stiffly.

The soft, rich chuckle that greeted her statement confused Michele. "I don't doubt it for a minute," Clarice assured her.

"I'm glad you realize that I . . . I have quite a background in research," Michele said uncertainly. "As a matter of fact, I must have been the most highly qualified applicant, because Mr. Hollister didn't really want to hire a woman." It was important for her job security that Mrs. Blaylock understand that.

"You don't say?" Clarice murmured cynically.

"I'd be happy to have you examine my résumé," Michele told her doggedly.

"I already have," the wife of the president of Blaylock assured her, making Michele even more uneasy. "For such a young woman, you've accomplished a great deal."

"Thank you," Michele answered warily.

"I'd like to talk to you further about your work. As a matter of fact, that's why I'm calling. Mr. Blaylock and I would like you to come for dinner on Friday night."

Put that way, the invitation was a royal command, one that Michele couldn't very well refuse. She felt renewed sympathy for the early Christians who had been invited to a feast—for the lions.

Offering a feeble protest that she knew was doomed, Michele said, "That's very kind of you, but I'll have to see if I can get a baby-sitter. I have a young daughter."

"So I've been told. I'm sure you can find someone, though." Clarice dismissed it with the carelessness of one who has never found servants a problem. "Will seven-thirty be convenient?"

"I . . . yes, that would be fine."

Better to get it over with now than to have it hanging over her head. The sooner she convinced Mrs. Blaylock that she was no threat, the more peaceful her life would be. Besides, Michele had to admit she was curious about the woman. It might even be an interesting evening. Clarice's next words took care of that notion.

"Drake will pick you up," she said.

"No!" Michele cried sharply, before she could stop herself. "I mean I . . . I have my own car. It would be out of Mr. Hollister's way."

"Nothing is very far in this little town," Clarice replied, with a flick of disdain. "That's settled then. We'll see you on Friday at seven-thirty."

Michele hung up with a distasteful feeling of having been manipulated. If she'd known Drake was coming, she would have found some way of refusing. It was bad enough to know she was being summoned for inspection. Did Mrs. Blaylock want to see them together so she could decide how far things had progressed?

If the situation weren't so insupportable, it might have had elements of humor. Watching Drake walk a tightrope would be very gratifying. He had to pay Clarice enough attention to reassure her without arousing her husband's suspicion, and his manner toward Michele had to be just the proper mixture of courtesy and disinterest—neither of which he'd shown her so far. Michele's grim smile faded. Damn Drake Hollister anyway! She didn't want to be involved in his sordid affairs.

Her ill humor was evident when Drake called on the interoffice phone a little later.

"Is something wrong?" he asked.

Michele went right to the point. "I suppose you know that your . . . that Mrs. Blaylock invited me to dinner tomorrow night."

"What's the matter, don't you have anything to wear?" he teased.

Michele ignored that as being unworthy of an answer. "She very kindly offered your services, but they won't be necessary."

"Maybe you'd better tell me what those services are," he remarked innocently. "I always like to do what's expected of me."

Michele gritted her teeth. "I think you'd better knock off the innuendos, Mr. Hollister. You might forget yourself and continue them at the Blaylocks'."

Drake seemed to be laughing at a private joke. "Do you really think that's likely?"

"No, I suppose not," Michele answered coldly. "What I was trying to say was, you needn't pick me up tomorrow night. I'd prefer to take my own car."

"But my . . . that is, Mrs. Blaylock," he mocked Michele's earlier slip, "has instructed me to call for you. I try never to disagree with her on trivial matters."

Michele threatened to choke on her indignation. "Well, thanks a heap! It's nice to know what you think of me."

"I wasn't aware that you were the subject," he commented artlessly. "I thought we were discussing transportation to a dinner party." Before Michele could explode, Drake said, "I'll pick you up at seven-fifteen, that will give us plenty of time to get to the Blaylocks'." He hung up, leaving her to fume impotently the rest of the afternoon.

Michele's last escape route was sealed when she got home from work that night. It had occurred to her that if Flora were busy, she would have a legitimate excuse for phoning her regrets. There was no one else she could call on.

Corey greeted her with unwelcome news. "When Mrs. Pennington came to pick up Diane this afternoon, she asked if I could go home with them after school tomorrow and stay all day Saturday. Please say it's all right, Mommy."

Michele saw her last hope slipping away. "Are you sure you weren't the one who suggested it?"

"No, honestly, she invited me."

Michele couldn't bear to extinguish the happy anticipation on her daughter's face. "Well, I guess it will be all right."

The house seemed very quiet when Michele got home from work the next night. Even Fluffy's ecstatic greeting didn't dispel the emptiness. Was this the face of the future? When Corey grew up and left the nest, was this what she had to look forward to? Michele pushed the disquieting thought to the back of her mind. She had more immediate problems tonight.

The luxurious bubble bath she ran for herself was so relaxing that she stayed in it too long. When Michele wandered into the bedroom wrapped in a towel, a shocked look at the clock sent her scurrying. Fortunately her makeup didn't take long; just a touch of mascara on her long, thick lashes, and a slick of lip gloss that turned her mouth rosy. Michele's translucent skin didn't require anything else.

After hurriedly slipping into a simple red silk sheath that clung lovingly to her curves, she clasped a wide belt with a gold buckle around her small waist. There was no time to do anything elaborate with her hair, so she pulled the sides back with two little combs and let it cascade down in a rippling fall of shining waves. She had just stepped into a pair of high-heeled sandals when the doorbell rang.

Michele's heart gave a sudden lurch, annoying her greatly. This was just another evening, more difficult than most perhaps, but nothing she couldn't handle. Lifting her head high, she took a deep breath and went to open the door.

Spotlighted by the porch light, Drake looked more handsome than she had ever seen him. The dark suit called attention to his wide shoulders and narrow hips. Underneath the trappings of civilization was a supple, powerful male body capable of giving untold pleasure.

Michele's cheeks turned scarlet at the unbidden thought. "Won't you . . . would you like to come in?"

A flame lit Drake's blue eyes, turning them brilliant as they wandered over Michele's exquisite face and enticing body. "I'd like it very much, but I think we'd better go." He took the coat that was over her arm, draping it across her shoulders. When his long fingers lifted her hair over the collar, Michele shivered involuntarily. "We wouldn't want to be late, would we?" he asked.

"No, of course not," Michele murmured.

To her relief, he was on his good behavior, making polite conversation as they drove across town to the exclusive section where the Blaylocks lived. It was a neighborhood of large homes surrounded by well-tended acres studded with trees.

"You're in for a treat tonight," Drake commented. "Dinner at the Blaylocks' is a memorable experience." Ignoring Michele's pointed silence, he continued, "They have a fantastic French chef. I can't imagine how Clarice lured him to a little town like Greenfield."

"She sounds like a very persuasive lady," Michele commented dryly. "Of course I imagine she uses different tactics depending on the person—and what her objective is."

Drake's chuckle had a deep, male sound. "Don't you think that's true of all of us?"

"I wouldn't like to think so," Michele replied distantly. "It sounds rather devious."

His smile was mocking. "It seems to me you're very quick to believe the worst of people."

Before Michele could answer what she considered his completely unfounded accusation, they turned into a circular driveway set in a velvety green lawn. The large, Tudor-style mansion facing the drive was very impressive. It was three stories tall, with mellow brick walls partially covered with ivy. The bottom floor was brightly lit, and music floated out through the diamond-paned windows.

As Drake helped her out of the car, Michele unconsciously took a deep breath, preparing herself for the ordeal ahead.

Unexpectedly, Drake's arm went around her rigid shoulders. Drawing her against the lean length of his hard body, he smiled into her tense face. "I think you're due for a surprise."

What was that supposed to mean? Was he trying to prepare her for something? As Drake reached for the doorbell, Michele had the panicky feeling that she was about to take part in a compelling drama, without knowing what her lines were.

Chapter Four

*M*ichele and Drake were ushered into the Blaylock house by the first butler she had ever seen outside of the movies. He showed them into a long room that was furnished with elegance and taste.

Great bowls of flowers were artfully placed on polished tables, echoing the soft colors of the imported print covering numerous couches and chairs. Graceful French doors along the far wall led to a torchlit terrace that was like an outdoor living room.

Michele registered all these details before their hostess came forward to greet them. After that, Clarice Blaylock commanded her full attention.

The former actress was tall and willowy, with impeccably coiffed dark hair framing patrician features. If she was in her early fifties, as Flora said, she certainly didn't look it. The wine-colored silk caftan swirled around a still-sexy figure. With a reluctant feeling of admiration, Michele began to understand Drake's attraction to the older woman.

Clarice's trained voice was throaty as she greeted the newcomers, extending a slender hand dominated by a huge cabochon ruby surrounded by glittering diamonds. "It's so nice to meet you, Mrs. Carter." Her gaze was as frankly appraising as Michele's.

"It was kind of you to ask me," Michele murmured dutifully.

Clarice's dark eyes moved to Drake, her expression changing. "And of course it's always good to see you, darling."

He leaned forward, kissing her cheek. With his dark head poised over hers, Drake said mockingly, "But sometimes better than others, isn't that so?"

Their eyes met in a shared understanding as Michele stood by, appalled. How could they carry on like that right under her husband's nose? She stole an involuntary glance at the tall, white-haired man leaning against the mantel.

Simon Blaylock was big without being fat, although age had blurred his waistline somewhat. His ruddy face glowed with health, and the piercing blue eyes looked as though they missed very little. Except where his wife was concerned, Michele decided, noticing the fatuous expression directed at Clarice. Didn't he see what was perfectly obvious?

Simon approached the trio, clasping Drake warmly on the shoulder while conferring a smile on Michele. "I've been anticipating this meeting as much as my wife," he said with courtly manners. "Your credentials were most impressive."

"Enough to impress even Drake." Clarice directed an unreadable look at the younger man. "You did say that, didn't you, darling?"

Michele seethed with anger she didn't allow to show. The woman didn't believe it for a minute. She thought Drake had hired her for her big gray eyes! She slanted a controlled glare at him, but he was frowning at Clarice. Even Drake recognized that she was going too far. There were uncomfortable undercurrents in the atmosphere. Only Simon seemed oblivious to them.

"You two will have plenty of time to discuss the matter later—as I've no doubt you'll do at great length." He grinned at his wife and Drake as though they were favorite children. "Why don't you take Michele to meet the others?" Simon instructed his wife.

"You're right as usual, my dear," Clarice told her husband sweetly. Giving Drake an entirely different look she said, "But don't think you've heard the last of this."

Although Simon Blaylock chose to take it as a joke, Michele felt chilled. She prided herself on being a thoroughly competent professional. Could her job actually be jeopardized by a jealous woman? It took an effort to force her attention back to the other couple in the room.

Tim and Polly Fenwick might have been brother and sister. They had the same light brown hair and young, guileless expressions. They were like two grown-up Barbie dolls, Michele thought, wholesome and friendly.

Polly's hazel eyes roamed over Michele with interest. "You're as lovely as Tim said you were."

It was a nice compliment, but Michele could have done without it in Clarice's hearing. "He was just being kind," she assured Polly. "Those white lab coats aren't exactly the last word in chic."

"Men don't care how they look at work," Clarice noted impatiently. "Why should women?"

"Because they have a natural advantage—they're prettier." Tim's eyes were filled with merriment as he glanced at his wife. "Not that I ever notice, naturally. I leave the ogling to bachelors like Drake."

Polly smiled fondly at him. "You're a big faker, but I don't mind—as long as you restrict yourself to looking. Besides, Drake is more Michele's type. Don't you agree, Clarice?"

Michele realized what a great actress the older woman was when Clarice gave her a smile that might have been genuine. "You'll have to watch out for Polly, she's an inveterate matchmaker."

Michele gratefully seized the golden opportunity that had been presented to her. "I'm afraid she's doomed to failure with me. Between my daughter and my work, I don't have time for men."

Clarice's raised eyebrows indicated cynicism, but before she could comment, Polly said, "Tim told me about your little girl. Does she like Greenfield? It must be quite a change after Chicago."

"I was worried about that," Michele admitted. "Mostly because we didn't know a soul here. But my neighbor has been very kind, and Corey has made friends in school."

"That's a pretty name," Polly said softly. She reached for her husband's hand. "I hope our baby is a girl, although I suppose that's selfish of me. I guess Tim wants a son, even though he doesn't say so."

The love on his face was blinding. "All I care about is that you're okay."

"She's going to be fine, and the baby is too," Clarice said briskly. "Simon and I have waited long enough to be godparents."

"I can just imagine how you're going to spoil her," Polly

teased. "And when she's utterly impossible, you'll get up and go home."

"That's the province of godparents," Clarice asserted. "I didn't have time to spoil my own, so now I'm going to indulge myself."

Michele tried to keep the surprise out of her voice. "You have children?"

"A grown son." Clarice laughed, her dark eyes sparkling. "Just don't ask his age because I barely admit to being that old myself."

"You're ageless, Clarice," Polly told her fondly. "You could go back to the theater tomorrow."

"What's all this subversive talk?" Simon and Drake had joined them. The older man cupped his wife's chin in his palm, gazing down at her admiringly. "Nothing and nobody is going to take this lady away from me."

Michele admired Clarice's performance as the actress exchanged a long, loving look with her husband. "Why would I want to get away?" she murmured in a throaty voice.

"That sounds remarkably unliberated," Drake commented sardonically.

Tim grinned. "Here it comes—round forty or fifty. It's at least that, isn't it?"

"You might as well know, Michele, that my wife and Drake wage the battle of liberated woman versus male chauvinist every time they're together," Simon said. "Neither ever convinces the other, but that doesn't deter them."

"All the zest would go out of life if they ever agreed." Tim chuckled.

"You make it sound as though we just enjoy arguing," Clarice protested. "I happen to think women's rights are a matter of great importance."

"All of which you have in great abundance," Drake commented derisively.

"What difference does it make if I benefit personally? It's a simple matter of justice," Clarice stated firmly. "Why shouldn't a woman get equal pay for an equal job?"

He frowned at her. "I've never denied that."

"No, you just don't want to hire one in the first place!"

"That's not fair. I only—"

"Have an hors d'oeuvre." Simon broke up the budding argument, indicating the uniformed maid offering a tray of tempting morsels. His smile included both of them. "What is it kids say?—lighten up. Polly and Tim are used to your antics, but Michele is going to think this is a serious disagreement."

"It is," Clarice asserted. She smiled warmly at Drake. "How anyone as utterly charming in every other way can have such a blind spot is beyond my comprehension."

He grinned back at her. "And how anyone as completely bewitching can have such a stubborn streak baffles *me*."

Clarice raised an arched eyebrow. "I wouldn't mention the word stubborn if I were you. You still haven't admitted I was right and you were wrong."

Drake's eyes flicked briefly to Michele. "It's too early for the final results to be tabulated."

Suddenly Michele realized that this was no longer an abstract, ongoing controversy. That inadvertent glance of Drake's was revealing. Were they actually arguing over her? Was it possible that Clarice was her unknown friend at court? If that were so, it changed the whole picture. Clarice wouldn't have insisted that Drake hire her if the two were having an affair. Even as the thought brought a strange satisfaction, Michele realized that her reasoning was faulty.

The profession of research chemistry was apt to conjure up images of earnest women with untidy graying hair and thick glasses. Suppose that's what Clarice expected to get? There were just too many unexplained insinuations. It was all very confusing. Michele suppressed her turbulent thoughts as she realized that Simon was addressing her.

"As you can see, Blaylock is like a big family—we even have our little squabbles."

Clarice linked her arm through Drake's. "But we always kiss and make up, don't we, darling?"

His firm mouth twitched at the corners as he glanced at Michele's set face. "In a manner of speaking."

"We're very glad that you joined us, Michele," Simon continued. "I hope you'll enjoy living in Greenfield."

"Thank you, I'm sure I shall," Michele murmured insincerely. "As long as my daughter Corey is happy, that's really all that matters."

"Drake says she's a dear," Clarice remarked.

"He's been very kind," Michele admitted, thinking again what a complex man Drake was.

"Yes, he's very fond of children." Clarice laughed. "That might be the only way some determined woman will get him to the altar."

"I thought I was supposed to be the matchmaker," Polly teased.

"When the right girl comes along, Drake won't need anyone's help in making up his mind," Simon stated.

"Dear romantic Simon," Clarice patted his cheek. "He believes for every man there's a woman."

"I hope more than one," Tim chuckled. "Otherwise, Drake has made off with a lot of other men's property."

"Will you tell me how I got to be the subject of

conversation?'' Drake complained. "Why don't you all turn your talents to Michele? She might welcome them more than I."

"You really *are* a male chauvinist, aren't you?" Michele's eyes flashed gray fire. "What makes you think I either want or need a man?"

"Good for you!" Clarice bobbed her head emphatically. "The days of the helpless shrinking violet are over. In case you men haven't noticed, there's been a sexual revolution."

Drake held up his hands. "If I may be permitted a word in my own defense, I merely meant that the role of a single parent must be difficult."

"I can handle it," Michele assured him grimly. "Just as I can handle working in a man's world."

Simon touched his wife on the shoulder, indicating the patient maid standing in the doorway. "I think dinner is served. And not a moment too soon," he told Drake. "You're lucky they're letting you eat with us."

"Only to keep the numbers even," Clarice informed him loftily.

Although Michele was still stiff with resentment, the others dismissed the subject as they strolled into the lovely dining room that looked like an illustration in an expensive magazine.

A gleaming mahogany table was set with white cutwork linen placemats holding Coalport service plates in an intricate floral pattern of pink and maroon. They were flanked by sterling flatware and sparkling crystal wineglasses. The color scheme was carried out in a low silver bowl filled with blood red roses, white stephanotis, and pink daisies. Tall candles cast a soft glow, and muted music formed an unobtrusive background to the effortless conversation. Michele couldn't help relaxing in the beautiful atmosphere.

After the wine had been poured Simon raised his glass to Clarice, who was sitting at the opposite end of the table. "I wish to propose a toast to my wife, who is at least a part-time magician. How she ever lured a chef like Jacques to Greenfield, I can't imagine."

"It wasn't at all difficult," she assured him. "Every month I just cash a small annuity."

He shook his head. "Money buys a great deal, but not devotion. I, above all men, know that, my love."

Michele turned troubled eyes on her host. What was he saying? Clarice had turned out to be so different from what she expected, so natural and unaffected. Yet Simon seemed to be implying something else. That Clarice had married him for his money? In that case it was possible after all that she and Drake were involved, in spite of their arguments.

"Still have reservations?" Drake's low voice sounded close to Michele's ear. "You're a hard lady to convince." Turning to Simon, he said casually, "Tell Michele about your courtship of Clarice. Women love romance."

Simon smiled reminiscently. "It was a rocky road, I can tell you. Clarice's friends were telling her she'd be a fool to give up her career, and my friends warned me I'd never keep such an exotic bird in a small cage like Greenfield."

Michele smothered a gasp as Clarice added dryly, "They also said I was marrying you for your money."

Simon gave her a rueful look. "They didn't know I'd already tried to buy you, and it didn't work."

"Now who's being the dramatic one in the family?" Clarice teased her husband. "It wasn't really like that," she told Michele.

"It was a blatant bribe and I'm not ashamed of it," Simon asserted. "I'm just sorry you wouldn't take it. We could have had an extra year of marriage."

"We had some memorable visits anyway," Clarice answered softly.

Something electric flared between them as they stared into each other's eyes, oblivious to the others for the moment. Michele's throat felt constricted as she recognized real love. Whatever conclusions she'd drawn had been false.

"Don't keep Michele hanging," Polly protested. "Tell her the rest of the story."

"Clarice was under contract to do a play for a producer who was all washed up," Simon continued. "He'd had a string of hits, followed by three disasters. Nobody would even take his phone calls—until he got Clarice's name on a contract."

Michele looked at the older woman in perplexity. "But you must have been able to pick and choose. Why would you take a chance with someone who was on the skids?"

"He was an old friend, and I was his last hope," Clarice answered simply.

Drake's blue eyes were filled with admiration. "If you're very fortunate, you'll find out what friendship means to Clarice."

"Really, don't you think you're all overdoing it?" she asked wryly. "I'm tempted to scoop the roses out of the bowl and stand up and take a bow."

"Don't listen to her," Simon ordered. "She *was* taking a chance; everyone advised against it. I wanted to buy up her contract, but she wouldn't let me. I even offered to back the show if she'd leave and marry me."

"Was it a flop?" Michele asked uncertainly.

"No, that's the romantic part," Polly contributed eagerly. "The play won a Tony award, but Clarice left as soon as the rave reviews and advance ticket sales showed it was a hit."

"Now that Michele has heard the story of our lives, don't you think we should pay attention to Jacques's magnificent creation?" Clarice asked dryly.

Michele was having trouble switching her attention to the huge silver tray that held a clutch of golden brown pheasants nestled on a bed of wild rice. The small, dark Frenchman had brought in the main course himself, proudly displaying his artistry. But Michele's praise was mechanical. She was too confused by the collapse of all her preconceived ideas.

Drake's sardonic voice was pitched too low for the others to hear. "Don't tell me I detect doubt on that lovely face? Surely you can't be admitting you were guilty of rushing to judgment?"

"If I was, you aren't exactly blameless yourself." She scowled at him. "You have a lot of explaining to do, Drake Hollister!"

"Gladly." He smiled into her angry eyes. "Shall we save it until we're alone? Just in case we can't think of anything better to do." The look on his face was wholly male.

Michele gritted her teeth. "I hope you're not getting any ideas, because I haven't changed my mind about *you*."

"That's because you don't know me well enough yet," Drake answered calmly. Raising his voice he said, "Polly, tell Michele how lovable I am."

"That wouldn't do any good," Tim joked. "Polly sees a little good in everyone."

Clarice's eyes were speculative as they rested on Michele

and Drake. "As long as you're not looking for husband material, he's really quite pleasant to have around."

Drake raised one eyebrow. "That's what's called damning with faint praise."

"You do want me to be truthful, don't you, darling?" Clarice drawled.

"How is the poor guy going to answer a question like that?" Tim chuckled. "I think you ought to get off Drake's case. If you want to straighten out some bachelor's life, why don't you pick on George Browder?"

Clarice's generous mouth turned down at the corners. "That dreadful man. I can't for the life of me see why you keep him on, Drake."

Drake's face became expressionless. "He's competent at the job he's doing."

"George Browder has the approximate appeal of an open grave," Clarice stated distastefully. "How do you stand him, Michele?"

"We haven't had any problems," Michele replied carefully, conscious of Drake's penetrating regard.

"It's only a matter of time," Clarice assured her. "The man's a troublemaker. He'll cause a lot of grief some day."

"I think you're exaggerating." Tim tried to put in a good word for a colleague. "I'll admit George wouldn't win any personality contests, but he isn't vicious or anything."

Clarice remained unconvinced. "Polly isn't the only trusting soul in your family."

"This is a dinner party, my dear, not a board meeting." Simon's comment was made gently, yet with firmness behind it.

When Clarice accepted his directive with only a slight grimace, Michele looked at her host with renewed interest.

He had seemed a rather passive figure until now, letting his wife and Drake share the center stage. Suddenly Michele realized it was through choice, not weakness. Simon and Clarice Blaylock were indeed a fascinating couple. There was only one more thing Michele wanted to know.

"Did you find it difficult to adjust to small-town living after the glamor of Broadway?" she asked Clarice.

"It would be foolish to say I don't miss some of the things New York has to offer. But I've made a full life for myself right here. Anyone who finds life dull, no matter where she lives, is either lazy or stupid."

Polly grinned at Michele. "Clarice is a demon organizer. She'll have you on one of her committees before you can think of a way to decline gracefully."

Clarice was eyeing Michele speculatively. "As a matter of fact, I was thinking of several things she might be interested in—the new research library as a start."

"Leave her some time to help me with the nursery," Polly pleaded. "I really could use your advice, Michele."

A warm feeling flooded Michele at this evidence of acceptance. She had felt so alone, counting Flora as her only friend. This one short evening had opened up a whole new vista. Her eyes were shining as she turned and saw Drake watching her, an enigmatic expression on his handsome face.

Michele's euphoria faded. There was still Drake—her nemesis. In spite of his polished charm tonight, she wasn't fooled. Drake was a very macho man. He had been forced to bend to Clarice's will, but he would never accept Michele. Looking at the deceptively relaxed pose of that long-limbed, lithe body, she felt a shiver of apprehension. If he confined his subtle warfare to the laboratory, Michele knew she could hold her own. It was his extracurricular attacks that were the dangerous ones.

Driving home after the party Michele felt her tension building, although Drake's behavior couldn't be faulted. He was pleasant without being personal. It didn't reassure her. Would he have the nerve to try to kiss her when he walked her to the door?

She stole a look at his strong profile, sharply etched by the light from the dashboard. Without wanting to, Michele noticed how well shaped his dark head was. The high cheekbones and clean jawline resembled the sculpted likeness on a Roman coin. Her eyes were drawn inexorably to the firm, chiseled mouth. Michele knew intuitively that it would be warm against her own, parting her lips with persuasion, not demand. She drew a sharp breath, wrapping her arms around her body.

Drake turned his head to glance at her briefly. "It's surprising how soon the nights turn chilly. Are you cold?"

"No, I . . . no," she concluded lamely.

"What is it, Michele? You're very quiet."

"I was just thinking . . . about the Blaylocks. They're quite unique."

Drake grinned. "I told you that you were due for a surprise."

"You set me up for it." She scowled, remembering Drake's deliberate deception. "Why did you lead me to believe that Clarice—that you and she—"

"Were having an affair," Drake finished calmly. "I didn't. It was entirely your own fabrication."

"Well, you said—" Michele stopped, trying to remember exactly what had made her so certain.

"I said she was a lovely lady and you reminded me a lot

of her." He stopped the car in front of Michele's house, going around to open her door.

"There was a lot more to it than that," she declared.

"Tell me how I incriminated myself?" He walked her up the path, taking the key from her clenched hand.

Michele was so indignant she didn't even realize he had followed her inside. "You knew perfectly well what I was thinking! You could have set the record straight if you'd wanted to."

"Unless you're asked, it's a little difficult to come right out and say, 'I'm not having an affair with my boss's wife.'"

Michele's mind scurried frantically, trying to find justification for her suspicions. With a sinking feeling, she realized that her certainty was based more on a desire to believe the worst than on fact. Flora's good-natured gossip, plus Michele's own wariness of Drake's blatant masculinity, had led her up the garden path. There was no way she was going to own up to it, however.

Thrusting out her rounded chin, she glared up at him. "What was I supposed to believe when you admitted that you even dressed to please Clarice? You said you wanted to keep her happy."

"That's not exactly what I said, but we won't quibble." He tucked a shining strand of hair in back of her ear in a gesture that was subtly sensuous. "I once told you I'm a man who likes to give pleasure."

Michele was suddenly aware that they were alone in an empty house. How had she allowed this to happen after vowing to be on her guard? Michele forced herself to relax. She was a mature woman, and Drake was a civilized man who would certainly accept no for an answer. Not that he had made any real move. Men and women sparred like this all the time. It was only because of her own inexperience that she was making such a big deal of it.

Michele moved gracefully away. "You'd give me great pleasure if you'd leave now. It's been a long day."

He leaned against the door, regarding her with concealed amusement, as though he knew how he affected her. "You owe me a saucer of milk."

"Surely you can't want milk after all that wine."

"I'd settle for coffee," he admitted. "You also asked me in when I came to pick you up. Surely you're not going back on *two* offers?"

"I was only being polite, and you don't want coffee anyway."

"I wouldn't mind a cup, but what I'd really like is to spend some time with you."

"We were together all evening."

"That isn't what I meant and you know it. I want to get to know you." His eyes narrowed appraisingly. "You're such a private person, Michele. I catch these tantalizing little glimpses that make me want to find out more."

Michele avoided his penetrating regard. "I'll make some coffee," she murmured.

Drake crossed the room swiftly. His firm grip on her slender shoulders prevented escape. "You're slipping away again." He searched the lovely face that held a hint of panic. "Why won't you let anyone get close to you, Michele—or is it only me?" he concluded softly.

Michele was nerve-shatteringly aware of the tall man standing so close that she could feel the heat of his body. One step would put her in his arms. The temptation was swift and inexplicable. When a soft sigh escaped her parted lips, Drake caught his breath sharply. The increased pressure of his hands on her shoulders released Michele from the spell.

She reacted like a frightened doe, turning quickly toward the kitchen. "Will instant coffee be all right?" she asked breathlessly. "I think it's all I have."

To her great relief he let her go, although he followed her into the kitchen. Lounging against one of the tall, built-in cabinets that separated the kitchen from the breakfast area, Drake rested his chin on his crossed arms, watching Michele's hectic activity. She avoided looking at him as she got out the teakettle and filled it with water, aware, nonetheless, of those fathomless blue eyes that seemed to be searching out her innermost secrets. It made her so nervous that the cups she was reaching for clattered in their saucers.

With the silent, lithe movement of a leopard, Drake was at her side. Michele stiffened instinctively as his arms went around her, drawing her tense body against the unyielding hardness of his own.

When she raised her head to protest, Drake's mouth covered hers, taking her breath away. He ignored the soft sounds of denial, gently tracing her trembling lips with the tip of his tongue. She quivered as he deepened the penetration, probing the moist, secret place in a sensuous exploration. The confident male aggression demanded a response that Michele was powerless to refuse.

Her body became pliant in his arms. The strong column of his thighs absorbed the weight of her suddenly nerveless legs, making her achingly aware of his masculinity. With a sigh of surrender, Michele wound her arms around Drake's neck, murmuring his name as she returned his kiss with pent-up passion.

His arms tightened for a moment, his fingers tangling almost fiercely in her long, silken hair. Then, inexplicably, he dragged his mouth away, pressing her head against his solid shoulder and touching his lips to her temple in a featherlight caress.

After a long moment, he said gently, "Now you can relax."

She looked up at him in bewilderment, wondering numbly why he was rejecting her. "I . . . I don't understand."

He removed his arms, tipping her chin up and smiling ruefully into her dazzled eyes. "Ever since we left the party you've been worrying about whether I was going to kiss you. Now you don't have to think about it anymore."

Michele's brain was starting to function again, leaving her appalled at her own unbridled response. How could he have breached her defenses so easily? Anger started to burn brightly as she realized that, to make matters worse, it had only been a joke to him.

Her cheeks were flaming as she jerked her chin away. "That's the most insufferably conceited thing I ever heard!"

His raised eyebrow mocked her. "You mean you weren't wondering? That kiss was all a waste?"

"It was worse than that. It was . . . it was insulting!"

"Strange," he mused. "I could have sworn you were enjoying it."

"Get out of my house, Drake Hollister!" Michele stormed. The teakettle chose that moment to whistle hysterically, echoing her mood.

"I haven't had my coffee yet," he replied calmly.

"You don't honestly think I'd sit down and have coffee with you now?" Michele's outrage was reflected in every line of her taut body.

Drake's firm mouth tilted in a taunting smile. "Unless you want me to think I disturb you so greatly you don't trust yourself around me."

"That's the most . . . I . . . you have to be kidding!" she was almost stuttering with rage.

"In that case we'll have a quiet chat and get to know each other better."

Michele watched helplessly as he reached for the jar of instant coffee and spooned some into each cup. "I don't *want* to know you better," she wailed.

"Because I'm your boss and you don't believe in mixing business and pleasure?" He picked up the cups and started for the breakfast room, leaving her no choice but to follow.

"That's one reason. Another is that we're like components of a combustible mixture. There always seems to be an explosion when we're together."

"Why do you think that is, Michele?" he asked softly.

She sensed the trap, refusing to walk into it. "It has nothing to do with sex. I'd feel the same about any other male as chauvinistic as you."

"How about one who isn't?"

"What do you mean?"

"You've been widowed for four years. How many men have you known in that time?"

Michele gasped, color flooding her fair skin. "How dare you ask me a question like that?"

"It's remarkably personal," he agreed. "But a normal woman would tell me to mind my own damn business, not react as though the very idea was abhorrent."

Michele's gray eyes darkened to pewter. "Are you saying I'm not normal?"

"That's a hard question to answer." He searched her

lovely, flushed face, his gaze lingering on the soft mouth that was compressed now. "I know you aren't frigid. It was a possibility that had occurred to me."

"So you conducted an experiment to find out!" she cried angrily.

He ignored her anger. "What was your husband like, Michele?"

Frustration threatened to overwhelm her. "Why are you asking me all these personal questions?"

"What was he like?" Drake waited inexorably.

She stared into her cooling coffee, resisting the memories that arose. But Drake was implacable. "I told you. He was a college history professor."

"That would make him quite a bit older than you," Drake mused. "How did you meet?"

Michele sighed. Since he was obviously going to pursue the subject, she might as well get it over with. "I was one of his students. It was in my junior year. We started to go out together, and at the end of the term we were married." If she thought that would satisfy Drake, Michele was mistaken.

"Did you finish college? You must have," he corrected himself, "to get your degree in chemistry."

"I did, but not right away. By the time school started again in September, I was pregnant with Corey. It wasn't until she was a year old that I went back for my diploma."

Drake's eyes narrowed. "Was it ambition that drove you—or your husband?"

She found that bitterly amusing. "It was entirely my own idea. Gary would have preferred that I stay home."

That was putting it mildly. It didn't begin to hint at the acrimonious quarrels they'd had. Gary couldn't understand why Michele needed anything but him to fill her world. He had even considered the advent of Corey to be solely Michele's fault.

Gary Carter had been a narrow, petty man, in spite of his degrees. He had lived all his life in the cloistered atmosphere of a small college, where his vanity was fed by the adulation of his female students. He'd been a romantic figure on campus, feeding the legend by dressing the part in silk ascots and tweed jackets with a pipe sticking out of the breast pocket. Michele was only one of the co-eds who had routinely developed a crush on him. But her haunting beauty had caught his eye.

She'd been only twenty, too young to distinguish between infatuation and love. And too inexperienced to know anything about sex. The physical side of her marriage had never been spectacular, and as she struggled toward her own identity, it had deteriorated into a duty—an obligation Gary had exacted whenever Michele needed to study for an exam, or if he considered that Corey had claimed her attention unduly.

"Was he a father figure, Michele? Is that why you run from younger men?" Drake persisted.

"I can assure you I never regarded him as a father," she stated grimly.

"But I notice you don't deny running away from love. Hasn't there been anyone in four years who succeeded in melting the wall of ice you've encased your emotions in?"

Michele thought of the dates she'd had, of the revulsion she'd felt when they had made advances to her. It always conjured up Gary's selfish lovemaking. Until tonight. Where had that flame of responsiveness come from—that molten feeling of being on the brink of an ecstasy she could only guess at?

Michele shivered away from the recurrent feeling, averting her eyes from the disturbing, virile male across the table. "That's the last word I intend to say on the subject," she told Drake firmly. "I've satisfied your idle curiosity, even though I had no obligation to. Now I'd like you to leave."

To her great relief, he stood up. "Is that what you think it was, idle curiosity?"

Maybe not, Michele realized belatedly. Maybe Drake was looking for a chink in her armor, any weak spot he could use against her.

He watched the play of emotions over her face. Linking his arms loosely around her waist, he held her when she would have broken free. "No, my dear, nothing about you is trivial. I want to find out everything there is to know— most of all, what happened to make you so afraid to live."

She gripped his forearms, feeling the muscles underneath the rich material of his jacket. "No one has ever accused me of being a coward. I've faced more than you'll ever have to, and I've come out a winner."

"It depends on your definition of winning. If cutting yourself off from all human response is winning, then I guess you're a success."

"I have a daughter whom I love very much," she protested, renewing her efforts to get away. The same strange magic was working its spell, fanning the embers that still smoldered from their last encounter.

"You know what I'm saying." His head descended until his lips were just inches from her face. "What about this?"

Michele stared at his mouth with a mixture of fear and fascination. When he was so close that his features were just a blur she closed her eyes, unable to fight the magnetism that was drawing her into a vortex of emotion.

His lips touched her closed eyelids gently before trailing

a path of fire across her cheek. Michele turned her head restlessly, blindly seeking his mouth as a flower turns to the sun. She twined her arms around his neck, running slim fingers through his crisp dark hair, holding him so her lips could capture his elusive ones.

He drank in the nectar of her mouth, wrapping his arms around her in a tight embrace. Moving against her sensuously, Drake cupped one taut breast. His fingers caressed the hardened tip, making her gasp with pleasure.

Michele was lost in a stormy sea of sensation, completely enveloped by this man who had the power to arouse her to heights she had never even guessed at. She was treading a path to the stars, when suddenly Drake groaned, deep in his throat. Putting her away from him, he bent his head and closed his eyes briefly, his breathing ragged.

"Drake?" It was a soft, heartbreaking plea.

He folded her in his arms, gently this time. "There's no secret about how much I want you, honey, but I'm not a complete cad. You've been without a man for a long time, and I just happen to be the one who broke through the barrier." He stroked her hair tenderly. "But that's not good enough for either of us. Someday I hope you're going to want me for the right reasons." Smiling into her dazed face, he kissed her trembling mouth. "Good night, Michele."

She watched his swift exit without being able to utter a sound.

Chapter Five

Michele slept late the next morning because she had almost no sleep the night before. After Drake left she had paced the floor, a seething mass of conflicting emotions.

At first, blazing anger had consumed her. The colossal conceit of the man, to think she would fall into bed with him if he merely crooked his little finger! Michele had banished the memory of her impassioned response, just as she had denied the evidence of her aching body.

It was easier when she was angry. After the tempest had come something almost like fear. Was Drake correct about her relationships with men? Her disastrous marriage had left a deep wound, Michele knew. Was it traumatic enough to have made her indifferent to the entire male sex? If that were so, what would account for her instant awareness of Drake? She had met other men as handsome, men who were a great deal more anxious to please.

With a sinking feeling, Michele had faced the fact that Drake was special. He was a charming meteor who had crossed the path of many women—and would encounter many more. He said he liked to give pleasure, and Michele could well believe it. He would be a practiced lover, bringing untold ecstasy—until he moved on to the next affair.

A long shudder had wracked Michele's slender frame as she rejected the idea. What was a casual affair to him could well destroy her. Drake had penetrated her defenses tonight, but he must never be allowed to do so again.

When she had finally fallen asleep, Michele's dreams had been troubled. Drake dominated them, murmuring endearments that made her twist restlessly in bed. He was a shadowy sorcerer, tantalizing her by holding out his arms, only to vanish when she reached them.

The dream evaporated with the morning light, leaving a leaden feeling, and a disinclination to face the day.

After showering and brushing her teeth, Michele called Diane's mother to say that she would be by shortly to pick up Corey.

"The girls made plans for today. Couldn't Corey stay?" Mrs. Pennington coaxed.

"I don't want to impose," Michele told her. "It was kind enough of you to invite her to spend the night."

"We loved having her. Corey is a dear child, and she and Diane get on beautifully."

After they had agreed that she would pick up her daughter at about five o'clock, Michele was left at loose ends. It was good that she wouldn't have to pretend to a cheerfulness she didn't feel, but the day stretched out as an arid wasteland. The telephone call a short time later was most welcome.

"I hope you weren't just being polite when you said you'd help me with the nursery," Polly said, after they had discussed the Blaylock party thoroughly. "It looks so . . . so sterile. If you're not doing anything today, would you come over and make some suggestions?''

Michele accepted the invitation gratefully. She had liked Polly instantly and welcomed the chance to get to know her better.

The Fenwicks' house was a rambling, two-story residence that was old, but comfortable. It was furnished in early American, the mellow, maple wood tables and ruffled-chintz-covered furniture giving it a warm, homey feeling. Michele's praise was sincere.

"We just love it," Polly acknowledged. "But the nursery defeats me. It has all the character of a department-store display."

When she led her to it, Michele knew what Polly meant. The big, airy room overlooked the back yard. It was flooded with sunshine from two large windows that also let in the cheerful sound of birdsong and the scent of flowers from the garden below. A brand-new crib and a chest of drawers were decorated with enchanting nursery rhyme cutouts, but the effect was still static.

Michele eyed the stark white walls and pristine net curtains thoughtfully. "I think you need some color in here."

"We didn't know whether to paint it pink or blue, so we took the safe way out," Polly explained.

"You could use yellow, that's neutral ground. And I think a valance and some side panels over those curtains would work wonders. They have such darling material now. You could use the same fabric to cover the cushions on that rocker." Michele looked at Polly questioningly. "Do you sew?"

Polly nodded. "I even have my own sewing room. Tim fixed up one of the smaller bedrooms for me."

"Then the whole thing wouldn't cost very much at all—just a couple of gallons of paint and a few yards of fabric. While you were running up the curtains, Tim and I could paint the walls. It's a cinch with those roller things."

"You're a dear to offer." Polly's eyes were shining. "Could we do it today?"

"I'm game if Tim is. While we're picking out the material, he can get the paint."

"Well, there goes my tennis game." Tim laughed ruefully.

"You might as well get used to it," Michele advised. "Once you're a father, your life changes drastically."

"I only hope my carefree bachelor friend Drake will understand when I break the date," Tim sighed.

"He can always call one of his girl friends," Polly told her husband unfeelingly. "They'd drop anything for the chance to parade around in front of him in one of those cute little tennis dresses."

It didn't particularly thrill Michele to hear it, but she knew Polly was correct.

Tim joined them in the car after a short phone call. "Guess what? Drake is going to help. With all of us working, we ought to zip through that room in nothing flat."

Michele's protest died on her lips. What reason could she give for objecting to Drake's help? The idea of seeing him again, especially so soon after last night, was insupportable, however. She'd just have to back out some way.

"It sounds as though we're going to be tripping over each other," she remarked casually. "Maybe I'll just leave it to the men. I have some cleanup work of my own that still needs doing."

"Oh no, Michele," Polly exclaimed. "We need you to supervise. The guys will find a way to goof off if someone doesn't crack the whip over them."

"You could do that," Michele pointed out.

"I'd be outnumbered. Besides, this way it will be like a party. Tim can barbecue hamburgers after."

"I can't stay. I have to pick Corey up at five."

"Bring her," both Fenwicks urged.

Michele shook her head. "She's had a busy two days. I'm going to see that she gets to bed early tonight."

"Well, we'll talk about it later. Tim, if you get through first, meet us in the fabric store," Polly instructed.

They had reached the village, leaving Michele no chance to argue further. With a feeling of frustration, she followed Polly into the shop.

Picking out material took her mind off Drake for the moment. There were so many adorable prints to choose from that she and Polly had a hard time deciding. They finally settled on a colorful, unisex pattern of tin soldiers saluting gingham-clad dolls.

On the way home, Michele was as enthusiastic as Polly over the project, until she spotted Drake's white Ferrari in the driveway.

"Glad to see you, buddy," Tim called. "Are you prepared to take orders? Today will give you some idea of what it's like to be married."

Polly eyed her tall husband critically. "You mean instead of spending the day in honest labor, you'd rather be like Drake, out chasing girls?"

"I wouldn't answer a question like that if you applied thumbscrews," Tim chuckled.

"Shame on you for maligning my character, Polly."

Drake strolled over to the car. "After I've given up the whole afternoon for you too."

"Don't think I'm not grateful. You and Michele are both beautiful."

Drake ducked his head in the window to look at Michele in the back seat. "Well, at least *she* qualifies." His blue eyes roamed over her admiringly. "You're looking very chipper today, Michele. Evidently the coffee didn't keep you up last night."

"Not at all," Michele asserted. "I fell asleep the minute my head touched the pillow."

Drake's mouth twisted in a mocking smile. "You're very fortunate. I had a lot of trouble getting to sleep."

"It must have been the wine with dinner," Polly told him. "It affects me that way too."

Drake's eyes held Michele's. "Do you think that's what it was, Michele?"

"Why ask me? Maybe your conscience was bothering you." She scrambled out on the driver's side, unable to bear his sardonic gaze any longer.

"He doesn't have a conscience," Tim joked.

Drake had sauntered after Michele. He stood over her, the subtle scent of him reminding her inexorably of the night before. "You know that isn't true, don't you?" The low voice was pitched for her ears alone.

The only thing Michele knew was that she had to get away from this tormenting man. Not content with humiliating her last night, he had the tastelessness to remind her of it.

As she turned blindly toward her car, Polly said, "Come on, fellows, stop clowning around or we'll never get started. Michele, where are you going?"

Michele paused with a hand on her car door. "I . . . well, I thought I'd go home and get into my work clothes." When she got there she'd phone with some sort of excuse.

Polly cut off that escape route. "You don't have to do that. I'll give you one of Tim's old shirts."

"That's right, don't let her get away," Drake advised smoothly. "It's the last we'd see of her today."

"Michele wouldn't run out on us," Tim said. "This whole project was her idea." He grinned at Drake. "You can blame her for lousing up your Saturday."

"For all you're accomplishing, you might as well have played tennis," Polly complained impatiently. "Come on, Michele, I'll get that shirt for you." She looked appraisingly at Drake. "I see you came prepared."

Michele noticed for the first time that Drake was wearing well-worn jeans. Their seams had whitened from many washings, and they had shrunk until they molded to his narrow hips and long, muscular legs like a second skin. She averted her eyes quickly, but not before Drake had caught her comprehensive scrutiny.

"You see, I do wear jeans like other people," he teased.

Not precisely, Michele thought. Other men didn't look as breathtakingly masculine—nor did they have this effect on her. How on earth was she going to get through this ghastly day?

It was a little better after they started to work. Tim moved Polly's sewing machine into the nursery, and they all concentrated on their individual tasks. The stereo was playing softly, and Michele felt her knotted muscles gradually begin to relax. The effortless swish of the roller was soothing as she moved it in time to the music.

"Doesn't all this good, honest work make you feel

righteous?'' Tim asked suddenly. ''You bachelors don't know what you're missing. When your apartment needs painting you just tell the landlord. No personal satisfaction. Of course the same holds true when the plumbing acts up.'' He laughed. ''I guess you know what you're doing after all, friend.''

Drake dipped his roller again. ''As a matter of fact, I've been thinking about buying a home.''

Tim stared at him. ''I was only joking. Why would you want to be tied to a house?''

''I'm thirty-six, don't you think it's time I put down some roots?''

''But you said you were a troubleshooter,'' Michele exclaimed. ''That you moved from place to place.''

''Perhaps it's time I stopped,'' Drake answered calmly.

Tim's eyes narrowed appraisingly. ''Are you trying to tell us something?''

''What do you mean?'' Polly looked bewildered.

''Is Simon quitting?'' Tim asked. ''Are you taking over the company?''

''Of course not,'' Drake replied impatiently. ''He wants to take it a little easier and spend more time with Clarice, maybe go to Europe for a month or two. Why shouldn't he? He's earned it. But he's certainly not retiring. Not yet.''

A slow smile spread over Tim's open face. ''Congratulations, old buddy.''

Drake sighed, putting down the roller and wiping his hands on a rag. ''I know I don't have to warn you not to go spreading any rumors, Tim.''

Michele sat back on her heels, scarcely hearing Tim's assurances. In the back of her mind, had she been counting on the fact that Drake would someday move on, removing his threatening presence? If that were true, it appeared the problem was tossed back in her own lap. How long did she have before he took over as head of the company? Because that would surely be the day she was dismissed.

Drake gazed down at Michele's troubled face, one eyebrow lifting derisively. "It seems that when I told you our association wouldn't be permanent, I was a little premature."

She returned his gaze steadily. "If I last that long."

"Dissatisfied already, Michele?" he asked softly.

"No, everything is the way I expected it to be." She sighed. Drake held all the cards. In addition, he was ruthless and determined. It was only a matter of time, but he said Simon's retirement wasn't imminent. That would give her breathing space. Under the circumstances perhaps she ought to look for another job, except that it would be cruel to uproot Corey again after such a short time. No, she'd have to hang in there, no matter how difficult Drake made it.

Polly returned to the subject that interested her more. "Have you started house hunting yet?"

"Not really, although Clarice told me about a place that just came on the market. It's around the corner from them, the big white house with the Georgian columns."

"But that's enormous!" Polly gasped. "Why would you want anything that huge?"

Drake shrugged. "I can always close off the rooms I don't use. Besides, I'm tired of being cooped up in an apartment."

"I was going to offer to help decorate, but that place is too elegant for a do-it-yourself job," Tim remarked. He stood back and looked at his handiwork. "Still, this isn't coming out half-bad if I do say so myself."

Polly's eyes were sparkling as she surveyed the partially finished wall. "It's fantastic, exactly what this room needed —a little color. Michele, you're a genius!"

"Maybe I can start a career as a decorator if all else fails," she answered, without looking at Drake.

"You must have done wonders with Corey's nursery," Polly enthused. "Was it pink?"

Michele smiled reminiscently. "Pink and white. I waited until the doctor was ninety percent sure, and then I painted the walls. You have no idea how difficult it is to get up and down a ladder when you're eight months pregnant."

"You shouldn't have been doing that!" Polly was shocked. "Why didn't you let your husband do it?"

"He . . . uh . . . he wasn't home much." Michele was aware of Drake's silent scrutiny. With a feeling that he was seeing entirely too much, she added hurriedly, "Gary was teaching some night classes at the time." It wasn't true, but Michele hoped it would lead Drake off the track.

That had been a bad time. When she'd first discovered she was pregnant, Gary had tried to persuade her to have an abortion, on the grounds that she was too young for a baby. When she'd refused, they'd had some blazing arguments, yet they weren't as hurtful as his later conduct. At least she could believe at first that Gary's concern had really been for her.

But his anger had turned into resentment. As Michele had grown bigger and more ungainly he'd found his entertainment elsewhere, leaving her home alone. That was when Michele had known she'd have to make a life for herself.

"You've really had it rough, haven't you?" Tim asked softly. The same compassion was reflected on all their faces.

"Not really." Michele raised her chin. She didn't want their pity. "Corey and I have done all right." She stood up abruptly. "I think I'll take a breather."

Tim climbed down from the ladder. "Me too. We won't be able to finish today anyway. It will take another can of paint."

"Oh, Tim, couldn't you go get it now?" Polly wailed. "Then tomorrow the walls will be dry and we can hang the curtains."

"Slave driver." He smiled as he ruffled his wife's soft hair. "Okay, you win."

"I'll go," Drake offered.

"You're a love," Polly told him gratefully. "Would you go with him, Michele?"

"It doesn't take two people to buy a can of paint," she protested.

"No, I'd like you to get something at the fabric store for me." Polly looked critically at the gaily patterned curtains that had taken shape under her skilled hands. "These need a finishing touch. I think that ball fringe they had at the shop would be the perfect thing. Will you stop in and get me some?"

Every nerve in Michele's body cried a denial. "Why don't you go with Drake? I might get the wrong color."

"I want to stay and work on these." Polly snipped off a scrap of material. "Here, match it to the yellow in this."

Drake put his arm around Michele's shoulders, leading her to the door. "Come on, let's get out of here before she has us do the marketing."

"Hey, that's an idea. I need some hamburger buns," Polly called. "Tim's going to barbecue tonight. It's a reward for all your labor. You'll change your mind and stay, won't you, Michele?"

"I really can't, Polly."

"I'll have to take a rain check too," Drake said.

"Well, all right." Polly accepted defeat reluctantly. "But don't forget, I owe you one."

"We'll remind her, won't we?" Drake asked Michele.

Not if she could help it, Michele vowed grimly.

As she settled into the bucket seat of the low-slung sports car, Michele was like a fighter waiting for the bell. She envied her opponent his ease. Drake was completely relaxed, long legs stretched out, his muscled thigh almost touching her own. She moved carefully to avoid any contact.

"I'm not contagious." He turned his head to smile mockingly at her. "Only habit-forming."

"Not to me you're not!"

"How can you say that? We're practically going steady— last night, and again today. Who knows where it will lead."

Michele stared straight ahead. "To the paint store and back."

Drake grinned mischievously. "That means we're going around together."

Michele's eyes were smoky gray as she twisted around in the bucket seat. "This is as good a time as any to settle things between us. Today was just an unfortunate accident. I never expected to see you again outside of the lab. I don't *want* to see you. Is that clear?"

"Not really. Why are you so afraid of me, Michele? Or is it your own emotions you don't trust?"

"Don't use that stale line on me!"

"Last night you—"

"Don't mention last night!" she interrupted frantically. "Haven't you humiliated me enough?"

He turned his head to take a long look at her distressed

face. Then Drake pulled over to the side of the road, turning off the motor.

"Why are you stopping?" Michele cried. "Take me back immediately or I'm getting out of this car." She fumbled with the locked door.

He reached out and captured her hands, holding both of them in a firm grip. "Not until we talk about this. How did I humiliate you, Michele? By not staying with you?"

"No! Of course not!" Her ivory skin flooded with color as Michele's long lashes fell, her hands struggling like little birds trying to escape.

Drake wouldn't release her. "Was it humiliating that I found you attractive?"

Michele couldn't answer, couldn't even look at him. He knew perfectly well what she was ashamed of.

Drake stared at the shining crown of her head. Then his palms framed her face, gently lifting it to his. "You have nothing to reproach yourself for, honey. You're a warm, passionate woman, whether you know it or not."

"I never acted like that before," she whispered. "Not with anyone."

One hand curved around the back of her neck, massaging the tense muscles under the spill of golden hair. "Doesn't that tell you something?" he murmured.

Her lashes flew up as she looked at him for the first time. "It isn't what you think."

Drake's eyes were brilliant. "There's something very potent between us, Michele."

"Just sex," she answered dully, admitting what she couldn't very well deny. Even now her body was quiveringly aware of every hard, lean inch of his. She wanted those long fingers to caress her bare skin, that heavenly mouth to devour her. A shuddering sigh shook her slender frame. "You were right about me. I haven't been with a man since my husband died."

"I'm sure you've had opportunities," he said softly.

She shrugged that off. "Yes, but I've never wanted—" Michele stopped, appalled as she realized she was confirming Drake's contention.

His fingertips traced an unbearably sensuous path over her cheek to her trembling lower lip. "Sex is a very powerful bond between a man and a woman."

Michele could feel herself turning to liquid inside, melting under his frank desire—and her own. She fought it valiantly. "It isn't enough! You said so yourself." If only he wouldn't touch her!

But Drake continued to stroke her satin skin with tactile enjoyment. "Why don't we take it slow and easy, and see what develops. I won't rush you, Michele, and I won't pressure you. You have to want whatever happens as much as I do." He released her at last, turning on the ignition and wheeling the powerful car back on the road to the village.

Michele picked out Polly's fringe in a daze. Did Drake mean what he said? Could he be counted on not to subject her to any more of those devastating seductions? She didn't believe it for an instant. Away from his hypnotizing magnetism, Michele started to think clearly.

Either he was setting her up for a love affair that would destroy her so completely when he ended it that she would leave town, or he planned to enslave her so totally that she wouldn't notice she was being eased out of her job. By the time Drake joined her in the fabric store, Michele's armor was firmly back in place.

If he noticed, it wasn't evident. Drake was completely

natural as he maneuvered through the Saturday-afternoon traffic, chatting about inconsequential things. Michele was concentrating so fiercely on keeping her cool that she didn't notice where he was heading.

"You're going the wrong way," she pointed out, when it became evident to her.

"I want to make a short stop first."

"But Tim is waiting for the paint."

"He has enough to work with until we get back."

Drake turned into a driveway set between two tall hedges that blocked any view from the street. It led to the most beautiful house Michele had ever seen. It was large yet graceful, with stately white pillars spaced along the front. Manicured green lawns bordered by flower beds formed a lush setting that spread over more than an acre.

"Is *this* the house you're considering?" Michele gasped.

He stopped the car in the driveway, gazing around with admiration. "It's a beauty, isn't it?"

"But it's huge! How could you even think of living alone in a place like this?"

His eyes brimmed with amusement. "Perhaps I won't always be alone."

"I see," she answered stiffly. "But surely an apartment is adequate for your activities—unless you throw orgies on a regular basis."

Drake threw back his dark head and laughed, white teeth gleaming in his tanned face. "Has anyone ever told you that you have a very prurient mind?"

Before Michele could issue an angry denial, the front door opened. The young woman who emerged was tall and leggy, her generous curves emphasized by the tight sweater she wore with her tan suit.

As she came down the steps, her eyes lit up with

pleasure. "Drake, what a nice surprise! How did you know I was here?"

"Just a happy coincidence," he replied easily, getting out of the car. Drake introduced the two women, then asked, "Is your real-estate company handling this property, Marilyn?"

The dark-haired woman nodded. "It just came up for sale and I was checking it out. The man who owned it was transferred suddenly. I think someone could make an excellent buy."

"I'd like to look at it."

The woman's brown eyes widened. "For yourself, Drake?"

He sighed. "I know—it's too big for me. If you don't mind though, I'd like to go through it all the same."

"Well, sure. The only thing is, I'm late for an appointment. Can I just give you the keys and leave you on your own? You can return them when you pick me up tonight."

After Marilyn had driven off, Drake opened the car door for Michele. "Come on, let's take a tour."

She got out reluctantly, filled with a vague sense of annoyance. "Are you sure it's all right? Maybe your girl friend wouldn't like an unauthorized person tagging along," she remarked waspishly.

"I'll vouch for you." He grinned mischievously. "She trusts me."

"Then she isn't very bright!"

Drake raised one eyebrow. "It sounds as though you didn't like Marilyn."

"I neither like, *nor* dislike her," Michele replied grimly. "What do you want, an endorsement? Fine, you've got it. I hope you have a peachy time tonight. Now, are we going to inspect the house or stand here all day discussing your love life? I want to get back even if you don't." Michele strode purposefully to the front door, followed by her thoughtful companion.

A wide entry hall was dominated by a crystal chandelier that tinkled faintly in the slight breeze. On one side was a huge living room, on the other, a dining room almost as large. Planked floors had been polished until they gleamed like caramel-colored satin.

Michele's rancor vanished as she gazed around the gracious rooms. "Oh, Drake, it's heavenly! Look at that view through the French windows. You could be on a country estate—or in a park."

"It is nice, isn't it?" Drake's satisfaction was quiet, but evident.

They wandered through the downstairs, eventually arriving at the kitchen, which was a cook's delight. It had been completely modernized and fitted with all the newest equipment. The color scheme was a cool blue and white, with French country wallpaper picking up the shades of the counters and inlaid flooring.

Michele ran her palm over the smooth surface of a square, butcher-block chopping table. "It seems a shame to waste this glorious kitchen."

"On a mere man?" Drake finished. "Talk about your chauvinists—they come in all sexes. What makes you think I can't cook?"

"Can you?"

"No," he admitted with a grin. "But once again you jumped to conclusions." He took her hand. "Come on upstairs, let's look at the bedrooms."

Where you know exactly what to do, Michele thought grimly.

There were several bedrooms, all large and airy, but the master suite was the *pièce de résistance*.

A marble-floored bathroom fitted with rose quartz faucets over a sunken tub was reached through a dressing area as large as a medium-sized room. Mirrored doors led to the bedroom, which was completely carpeted in white.

"You could certainly hold one of those orgies you mentioned in here," Drake remarked mockingly. "This place could accommodate a circular bed—complete with stereo in the headboard and black satin sheets, of course."

Michele knew he was teasing, but she couldn't help protesting, "You wouldn't furnish it in modern, would you?"

"I hadn't thought about it. Why? What would you do?"

She didn't even have to think about it. "I'd put one of those wonderful old four-poster beds over there against the far wall. With two little chairs and a round table covered with a skirt that matched the bedspread, between the French windows." She turned toward the charming fireplace framed by a carved white mantel. "And I'd have a Chinese throw rug in front of the hearth, with a couch facing the fireplace." Her eyes were wistful and far away. "On winter nights you could sit here and watch the flames and just dream."

Drake's hands gripped her arms, giving her a small shake. "I'm not a dreamer, I'm a doer. Wishing for things doesn't make them happen."

"I know," Michele agreed sadly. "But everyone has to indulge herself sometimes." She mustered a smile. "It's the aspirin of the spirit."

He searched her upturned face. "Is reality so painful, Michele?" Drake asked gently.

"No, of course not." She moved toward the door, out of range of the tall, handsome man who disturbed her in so many ways. "If you've seen enough, we'd better be getting back."

The return trip was uneventful. Either Drake had decided to be on his good behavior, or he had tired of baiting her. Michele decided to take no chances.

When they got to the Fenwicks', she handed Drake her package. "Would you take this to Polly for me? I have to leave."

He didn't urge her to stay, confirming Michele's suspicion that he was tired of the game. Smiling pleasantly, Drake said, "Good-bye, Michele, it was nice being with you."

The Pennington house was alive with the sound of children's voices, music and laughter. Michele could see why Corey enjoyed being there, but she couldn't understand why the Penningtons needed another child around.

"Corey is no trouble at all," Mrs. Pennington assured Michele when she voiced the opinion. "She and Diane get along like sisters. I hope you'll let her visit often."

"We'd like to have Diane too," Michele said. "Although I'm afraid our house will seem rather quiet to her."

Jane Pennington laughed. "She'll welcome the change." She hugged Corey. "Come back again soon, honey."

Corey fizzed with excitement all the way home, singing the praises of the whole Pennington clan. Fluffy was waiting with an ecstatic greeting, bouncing like a rubber ball in her rapture at seeing them. While Corey took her for a walk, Michele started dinner.

After her bath, Corey was visibly drooping. She offered only a token protest at having to go to bed.

Michele washed the dishes and emptied the garbage, unconsciously dragging out the chores. By eight o'clock there was nothing left to do.

She wandered into the small living room, trying not to notice the silence. That was the hard part—the lonely nights. The whole world seemed to be made up of two-somes. Polly had Tim, Clarice had Simon—and Drake had the enticing Marilyn. Were they out dancing now, her voluptuous body moving sensuously against his in a pre-view of what was to come?

Michele stood up abruptly, snapping on the television to dispel the awful quiet—and her thoughts.

Chapter Six

Sunday was a beautiful day, dispelling Michele's gloom of the night before. She breezed through the morning's chores with Corey's help, making beds and straightening the house. But by late morning, when everything was done, Corey became restless.

"I don't have anything to do," she complained.

"You can help me weed the flower beds," Michele suggested.

"That's no fun. I wish I had someone to play with." Corey heaved a dramatic sigh. "I wish I had some brothers and sisters."

"Well, you don't," Michele advised her crisply. "You'll have to learn to amuse yourself at times."

Corey's eyes were speculative. "Would you have to be married to have more children, Mom?"

"It would certainly help," Michele remarked dryly. Before Corey could pursue the subject, she opened the back door. "I'll be in the garden if you change your mind."

Sheer boredom brought the little girl out a short time

later. Her listless efforts were more of a hindrance than a help, however. Most of all Michele minded the long face and sighs of self-pity. She was rapidly losing patience when Corey let out a happy shout.

"Mr. Hollister!"

Michele stiffened automatically. It couldn't be! The man was persecuting her. She sat back on her heels, glaring at the unwelcome sight of her daughter greeting Drake like the answer to a prayer.

"I was hoping you'd come over today," Corey cooed, displaying a social precociousness that appalled Michele.

"It must have been ESP," he answered solemnly. "I thought you and your mother might like to go to the county fair with me."

"Yippee!" The little girl threw her arms around Drake's waist, amazing Michele.

Corey wasn't usually demonstrative with men, having had little experience being around them. Like me—Michele thought unavoidably. Was Corey beginning to feel the lack of a father figure in her life? The idea dismayed Michele; there was so little she could do about it. Except keep her away from Drake. He was certainly not the right influence.

"Can Diane come too?" Corey was asking excitedly.

"I don't know why not, if it's all right with her parents."

"Corey, we can't—" Michéle's admonition was given to thin air. Her daughter had vanished into the house. She stood up, her gray eyes flashing fire. "You might have asked *me*."

"I did." Drake thrust his hands in the pockets of his black slacks. The checked gingham shirt he wore with them was open at the throat, disclosing dark, curling hair.

"You know what I mean," Michele said angrily. "Now you've gotten Corey all excited."

"Is that bad?" he asked mildly.

"You should have asked me first," she maintained stubbornly.

"You would have said no. I've had to threaten or trick you into being with me every time the occasion comes up." One eyebrow raised mockingly. "I have a recurrent dream that someday I'll ask you to go somewhere, and you'll accept without arguing."

Michele stared defiantly back at him. "I thought you never dreamed. Isn't that just for the weak?"

"I find you've changed my thinking on a lot of things, lady," he answered softly, something flickering in his clear blue eyes.

Michele's gaze dropped to his well-shaped mouth, noticing, without wanting to, the sensuous fullness of his lower lip. She knew its feel, the firm persuasive pressure it could exert. In one comprehensive glance she was conscious of everything about him, the turned-back cuffs that revealed his hair-roughened forearms, the short, well-kept nails on his capable hands.

"It's okay, Diane can go!" Corey came running out of the house. "I told her we'd pick her up in fifteen minutes."

Michele drew a deep breath. "No, I . . ." She was conscious of Drake's enigmatic gaze. Once more he had outmaneuvered her. How could she disappoint the children? "I have to get cleaned up first," she finished.

"Hurry up," Corey pleaded. "We don't want to miss anything."

Drake smiled. "Don't worry, I won't let you miss a thing."

The words were for Corey, but he was looking at Michele. Was it a threat or a promise, she wondered? Her mind skittered away from the benefits he could bestow.

Michele changed quickly into a navy skirt with a matching cardigan over a pale blue silk blouse. She chose a pair of low-heeled pumps, mindful of all the walking they would do.

As she ran a brush through her long blond hair, taming it into a silken fall of pale gold, Michele experienced a sudden feeling of anticipation. The day that had stretched out so uneventfully now promised to be fun. It was childish to resent Drake for doing something so nice for Corey. This whole outing was really for her, Michele realized.

The fairgrounds on the outskirts of town were crowded. Happy children raced from place to place, followed by slightly distracted parents. Young couples walked hand in hand at a slower pace. As they strolled after the excited girls, it seemed entirely normal for Drake to take Michele's hand.

The children were determined not to miss a single thing. They visited every display, cooing over the rabbits and baby chicks proudly displayed by 4-H club members and salivating over the homemade cakes and pies. Drake solved that problem with hot dogs and corn on the cob, followed by cotton candy.

"They'll be sick," Michele protested.

"Nonsense. Red-blooded American children can digest tacks," he asserted.

"If you just happen to be wrong, can I call you in the middle of the night to come over and hold Corey's head?"

A faint smile played around Drake's mouth as his eyes held hers. "You can call me anytime."

"You probably wouldn't be home," she replied tartly, remembering whom he had been with the night before.

The girls had saved the best till last—the amusement area with its souvenir stands, rides and games of chance. They pleaded with Michele and Drake to accompany them on the ferris wheel, squealing in mock fear as their gondola swung gently back and forth. When it stopped at the very top, the little girls' joy was complete. They looked over the side, waving to the less fortunate below, much like benevolent monarchs acknowledging their subjects.

The corners of Drake's eyes crinkled in amusement. "Ah, to be seven years old again."

Michele turned her head to look critically at the sophisticated man next to her. Even in casual clothes there was a subtle elegance about him. Although he seemed to be enjoying himself, she knew this wasn't his normal milieu.

"Somehow I can't imagine you as a little boy."

"I was," he assured her. "I played cowboys and Indians and space invaders. I also teased little girls."

"That I can believe," she replied dryly.

"I thought you might. I just threw it in to prove I was normal."

"You seem so invulnerable. Did you ever fall down and scrape your knee?" she persisted.

"I was the one who made the Band-Aid company what it is today," he boasted.

"Did you cry?"

"It wasn't considered manly," he admitted. "Kids have it much easier today. I applaud the enlightened attitude that lets boys express their emotions. They don't grow up as inhibited."

Michele had reason to remember Drake's compelling sensuality, his ability to generate pleasure and respond to it. She raised a skeptical eyebrow. "You don't seem to have grown up repressed."

He gave her a wide grin. "You never know how much more confident I might have been."

"It doesn't bear thinking about!" Michele exclaimed in mock horror.

Drake laughed. "Tell me about yourself. What kind of child were you?"

"Normal—in spite of what you think," she couldn't resist adding, his earlier criticism still rankling.

"I don't doubt it for a minute." His eyes caressed her delicate face. "You must have been enchanting."

"If you like skinny little kids."

"My, how you've changed," Drake murmured.

She was very conscious of his admiring eyes on her small, high breasts. It was like a tangible caress, sending a tiny shiver up her spine. "I also wore braces," she remarked tartly.

"It was worth it." He traced the shape of her full lower lip, gently tugging it down. A long forefinger slipped suggestively inside, slowly sliding over her even teeth.

The audaciousness of it made Michele draw a sharp breath. She bit his finger sharply.

"Ow!" Drake yelped. "That hurt."

"It was supposed to," she answered complacently. "That will teach you not to take liberties."

Drake's yelp had attracted the attention of the little girls. They were regarding Michele with shocked surprise.

"My mother gave me a spanking once for biting my brother," Diane observed primly.

"It's an interesting idea," Drake murmured in Michele's ear. "I owe you one."

She ignored him, addressing the girls. "We all know that biting is wrong, but Mr. Hollister and I were just playing."

"I didn't know grown-ups played games." Diane wasn't completely convinced.

"All the time," Drake assured her. "It's called the battle of the sexes."

"Will you stop confusing them?" Michele asked irritably.

Drake grinned. "They might as well learn early."

"Not necessarily. By the time they grow up, perhaps things will have changed for the better."

"I hope it's the battle part you hope to eliminate, not the sex," he teased.

Michele was conscious of two pairs of wide eyes watching them. "Do you mind if we continue this conversation at a later date?" she murmured to Drake. "I don't think a ferris wheel is the place for a lesson on sex."

"Okay, but when I reopen the subject, don't forget it was your suggestion."

After they had ridden on a few more rides, Corey had to use the ladies' room. Of course Diane had to accompany her, and the two little girls bustled off. Michele knew better than to offer to go with them. That was for babies. But when it seemed to take an inordinate amount of time, Michele decided she'd better check.

Their sweet little piping voices carried to the anteroom, stopping Michele in her tracks.

"I think your mother likes Mr. Hollister," Diane was saying confidently.

"I like him too," Corey answered.

"Not *that* way!" Diane was scornful of her friend's naïveté. "You know what I mean."

"Oh." After a short silence and much splashing, Corey remarked thoughtfully, "I don't know, Mommy doesn't care much for men."

Michele was appalled. Was it that obvious?

"She likes Mr. Hollister." Diane seemed sure of her

facts. "Maybe they'll get married and then you'd have a father too."

"I already had one. He died."

"I think you can have two, only the second one is called a stepfather."

Corey was hesitant. "I don't know if I'd like that."

"Sure you would. Then Mr. Hollister would move into your house."

"That would be neat!" Excitement vibrated in Corey's voice. "Do you really think he might?"

"Well, maybe." Doubt suddenly assailed Diane. "Except that my father said Mr. Hollister would be crazy to get married. He said Mr. Hollister had it made in the shade. I don't know what that means, but my mother got mad when he said it."

Michele had heard enough. She beat a hasty retreat, color flaming in her creamy skin.

"Are they all right?" Drake frowned, looking at her pink cheeks.

"They're fine," she answered shortly.

He sensed something amiss. "Would you like to tell me what's going on?"

Michele's annoyance burst its bounds. "It might interest you to know that your exploits have reached the ears of even a seven-year-old!"

He was honestly puzzled. "Could you make that a little clearer?"

"No, I couldn't!"

The girls were coming and Michele had enough of a problem composing herself. Mindful of their speculation, she pulled her hand away when Drake tried to take it. He didn't persist, but his thoughtful eyes studied her as they followed the children.

Michele needn't have worried. Corey and Diane had no further time for the affairs of grown-ups. They skipped from place to place, finally stopping in front of a shooting gallery. The stuffed animals on display were the prizes for annihilating a row of moving men representing bandits. The proprietor of the booth was dressed as a cowboy.

When he saw the longing on the girls' faces, Drake accepted the rifle being urged on him by the pitch man. The bell that signaled a hit rang out so often that a small crowd gathered to watch the lean, intent man with perfectly coordinated muscles sight down the long barrel. When the gun was empty, Drake had a perfect score. He had neatly removed the heads of ten little clay men. A buzz of admiration greeted the end of his performance.

Michele added her praise. "Drake, that's fantastic! How did you do it?"

He shrugged. "I shoot skeet in the winter when it's too cold to do anything else."

"You're wonderful," she enthused.

"It's about time you noticed," he said, smiling.

When the proprietor lifted down a giant stuffed elephant, a dilemma presented itself. Drake solved it neatly by requesting two smaller toys, one for each girl.

"Shall I try again for you?" he asked Michele.

"No, I think you'd better quit while you're ahead," she decided.

Drake tipped her chin up, smiling down at her. "One thing you'll find out about me," he said softly. "I never quit until I get the prize."

The people swirling around them receded into the background as Michele stared up at him, tinglingly aware of the male challenge he was issuing. Would she be able to withstand it? Or would her own sexuality be the thing that ultimately betrayed her?

When someone jostled them accidentally, Michele snapped back to normal. She drew a shaky breath. "We'd better go after the girls."

As they caught up with Corey and Diane, someone called Drake's name. A gorgeous redhead, in a tight-fitting T-shirt with an emblem over one of her ample breasts, was waving excitedly to him. She was behind the counter of a booth draped in red, white and blue bunting.

"Hi, Shelley." Drake waved back, shepherding his little group in that direction. "What are you selling?"

When they got closer, Michele could see the sign on the counter that said: Kisses $1.00.

The redhead flirted long lashes at Drake. "Something I hope you're buying. It's for the hospital fund—a very good cause."

He reached in his pocket, taking out a five-dollar bill. "Very worthy," he agreed. When she reached out her arms to him, Drake laughed. "That won't be necessary. Just consider it a charitable donation."

"I'm not a charity case," the redhead pouted. Before Drake could answer, she put her arms around his neck, twining her fingers in his hair as she warmed to her work.

After what seemed like an eternity to Michele, Drake disentangled the woman's arms, amusement shining out of his eyes. "Your dedication to the cause is admirable."

She smiled seductively. "I still owe you four more."

Drake's own smile was sardonic. "I feel I got my money's worth the first time."

The two little girls were interested spectators. Michele was considerably less so. She took each one by the hand, marching them away from the booth. When Drake joined them, she was too angry to trust herself to speak.

"Where shall we go now?" he asked, as though nothing had happened.

"Home," Michele said decisively.

The girls set up an immediate outcry. "Oh no, Mommy, can't we stay a little longer?"

"No, I've—you've had quite enough."

Drake's eyes narrowed as he gazed at Michele's set face. To add to her outrage, he gave the children some money and sent them to play the ring toss game. When Michele turned on him furiously, Drake forestalled her.

"I have a feeling I already know what this is all about, but suppose you tell me," he remarked evenly.

"It's getting late," she answered distantly. "The children have school tomorrow."

"And it just occurred to you?" When Michele turned away, not deigning to reply, Drake pulled her back. "It couldn't be that you're angry over that little incident at the kissing booth?"

Michele's resentment boiled over. "Don't be ridiculous! You can kiss every woman in the fairgrounds as far as I'm concerned! And I wouldn't be at all surprised," she added waspishly.

Drake smiled unexpectedly, running the back of his knuckles lightly over her cheek. "I wasn't trying to, but I'm delighted that I succeeded in making you jealous."

"Jealous!" Michele was almost choking with indignation. "Don't flatter yourself, Mr. Hollister."

"Can you tell me any other reason for this display of temper?" he asked calmly.

"All right, you asked for it. You're right in thinking I'm angry—*damn* angry! But not for the reason you've given. I just think your behavior was disgusting in front of the children.''

Drake's face hardened. "You think their morals will be corrupted by seeing a man and woman exchange an innocent kiss?''

"If that was innocent, I'd hate to see you when you were applying yourself!''

"You already have, but let's not change the subject.'' Drake's voice was cold. "I'm afraid your values are seriously out of line.''

"Look who's talking!'' Michele exclaimed. "Perhaps the male viewpoint holds that it's all right to carry on in public, but I wasn't brought up that way. And I don't want my child to think it is.''

"Correct me if I'm wrong, Michele, but didn't you find my prowess with a rifle a few minutes ago quite admirable?''

"What does that have to do with anything?''

"Answer me. Didn't you consider it quite an accomplishment?''

"Okay, I did. What do you want, applause?''

"Scarcely. I just want you to think about it. I blasted the heads off ten little men, and you thought that was noble. But a meaningless kiss offends your sensibilities. Violence is okay, but not body contact, is that it?''

"You're twisting everything around,'' she protested. "Those little figures weren't real, there was no violence.''

"It was symbolic,'' he said simply.

"You don't say,'' Michele remarked sarcastically. "Well, your kiss was certainly real.''

"But not salacious, as you're implying. It was merely a high-spirited joke.'' He ran a big, square hand through his thick hair. "Don't you see, Michele? It's your attitude, rather than my actions, that is important. If you show that you think any contact between a man and a woman, any warmth, is distasteful, you're sending Corey a clear message. Do you want her to grow up as frightened of life as you are?"

"I am *not* afraid of life!"

"Just of men?" His smile was mocking.

Michele was stung into angry speech. "Since meeting you, I have to admit they aren't my favorite people."

"Men make up roughly half the population. Do you really want to cut yourself off from fifty percent of the people in the world?"

"No, only from you!"

He made a disgusted sound deep in his throat. "Okay, you've got it. Come on, I'll take you home." Drake's gaze was wintry as it swept over her defiant face. "You can climb back into your stockade, Michele. Just be sure to double-lock all your emotions so none of them have a chance to escape." He walked rapidly away from her.

Michele followed, seething. She struggled to keep righteous indignation dominant, refusing to listen to the small voice that suggested perhaps she had overreacted. Drake was the one who was wrong! He *had* made a public display of himself.

Drake strode up to the two girls. "All right, kids, we're leaving."

"We just started this game. Can't we finish, Mr. Hollister?" Diane pleaded.

His stern face relaxed. "Sure. Mrs. Carter and I will wait for you over by that bench." He turned to Michele with distant courtesy. "I hope that was all right. They'll only be a few minutes."

"Yes, of course," she muttered.

They waited in a heavy silence that tortured Michele's nerves, but didn't seem to bother Drake. He glanced out over the crowd indifferently, his expression a mixture of boredom and impatience. Under her discomfort, Michele felt a nagging sense of loss. The easy camaraderie between them had fled, the unaccustomed, comfortable feeling of being part of a couple instead of a single parent. Even while she realized it was an illusion, Michele had to admit she had enjoyed it.

It was a relief when Drake was hailed by a young couple, although his warmth toward them underscored his indifference to Michele. When he made the introductions, it was with cool politeness. Todd Johnson and his wife Mary both worked for Blaylock, so at least Michele had something to say to them.

After they left she attempted to keep the conversation going. "Flora tells me that most of the people at the lab are local."

Drake nodded. "A large percentage." That was all.

Well, if he wanted to act like a child, so be it, Michele concluded with annoyance. That was the last olive branch she was going to extend.

They might have been total strangers who happened to be standing next to each other. The arrival of the children broke up the tableau.

On the way home Corey said, "Can Diane have dinner at our house?"

"I can't," Diane broke in. "My grandmother is coming."

Corey was reluctant to see the day end. "Can Mr. Hollister come then?"

"No!" Michele answered sharply. Modifying her tone, she added, "He has a previous engagement."

"Mr. Hollister does *not* have a previous engagement," Drake bit out sharply. "Can't you even be honest with your own daughter?"

Michele cast a quick glance at the two shocked little faces in the back seat. "Please, Drake," she murmured.

"You're right." He sighed deeply. "What I meant to say was that your mother was just being polite, Corey. She doesn't feel like cooking after being out all day."

Although his voice was pleasantly matter-of-fact, Corey wasn't convinced. "She has to make dinner anyway."

Michele bit her lip, uncertain of what prompted her offer. "I do have a casserole in the refrigerator. You . . . you're welcome to join us if you like."

Drake turned his head to look at her for a long moment, his expression unreadable. "Are you sure, Michele?"

She experienced a mixture of dismay and exhilaration at his acceptance. "Yes, as long as you don't expect too much."

A mocking smile curved his firm mouth. "Do you say things like that on purpose?"

Michele was mindful of the small, listening ears. "I can open up a can of soup and make a salad," she hurried on.

"I'm sure you'll manage to make it a memorable meal," Drake remarked dryly.

When they got home Michele refused Drake's offer of help. "You said you couldn't cook," she pointed out.

"I can't, but I can keep you company."

"No thanks, you'd just be a distraction." At his lifted eyebrow, she added hurriedly, "I'm used to being alone in the kitchen."

"And everywhere else, Michele?" he asked softly.

She opened the refrigerator door, ignoring his question. "Why don't you go in the living room and read the paper? I'll call you when dinner's ready."

Michele prepared the meal automatically, her attention focused on the sounds from the other room. The murmur of Drake's deep voice, punctuated occasionally by laughter, formed a counterpoint to Corey's delighted chatter. It was such a comfortable sound—as though they were a family.

The feeling was reinforced when Corey dashed into the kitchen with an excited bulletin. "Guess what? Mr. Hollister fixed my record player. It plays fine now. He says the arm was just bent."

"That's wonderful, dear."

"Maybe he could fix that window that's stuck in my room."

"Mr. Hollister is a guest, Corey. Besides, I told you I'd take care of it."

"But you said it was stuck so tight it needed somebody stronger than you. Mr. Hollister is stronger." Corey danced out of the room, her words echoing in Michele's ear.

Dinner was pleasanter than she would have thought possible, perhaps because of Corey's presence. The little girl monopolized a good part of the conversation. Michele only half listened, absorbed in her own thoughts, but Drake seemed to be enjoying the novelty of it. He asked Corey about school, listening to her answers as though he were really interested.

"We're going to have parents' night next Friday," Corey volunteered. "If you came with Mommy, you could meet my teacher."

That caught Michele's attention. "It's only for mothers and fathers," she admonished sharply.

Corey caught the warning note in her mother's voice. Her lashes fell as she concentrated on her plate.

Drake changed the subject, his expression carefully blank. "I wonder if Polly got her curtains hung. We finished painting yesterday."

Michele's tense body relaxed. "It must look lovely. All that room needed was a splash of color."

"I just wish they'd waited till she was a little farther along." Drake's forehead creased in a slight frown. "It would be tragic if they had another disappointment."

Michele nodded. "But I can understand their need to think positively. Fixing up the nursery makes them feel like parents."

"Can children have more than two parents?" Corey asked unexpectedly.

Michele looked startled. "I don't know exactly what you mean."

"Well, if you got married again, I'd have two fathers, wouldn't I?"

"You'd have a stepfather." Michele avoided looking at Drake.

"Would he be mean like the wicked stepmother in 'Cinderella'?" Corey had evidently given the matter some thought. She waited earnestly for an answer.

"That sort of behavior is limited to the female of the species," Drake chuckled.

Michele shot him an annoyed look. " 'Cinderella' is just a fairy tale, Corey. You're old enough to know that."

Corey sighed happily, giving Drake a big smile. "Then I wouldn't mind having a stepfather."

"That should take a load off your mind," he murmured mockingly to Michele.

"If you're through with dessert, you may be excused," Michele instructed, in a voice that brooked no further discussion. "Come in and say good night after your bath."

Drake hooked one arm over the back of his chair, regarding Michele with amusement. "It seems your sister isn't the only one actively searching for a man for you."

"I don't know what got into her," Michele grated. "Yes, I do! It was Diane. They had a long conversation in the ladies' room."

"I wondered what happened to put you in such a state. Was it the fact that I was part of their plans?"

"It was finding out that you're a topic of conversation all over town," she snapped.

Drake searched his memory. "I can't recall committing any flagrant indiscretions."

"It's your steady stream of them. Diane's father informed her mother that—and I quote—you had it made in the shade. Mrs. Pennington, I might add, was not as appreciative."

Drake threw back his handsome head, laughing out loud. "It displeases wives greatly when their husbands express admiration for the bachelor way of life. If only they'd realize that spectator sports are rarely harmful."

"Perhaps not, but I should think you'd feel some concern over the fact that seven-year-olds are discussing your activities."

"They're merely parroting their parents—who, incidentally, should have better things to do." There was steel in Drake's voice as he added, "And I've done nothing to be ashamed of."

Michele realized they were drifting toward another argument, which would be fruitless. "Well, anyway, that's how the subject of stepfathers came up. You needn't take it personally."

"I didn't," he answered calmly. "I don't consider you marriage material."

Michele gasped as though she had been drenched with a bucket of cold water. Then pure rage flooded her. "That's extremely fortunate in light of the fact that I wouldn't marry you under a court order!"

Her anger didn't ruffle him. "I wasn't finished. What I was going to add was, until you get rid of some of your hang-ups you're not ready for wedded bliss."

The word *bliss* struck a grating note. Michele's laughter was harsh. "A lot you know about it—*or* me."

Drake's eyes were like blue laser beams, searching her soul. "I'm beginning to get the picture," he said softly. Before she could respond he got to his feet, picking up Corey's plate and his own. "Let's do the dishes."

"It isn't necessary," she answered stiffly.

He paused in front of her, examining her face intently. "Didn't your husband help you with that either?"

How could he possibly read so much in a few innocent words? Michele's lashes dropped, masking her confusion. "It won't take me long," she murmured.

"Not if I help," he agreed, piling the dishes in the sink and turning on the hot water.

"You'll get all dirty," she protested.

"That wouldn't be terminal." He held out his wet hands. "Roll up my sleeves."

When she couldn't dissuade him, Michele did as Drake instructed, feeling an unwilling sense of pleasure as her fingers trailed through the crisp hair on his forearms.

"Okay, I'll load the dishwasher while you clear the table," he ordered.

Michele was unaccustomed to anyone taking over her kitchen, but Drake had it neat in a surprisingly short time.

"It's just a matter of organization," he declared smugly when she complimented him.

Michele felt surprisingly lighthearted. "Are you denigrating women's work?"

"That's a loaded question which I respectfully decline to answer." He laughed.

After turning on the dishwasher she led Drake into the living room, expecting him to leave. Instead, he stretched out on the floor, resting the back of his head against the couch. Michele sat gingerly on the chair facing him. Before any tension could develop, Corey came in dressed for bed.

She hugged Michele, who whispered in her ear, "Don't forget to thank Mr. Hollister."

Corey knelt on the carpet next to Drake. "Thank you, Mr. Hollister," she repeated obediently. "I had a very nice time today."

"I did too." He smiled. "Does it rate a kiss?"

Corey hugged him enthusiastically, and Drake's arms closed around her. It twisted Michele's heart in a strange way to watch them.

After she had tucked her daughter in bed Michele returned to the living room, again expecting Drake to leave. Once more he surprised her. His eyes were closed and he seemed set for the night.

"Drake?" Michele called tentatively.

He lifted heavy eyelids, smiling sleepily at her. "Corey all tucked away?"

"Yes, she's probably dead to the world already. She had a big day. It was very kind of you," Michele said diffidently, mindful of all the abrasiveness that had flared between them.

"I got a kick out of it too."

She hesitated. "You look tired. Why don't you go home and go to bed?"

"In a few minutes." He patted the carpet next to him. "Come over and lie down next to me."

"No thanks, I'm comfortable right here." She seated herself on the edge of a big chair.

"You still don't trust me, do you?"

Drake looked deceptively harmless, his long body languidly relaxed on her rug. But Michele knew it was only an illusion. A giant cat might look just as innocent—until its prey was within reach. Then its coiled muscles would ripple as it sprang, its lithe body poetry in motion.

Michele gave herself a mental shake. Drake wasn't a jungle animal; he was a highly sophisticated man who had no need to pursue a woman who didn't want him. Still, there was no need to give the wrong impression.

"Of course I trust you," she said lightly. "How could I not after you came right out and told me I wasn't marriage material."

A mocking smile curved his mouth. "There are other relationships." His even teeth gleamed in a wide grin as she reacted the way he expected. "You're such fun to tease, Michele."

She forced herself to relax against the cushions. "I'll admit I'm not very good at playing games. I wonder why you even bother. It's probably the novelty. As soon as that wears off you'll move on to more productive pastures." She tried to look as though the prospect were pleasing.

"Don't count on it," he said lazily. "You're a very beautiful woman."

Her body tensed in spite of herself. "How can I convince you that you're wasting your time?"

He shrugged. "It's my time. Besides, there are fringe benefits. I told you I like children and dogs." He looked around. "By the way, where's Fluffy?"

Michele clapped a hand to her forehead. "I forgot all about her. Flora offered to keep her since we were going to be gone all day, but I should have picked her up."

Drake smiled, sitting up straight. "She's in good hands."

As soon as he levered himself to his feet, Michele sprang up as though jet propelled. "I'll see you to the door."

One dark eyebrow raised derisively. "That isn't a very subtle hint."

"Oh, I . . . I just assumed . . . I mean it is getting late and tomorrow's a work day."

"I guess you're right." He arched his back, stretching luxuriously.

Michele stared at his strong, athlete's body, feeling a tremor go through her. "I want to thank you for a lovely day, Drake," she said formally. "I really enjoyed it."

"Does it rate a kiss?" He reiterated his earlier words to Corey, putting his hands on Michele's shoulders and bending his dark head to her bright one.

She hesitated, gazing up at him uncertainly. There was something predatory about that hawklike face. His lowered lashes didn't quite hide the gleam in those brilliant blue eyes. Michele caught her breath, drawing back as his hands tightened imperceptibly. He released her immediately, the illusion of danger vanishing.

"Good night, Michele," Drake said pleasantly, with no obvious disappointment. "Thank you for dinner."

When she was alone, Michele chastised herself. Why did she have to make such a big deal about it? Why hadn't she just allowed Drake to kiss her good night so he'd know it didn't mean anything to her either? What made her so wary around him?

Drake's image was suddenly as real as if he were still standing there with the easy stance that showed he was in complete command of that broad-shouldered, lean-hipped body. There was a sort of leashed energy that challenged the imagination. Would he lose that air of dispassionate control when he made love? Would he murmur broken phrases of endearment, words of entreaty?

Michele wrapped her arms around her trembling body. It would be foolhardy *not* to be wary of this man. She knew exactly what she was afraid of.

Chapter Seven

M ichele felt entirely different about going to work on Monday morning. It was incredible that one weekend had changed her whole life. Last Friday she had felt alone in a sea of hostile strangers; now she had friends and a whole new outlook.

One thing hadn't changed, though. George Browder. He was even more hostile, if possible, than he had been at the close of the week. Michele soon found out the reason.

"I hear you were out in high society Friday night," was his opening shot.

"I had dinner at the Blaylocks'," she agreed. Keeping anything quiet in a small town like Greenfield was virtually impossible, Michele supposed, although there was no reason to be secretive.

"Did you take a good look around? The king and queen always make a point of entertaining the newest peasant, and then that's the end of it," he sneered.

Michele knew that wasn't so, but if it salved George's

pride she wasn't going to disagree with him. "They have a lovely home," she remarked neutrally.

"And a French chef. Were you impressed?"

Michele refused to be baited. "I thought Mr. and Mrs. Blaylock were both charming."

"I figured you'd like *her*—she's one of your kind. You girls stick together, don't you?"

Michele's patience was fraying. "I don't think either Mrs. Blaylock or I consider ourselves girls."

"What are you calling yourselves these days—ladies?" George seemed to find that amusing.

"Why don't you try *women?*" Michele replied evenly.

"You'll have to excuse me." His voice was heavy with sarcasm. "I'm not up on all the modern terminology."

"Just as long as you aren't equally confused in the lab." Michele knew her veiled threat couldn't be enforced, but it made her feel better.

"Any time you doubt it, you can complain to Drake," George answered confidently.

That would please him greatly, she knew. "I wouldn't bother Mr. Hollister with trivial matters," she remarked calmly, turning toward her office.

"Hi, Michele, how's the demon decorator? Did you have a good weekend?" Tim came in the door, bringing a breath of fresh air.

"Great, how was yours?" She grinned. "Did Polly give you time off for good behavior yesterday?"

"After I hung the curtains and touched up a few spots we missed on Saturday. The least you could have done was come back and finish what you started."

The lines around George's nose deepened as he listened to their banter. "I didn't know she knew your wife." He seemed incapable of using Michele's name.

"They're soul sisters." Tim laughed. "Both of them like to see a man working."

"At least I worked alongside you," Michele observed. "Which is what we'd both better start to do now. How is your test on that new nasal spray coming?"

Tim frowned slightly. "I'm not satisfied with it. One of the ingredients is too volatile; we'll have to look for a substitute."

They walked toward the supply closet, absorbed in discussion of the day's work. George stared after them, a baleful expression on his pinched face.

Although she was absorbed in an experiment, a part of Michele's mind waited for the phone to ring. Drake had popped up with such regularity over the weekend that she had grown accustomed to it—expected it, actually. But the tranquility of the lab remained undisturbed.

At lunchtime Michele's anticipation was heightened. On the way to the cafeteria her pulse rate quickened and her hands felt clammy. It was useless to tell herself she was behaving like a high-school girl on her way to meet the local football hero. The prospect of seeing Drake again, watching that slow smile warm his eyes at first sight of her, was like heady wine in Michele's veins.

Their eventual meeting replaced it with ice water.

Drake was walking down the hall with a man she hadn't seen before. When they all arrived at the lunch room at the same time, the man stood aside with a smile and a nod to Michele.

Drake turned his head with a slightly querying expression. "Oh, hello, Michele."

That was all. She might have been a stranger whose name he happened to know. After the initial shock, Michele was furious. Even if his interest in her over the weekend had been feigned, he could have pretended a little more warmth.

She selected her lunch quickly, wishing she had gone home instead. Michele was tempted to do just that until an unexpected greeting stopped her.

"Hello, remember me?" Mary Johnson was sitting at a table with several other women. "We met at the fair yesterday. Come and join us if you're alone."

There wasn't any way Michele could refuse. Under ordinary circumstances she wouldn't have wanted to, but after the recent encounter with Drake she needed time to compose herself. It didn't help when he and his companion took the table facing theirs. Drake was in her line of vision every time Michele raised her head. Not that he ever looked in her direction. Drake was completely absorbed in his conversation, oblivious to Michele's existence.

By the time she went back to work, her simmering anger had led to a resolution. She would never let down her guard with Drake again. How many times could she let him make a fool of her?

Usually the time flew by when she was working, but that afternoon seemed to drag endlessly. As she walked to her car at the close of the day, Michele felt limp. The sound of a familiar voice made her slender body stiffen.

"Had a hard day?" Drake fell in step, smiling down into her shadowed eyes.

After a quick glance, she tilted her chin and kept on walking. "Not especially."

He surveyed her rigid profile. "You look as though you need to relax. I'll buy you a drink."

"No, thank you. I have a child waiting for me."

"I don't suppose you'd like to invite me to your house for a drink?" he cajoled.

"You suppose correctly." They had arrived at her car.

As Michele reached out to unlock the door, Drake's hand closed over hers. "Do I detect a slight chilliness aimed my way?"

"That's very strange coming from you!"

His hands fastened on her shoulders, turning her so he could search her face. "What's wrong, Michele?"

"Not a thing. I'm just trying to follow your guidelines."

"What are you talking about?"

She had resolved not to give him the satisfaction of knowing his rebuff had hurt, but her resentment boiled over. "I told you I wasn't very good at playing games. I can't play hot one minute and cold the next."

Drake's blue eyes lit with laughter. "If you put as much passion into the first as you do into the second, I can hardly wait."

"You've mastered both techniques, haven't you?" she asked bitterly. "Your performance at lunch was faultless."

"So that's it," he said softly.

"That's exactly it! I've gotten a warmer greeting from my butcher."

He raised a dispassionate eyebrow. "You were the one who was so adamant about not giving anyone the wrong impression. Did you want me to tell you in front of everyone that I enjoyed holding you in my arms the other night? I did, you know."

"No, of course not!" she gasped. "I just . . . you didn't have to be so aloof."

Drake hesitated. "We both know you got your job on merit, Michele, but not everybody does. If I showed you undue attention it could lead to speculation which would be unfair to you. It might also generate petty jealousies. My job is to run this plant efficiently; I can't let my personal feelings blind me to that fact.''

It was a pretty speech which Michele didn't believe for a moment. Concern for her had nothing to do with it. Nor was there any chance that Drake would ever let his emotions get in the way of ambition—especially now when the whole company was within his grasp. He was very smooth about explaining things away, but he was still following his master plan—to seduce her for his own purposes. Remembering how nearly he had succeeded, Michele shivered.

"You're cold," Drake said. "Let's go out to dinner and discuss this. Flora will sit with Corey."

She stiffened away from him. "Your reasoning seems a little faulty. If you don't want people to think you're attracted to me as you *allege*"—she stressed the word to show she wasn't taken in—"why would you consider being seen in public with me?"

"I'm only answerable for my conduct at work—which has always been and will continue to be impeccable. My private life is my own."

"Well, I don't want to be part of it. There are too many rules involved. I might forget myself at the lab and speak without being spoken to," she said sarcastically.

Drake's expression hardened. "I've tried to explain something that should have been self-evident."

Michele's eyes sparkled with anger. "It was good of you to go to the trouble. Now that you know how dense I am, perhaps you'll finally leave me alone."

He stared down at her from his superior height, a muscle bunching at the point of his square jaw. "I once thought there could be something between us, but I see now I was wrong. You're determined to shut yourself away behind a tall fence. I've been able to scale it once or twice after great effort but frankly, my dear, I don't think you're worth the effort.'' His long legs carried him rapidly into the darkness.

Michele shook with rage all the way home. What right did he have to talk to her like that? It was a damn good thing she *was* cautious. It was men like Drake who made it imperative. He was just angry that his planned seduction had failed; at least now he'd give up. The conviction should have made her happier.

There were lights in the house when Michele turned into her driveway, sending a stab of apprehension through her. Corey should have been at Flora's. Michele braked to a sharp stop, running breathlessly into the house.

Corey and a young girl about eighteen or nineteen were sitting on the floor playing Monopoly. Neither Fluffy's barking nor the loud stereo seemed to bother their concentration. The whole atmosphere was unaccustomedly lively, so different from the quiet that usually greeted Michele.

Corey jumped up to hug her mother excitedly. "This is Carole, Mommy. She's going to take care of me."

"If your mother wants me to," Carole corrected with a smile. She had the scattering of freckles that went with her coppery hair. "Flora said she spoke to you about me, Mrs. Carter. I phoned Saturday and Sunday but there was nobody home, so I took a chance and came over this afternoon."

"I'm so glad you did," Michele exclaimed. "I need someone desperately."

Carole Spellman answered all of her questions satisfactorily. In fact she seemed too good to be true. After Michele outlined her requirements, Carole had some suggestions.

"I could also start dinner for you," she offered. "I might as well be doing something while I'm here. I can even stay overnight when you go out on dates so you don't have to worry about coming home early."

"Well, we'll see about that part," Michele temporized, knowing it wouldn't be necessary.

After they settled on a salary Carole left, with mutual expressions of delight all around. Michele's relief at solving her domestic arrangements helped ease her other frustrations.

It was the only solace she had all week. Nothing at work seemed to go right. Most of the problems were caused by George. After discovering that Tim had gone over to the enemy, he had become even more surly. It was inhibiting to both Michele and Tim. They could no longer banter freely, with George like a silent, vengeful spider evaluating their every word.

George's work was unsatisfactory also. He was dragging his feet over a product test that should have been completed days before, but Michele didn't like to call him on it so soon after taking charge. In the hope that professional pride would make him stop acting like a spoiled child, she decided to give him extra time.

Unfortunately, Drake didn't accord her the same privilege. He called her to his office one morning in the middle of the week.

Michele hadn't seen Drake since their encounter in the parking lot, and she didn't welcome the meeting. His cold formality on the interoffice phone warned that she was in for an ordeal.

"I've been expecting a report on that new hand cream." Drake's face was stern, his blue eyes wintry. It reminded Michele of her first interview.

"George is working on it now," she answered.

"He's *been* working on it for two weeks. It's a hand cream, not an artificial valve for heart transplants!"

Michele gritted her teeth. "I didn't know there were priorities where quality was concerned."

A pencil Drake was holding suddenly snapped in his hand. "Everything that goes out of this lab is thoroughly tested, but there are only so many procedures on a product of this kind." He proceeded to name them, surprising Michele anew with his knowledge. "It's either allergenic or it isn't. By this time George should have been halfway through the shampoo tests. What does he have to say about it?"

"Well, I . . . I haven't discussed it with him."

"Why not?"

Michele had a feeling Drake knew the answer to that. She took a deep breath. "I thought it would be better to wait and observe his methods, in order not to create any ill feelings."

"You aren't here to win friends, Mrs. Carter. And his methods are the same as anyone else's—only slower since you took charge."

Michele clamped a tight lid on her temper. She wouldn't let Drake maneuver her into an act of insubordination that would give him an excuse to fire her.

"I wasn't aware that we were on a tight schedule." A hint of bitterness crept into her voice. "That's something I would have appreciated being told. But now that I know the problem, you'll have your results—if I have to stay late and do it myself."

Drake frowned. "That isn't your job. As head of the department, you're supposed to know how to get the most out of your men." He leaned back in his chair, a mocking smile releasing his tight lips. "That isn't your favorite pastime though, is it, Michele?"

She stood up, hands held rigidly at her sides. "We all have to do things we don't want to do—and put up with people we don't like. If you have nothing further to say to me, I'll go back and do my job."

"I hope for your sake you can, Michele." There was an odd note in Drake's voice.

Knowing he was hoping she would fail put steel in her spine. She called George into her office as soon as she got back to the lab.

"When do you expect to finish the tests on that hand cream?" she asked without preamble. "You're a week behind schedule."

"You'll get it when I'm ready," he said insolently. "I don't do sloppy work."

"I'll get it by the end of the day, or I'll finish it myself. And turn it in with my own stamp on it," she added deliberately.

His face turned red with anger. "You'd like to take the credit, wouldn't you? Well, it won't work. Drake knows that product was assigned to me!"

"Mr. Hollister is the one who wants to know where the results are. I promised them to him—one way or another."

George clenched his hands impotently. "I told you, you'll get them when I think they're ready."

Michele guessed, rightly, that his defiance was mere bravado. As she expected, the finished report was on her desk by the end of the day. Getting it had taken its toll, however. She was tired and depressed by nightfall.

The one bright spot in her week was a call from Clarice.

"I'm having a committee meeting for the library fund on Saturday morning," Clarice phoned to say. "Polly and Jane Pennington will be here, and I'd like you to come, Michele. After the meeting we'll have lunch."

Michele accepted gratefully. She liked all the women involved, and she needed some interests outside of work.

Saturday dawned bright and sunny, but with a definite hint of winter in the wine-crisp air. Mindful of Clarice's dislike of jeans, Michele chose a powder blue wool dress. The tight bodice outlined her high, firm breasts, and the wide belt accentuated the narrowness of her small waist. Twirling in front of the mirror, Michele was pleased with the result. It was rather nice to get out of her usual uniform—tailored suits at work, and jeans at home. In keeping with her new image, she let her pale blond hair hang loose, brushing it until it shone like burnished gold.

Everyone was assembled in the den when she got to the Blaylock house. The attractive room was paneled in walnut and furnished with deep, comfortable couches and chairs. Clarice presided over the meeting from a leather-topped game table. After greeting Michele warmly, she opened the proceedings.

Halfway through the minutes Clarice exclaimed, "I don't know how they can play tennis in this weather!" The laughing voices floating in from outside were a distraction, even though all the windows were closed.

"Tennis players are fanatics." Polly laughed. "Just ask me—I'm married to one."

"Is Tim here?" Michele inquired.

"Practically all the time." Polly smiled fondly at her hostess. "Clarice and Simon are so good about letting people use their court."

Clarice shrugged. "What's the sense in having it go to waste? I should have had this meeting in the front of the house, though. They're especially exuberant today."

Michele wondered who "they" were. Was Drake here

too? She sighed as the pleasure seemed to go out of the day. In a small company town like Greenfield he was virtually unavoidable, whether in body or spirit. From then on Drake was at the back of her mind like a dull ache, preventing Michele from giving the meeting her full attention. She did her best to concentrate, telling herself that maybe Tim's partner was someone else. But her ears were attuned to the noises outside, and her eyes strayed often to the window.

"Well, I think that about wraps it up," Clarice remarked finally. "Do you think you'd be interested in joining our group, Michele?"

"Oh, I . . . it sounds very worthwhile." Michele wished she had paid more attention. "I'll certainly consider it."

"Good. We'll discuss it over lunch."

The dining-room table was as beautiful as it had been at dinner, but not as formal. The tall candlesticks weren't in evidence, and the floral centerpiece was a casual arrangement of white daisies and blue bachelor buttons in a straw basket. Blue delft service plates at each place held a large fluted shell filled with chicken salad.

"This looks perfect, Clarice. I'm so glad you didn't have quiche, or those gorgeous crepes with creamed mushrooms." Polly patted her stomach. "I'm getting big already."

"You look wonderful," Jane assured her.

"Hi, everybody." Tim stuck his head in the door. "Just wanted to say hello before we go down to Joe's for lunch."

"Would you like to stay here?" Clarice asked hospitably. "If you don't mind being surrounded by four gorgeous women, that is."

Tim grinned. "Best offer I've had all week."

When Drake appeared at his side, Clarice extended the same invitation. "Would you and Shelley like to join us for lunch?"

The redhead from the kissing booth! Michele held her breath, letting it out gratefully when she heard Drake refuse.

"That's straining the bonds of hospitality," he observed.

"Nonsense, it's only salad and rolls. Jacques can whip up three more."

"Thanks, but I think Shelley has her heart set on a hamburger. Besides, we don't want to break up your meeting." Drake stuck his head in the door, looking around the room for the first time.

Michele arranged her napkin on her lap, carefully smoothing the heavy linen.

"We're all finished with our meeting," Clarice answered. "But I won't urge you. Tell Margaret if you want something to drink later."

"On second thought, that chicken salad looks great," Drake remarked casually. "I think we'll take you up on it."

Shelley was less than delighted with the change in plans, especially when Drake seated her next to Clarice. He took the chair beside Michele.

"Are you only a threesome?" Jane asked. "I thought tennis players came in pairs, like Noah's selections for the ark."

"I'm afraid that was my fault." Shelley smiled through her lashes at Drake. "I was dying to play and I couldn't find a partner, so I horned in on their game."

"I admire your dedication," Clarice remarked dryly. "The only reason I can imagine for playing tennis in this weather is to wear one of those darling outfits."

Shelley had removed her warm-up jacket, displaying a tight-fitting top over a short white skirt. She glanced down at herself. "They are rather cute, aren't they?" she asked complacently.

"If you have the figure for it," Drake agreed, his voice leaving no doubt that Shelley fit the category. "So much more feminine than jeans, wouldn't you say, Michele?"

Clarice answered for her. "Jeans! They're an abomination!"

"I don't agree," Tim said. "They can be pretty sexy on the right woman. You should have seen Michele last Saturday."

Michele felt herself flush as everyone looked at her. She was especially conscious of Drake's mocking regard.

"Michele would look good in anything," Polly replied fondly.

Shelley's eyes narrowed as she noticed the expression on Drake's face. "Don't you think after a certain age, women should dress more suitably, though?" Her voice was deceptively sweet.

All of Michele's combative spirit rose to the fore. "You mean like Bermuda shorts for tennis instead of little-girl attire?" she asked, equally sweetly.

Polly snorted, attempting to turn it into a cough. Her change of subject was done diplomatically. "This chicken salad is delicious, Clarice. Does it have curry in it?"

Under cover of their hostess's reply, Drake murmured in Michele's ear, "Are those little claws retractable?"

Michele was indignant. Why was she always the one at fault? Well, this time she didn't have to take anything from him. "Is your girl friend's tongue permanently forked?" she asked in reply.

Drake's chuckle came from deep in his chest. "Not that I've been able to discern."

Michele knew what he was telling her. She had felt his exploration herself, that warm, masculine thrust that promised so much. "You'd certainly know, wouldn't you?"

"I suppose so." The reminiscent smile on his tanned face answered her question even more than the words.

Michele sat back in her chair, finding that Drake's arm was resting along the back of it. She forced herself not to change position. But when his long fingers started playing idly with the metal tab of her zipper under her soft tumbling hair, she turned her head to glare at him.

"Would you kindly behave yourself?" she asked in a controlled hiss.

"I was just fastening you up. You can always tell an unattached woman—she doesn't have a man to dress her." The rest of his observation was implicit in the suggestive tone.

Shelley was looking with displeasure at Drake's dark head, bent so close to Michele's that his warm breath feathered her ear. "Are you two telling secrets?" she called. "Or can the rest of us hear too?"

"We were just discussing a survey I've conducted," Drake answered smoothly.

"You mean like how many hours a day you watch television? Or what you like to do in your spare time?"

Drake smiled. "Not precisely, but something like that."

"The whole question of spare time will be academic for us once the baby arrives." Polly laughed ruefully.

"I won't notice any difference," Tim chuckled. "The future Fenwick heir can't keep me any busier than you do."

"Poor soul!" His wife made a face at him. "You know very well it's a man's world."

"I wouldn't have it any other way," Shelley declared.

As the other women regarded her with varying degrees of incredulity, Tim held up both hands. "No fair, we're outnumbered."

"Only by four to three." Shelley put herself firmly on the side she preferred.

Clarice looked at her dispassionately. "Wait until you compete for a job with a man—and he gets it because they tell you he has a family to support."

Jane nodded. "I had a friend who asked if she would qualify for the position if she married an unemployed man and adopted three children. She didn't get the job, but they all got a big laugh out of it."

"I don't know why a woman would want to do men's work anyway," Shelley maintained stubbornly.

"What exactly is men's work?" Clarice asked.

"Well . . . you know," Shelley answered vaguely.

"Don't you have something to contribute, Michele?" Drake asked softly.

"As a matter of fact, I do." She was careful to address her words to the redhead across the table. "You won't think men are so omniscient when one calls you on the carpet for something that wasn't your fault."

"Has that happened to you, Michele?" Drake's voice was silky.

"No, I . . . it was just an observation."

"But scarcely a valid one." No emotion showed on his handsome face. "Let's take a hypothetical case. Let's say you're the head of a department, and a man under you is goofing off. Whose job is it to whip him into line, yours or management's?"

"Hers, of course," Shelley crowed, deciding her side had made a point.

"I think I'd like to hear Michele's answer." Drake waited implacably.

"Well, it's . . . it would be mine," Michele replied. "But there could be extenuating circumstances."

"Such as?"

"Being new at the job," Clarice put in, her dark eyes holding comprehension.

Drake turned his attention to this new adversary. "Heads of departments are not supposed to require on-the-job training," he commented dryly.

"You're referring to men I imagine." Clarice warmed to their running battle. "It's quite a different thing when women inherit men who resent them merely for their sex."

"Presumably they know that's a possibility when they apply for the job. Real life isn't a birthday party—you don't get to invite only your best friends."

Michele felt she should take over her own defense. "I didn't expect it to be easy," she protested.

"Why, Michele, you're not taking this personally, are you?" Drake gave her a shark-toothed smile. "I thought we were talking hypothetically."

She wriggled out of the trap, making her voice casual. "It's just so similar to something that happened to me—in the past, of course."

"Of course," Drake concurred sardonically. "Were you able to solve the problem?"

She nodded grimly. "In spite of the male fraternity expecting me to fail."

"You malign my sex. Maybe some of them were hoping you'd succeed," Drake said softly.

But not you, Michele thought bitterly. Drake had made his position clear, in spite of his belated attempt to soften it.

Shelley felt she had been out of the conversation long

enough. "It's been my experience that you can get anything you want out of a man if you go about it the right way."

Clarice stared at her in faint disbelief. "We used to call that the starlet syndrome. I didn't know anyone subscribed to it anymore."

"I've always wanted to be in show business." Shelley was instantly diverted. "Meeting famous people, and going to all those glamorous opening nights."

"When you're working, the only opening night you go to is your own," Clarice advised her. "The theater is very inhibiting to one's social life."

Shelley looked unconvinced. "I'll bet you enjoyed every minute of it."

"Certainly I did," Clarice agreed patiently. "Unless you like what you're doing, going to work every day becomes as much a chore as making beds or changing diapers."

"I don't think I'm going to mind that," Polly commented softly.

"No, of course you won't." Clarice's expression softened. "But you mustn't try to do everything yourself. You're going to need some help in the house, including baby-sitters so you don't turn into a hermit."

"Maybe after a while," Polly temporized.

"I can help you there," Michele offered. "Carole Spellman would probably be glad to baby-sit. She takes care of Corey for me and I can recommend her highly."

"I wouldn't take her away from you," Polly protested.

"It's all right, I don't need her at night," Michele assured her.

"I think you're worrying about the wrong person, Clarice." Drake's expression was bland. "It appears that Michele is the one who plans to become a hermit."

"Not with that face and figure," Jane remarked. "I think

I have just the fellow for you, Michele. A new man just joined Jim's law firm.'' She turned to the others. "Don't you think Frank Goodwin would be perfect for her?''

A slight frown came and went just as quickly on Drake's broad forehead. "Michele doesn't welcome being fixed up with men. She was very vocal about it the other night.''

Clarice's eyes rested thoughtfully on both of them. "That was said in the heat of the moment. I think she and Frank would get on very well together.''

"I'll have him call you," Jane promised.

Michele felt like a tightrope walker on a very shaky wire. She was damned if she was going to confirm Drake's opinion of her as a sour man-hater, but she really didn't want Jane's friend to call.

Tim saved her the trouble of answering. He gave his wife a wide grin. "Looks as though you've lost your position as chief matchmaker.''

"Not necessarily." Polly exchanged an impassive look with Clarice. "I have someone in mind for Michele also.''

Michele felt things were getting out of hand. "I'd rather none of you went to any trouble. It's been my experience that these things never work out.''

Jane shrugged. "You don't have to marry the man. You can just go out with him and see what develops.''

"Exactly. And who knows? It might even be love at first sight," Clarice remarked.

Michele was beginning to feel pressured. She no longer cared what Drake thought. "I'd feel ridiculous going out on a blind date at my age!''

"That's right. Better the devil you know than one you don't," Drake advised, amusement coloring his murmured comment.

Jane didn't hear him. "I can understand how you feel.

Tell you what—I'll have a little party. It won't be as awkward for either of you if there are other people around.''

"I accept," Drake said promptly.

Clarice raised a perfectly arched eyebrow. "She hasn't told you the date."

"I'll have to see when Frank is available," Jane agreed.

Shelley's vapidly pretty face wore a pinched expression. "If you're through arranging Michele's love life, could we get back to our tennis game?"

Tim stood up. "I'm ready. Coming, Drake?"

Drake leaned back in his chair, crossing one muscular leg over the other, the brief white shorts displaying their length. "You go ahead. I'm needed here. I have to give Michele advice on how to trap Mr. Wonderful—tell her what turns a man on."

"Michele will do quite nicely without your assistance. Run along, Drake." Clarice's cool tone brooked no argument.

"I have to run too," Jane said. "It was a lovely lunch, Clarice. I'll be in touch, Michele."

"Me too." Polly got to her feet. "I have an appointment at the beauty shop."

"Don't rush off," Clarice said as Michele rose also. "Stay and have another cup of coffee with me."

"You probably have things to do."

Clarice assured Michele she didn't, leading her into the den. After the maid had brought hot coffee, they talked for a while about the library fund. Michele had even more trouble keeping her mind on it this time. Damn Drake Hollister anyway she thought. There must be some way to get back at him.

"How are things going at the lab?" Clarice asked, when the other subject had been exhausted.

"Just fine."

"No problems?"

"Nothing I can't handle."

"I admire your independence, but sometimes it helps to unburden yourself to a sympathetic listener," Clarice said gently.

"There really isn't anything to tell," Michele insisted. "George is a little difficult, but I understand everyone finds him rather heavy going. We had a small set-to that was resolved satisfactorily. I can handle *him*." She stressed the last word unconsciously.

"How about Drake?"

Michele's long lashes fell. She examined her cup with great interest. "I don't see a great deal of him."

"By choice?"

Michele nodded grimly. Suddenly her pent-up frustration burst forth, in spite of her resolve not to complain. "He resents being forced to hire me. Nothing I can do is going to change that. When he looks at me, all he sees is a blow to his macho pride!"

"I don't think Drake is that insecure," Clarice remarked. "He'll fight like a tiger to win, but I've never found him a vindictive loser."

Michele realized belatedly that Drake was a great favorite with both Blaylocks—besides being the heir apparent. No matter how committed Clarice was to women's rights, she was bound to give Drake great leeway. It had been a mistake to violate her own credo—never complain, never explain.

"I think you should get to know him better," Clarice urged.

"Perhaps you're right," Michele agreed politely.

There wasn't any point in arguing about it. She couldn't

tell Clarice that her fair-haired boy was a devil incarnate, with a full bag of Machiavellian tricks for getting rid of Michele.

A look of annoyance crossed Clarice's patrician features before being quickly banished. "You two have so much in common. It seems a shame to let an initial disagreement spoil what could be a very pleasant relationship."

"The only thing we have in common is our work at the lab—and a mutual desire to keep it at that," Michele answered tautly, not caring *how* fond Clarice was of Drake. She stood up, putting her cup on the coffee table. "I really must go. Thank you so much for everything."

Clarice walked her to the door, staring after Michele's slender, departing figure. A slight frown of concentration puckered her lovely brows.

Chapter Eight

*E*verything went more smoothly the following week. George had evidently awakened to the realization that his sabotage was reflecting on himself. He wasn't any pleasanter to be around but he did his work, and that was all Michele was interested in.

Drake maintained a discreet distance too, for which Michele was grateful. It enabled her to forget about him for hours at a time. The only annoyance was Jane's phone call late in the week.

"Did you think I forgot about you?" she asked.

"No." Michele tried to keep the resignation out of her voice. "I was sure you hadn't."

"Good. It just took me this long to pin Frank down. You've no idea how sought after a bachelor is in a small town like this."

"I suppose it's the same anywhere," Michele murmured. "Things haven't changed that much."

"You're right—they're disgustingly spoiled. Frank seems quite nice though, and he's anxious to meet you."

"I hope you didn't give me a big buildup," Michele cried in dismay.

Jane laughed. "Oh no, I just told him you had a sensational figure, long blond hair and beautiful gray eyes."

"Good Lord, I hope you're kidding!"

"What else could I say when he asked me? Anyway, I'm having a little get-together Saturday night. I gave Frank your phone number; he'll be calling you."

Michele felt a sinking sensation in her stomach. There was no way she could get out of it; Jane was giving the party for her. Besides that, she was the mother of Corey's best friend. Michele wouldn't do anything to jeopardize that relationship.

She sighed. "What time would you like me there?"

"I told Frank to pick you up at eight o'clock."

"I'd prefer to take my own car, Jane."

"Don't be ridiculous," her friend scolded. "You'll only be alone with him for a few minutes; that can't be too awkward. He's really very handsome. You're going to thank me."

Afterward, Michele was to wonder what would have happened if she had insisted. Would it have changed anything?

It wasn't until later that she thought about the guest list. It wouldn't have been polite to ask who was going to be there, and she couldn't very well have singled Drake out anyway. Was he coming, though? Probably, since he had invited himself. Michele began to feel better about having a date. Even if this Frank Goodwin had warts and a double chin, she was going to lavish wide-eyed admiration on him. At least when Drake was looking.

Michele dressed for her date reluctantly on Saturday

night. She was tempted to wear the worst mistake in her closet, and pull her hair back in a tight knot. But that would be rude to her host and hostess.

With a deep sigh she sat down at the dressing table, applying mascara to her long, thick lashes, and using a lipstick brush to outline her full mouth. She refused to do anything elaborate with her hair though, letting it hang loose to curl around her shoulders.

The exquisitely contoured face in the mirror didn't please Michele. Nor was she satisfied with the dress she chose, a beige jacquard silk with a high neck and a low cowl back. The soft fabric clung subtly to her curved body, the pale color complementing her light hair.

Her slight frown deepened. Although she hadn't gone to any great effort, it looked as though she had. Michele didn't want Frank Goodwin to think she considered this a special occasion.

Carole and Corey were lavish in their praise.

"You look sensational, Mrs. Carter." Carole's eyes gleamed with admiration. "Like you just stepped out of *Vogue* magazine."

"That dress is neato," Corey concurred.

"Is it new? Has your boyfriend seen it yet?" Carole asked.

"He isn't my boyfriend," Michele answered defensively. "I don't even know the man."

"A blind date?" Carole made a face. "Someone fixed me up on one once and it was a disaster." Realizing that was less than tactful, she added hurriedly, "But I'm sure yours will be fine."

Why did she have a feeling Carole was right the first time? Michele asked herself as she went to answer the doorbell.

Frank Goodwin should have allayed her fears. He was almost six feet tall, with even features topped by wavy, fair hair. A luxuriant moustache dominated his upper lip. Michele wondered irrelevantly if he had grown it to distract attention from his rather weak chin. She dismissed the thought immediately as being unworthy.

"Well, hello." Frank's greeting was drawn out to let his eyes travel over Michele from head to toe, lingering in between. "Jane certainly didn't give me a bum steer this time."

Michele restrained herself from asking if that was usually the case. She settled for inviting him in. "This is my daughter, Corey."

"What a pretty little girl. How old are you?" Frank asked, in the falsely bright tone usually reserved for two-year-olds with a learning disability.

Before she could answer, he noticed Carole. Her red gold hair was loosed from its usual long braid. With the bright cloud sweeping her shoulders, and a thin T-shirt and tight jeans molding her supple figure, she was an undeniably sexy sight.

Frank switched his attention instantly, taking inventory of every rounded curve. "And how old is this little girl?"

Michele felt a ripple of distaste. "When you get to me, don't expect an answer," she advised dryly, her eyes meeting Carole's in a look of mutual understanding.

As she returned from the bedroom with her coat, Carole murmured consolingly, "He's very good-looking."

Gary had been good-looking too. Where had that unbidden thought come from, Michele wondered? Frank was nothing like her departed husband except that they were both blond. Michele pinned a determined smile on her face. As Jane had pointed out, they wouldn't be alone long.

During the short ride, Frank asked questions that bordered on the personal, yet never quite crossed the boundary sufficiently for her to object. He seemed bent on compiling a complete dossier, even about irrelevant matters.

"Is Carole your baby-sitter, or does she live in?" he asked casually.

"No, she takes care of Corey for me until I get home from work."

"Does she stay over when she baby-sits?"

"She offered to, but I told her it wasn't necessary. Sunday is her only day to sleep in, and my daughter gets up very early."

Why would he ask a question like that? Suddenly Michele realized that Carole was the one Frank was really interested in. Relief flooded her, along with amusement. Carole was a lot better equipped to handle Frank's brand of male chauvinism. Young women today didn't put up with sexual harassment, no matter how subtle.

Michele felt the time had come to change the subject. She chose the one she thought would be his favorite. "How did you happen to settle in Greenfield?"

Frank's face wore a smug expression. "You noticed this little town isn't quite my speed—very perceptive of you."

"You aren't like any of the other people I've met here," she murmured ironically.

He took it as a compliment. "Neither are you, baby. I think we're going to get along just dandy."

Michele stifled a sigh. "You were going to tell me what you're doing in Greenfield. Where did you live before?"

"Several places," he answered vaguely. "The last one was Chicago."

"You're going to find it quite different here," she remarked. "*I* certainly did." Michele thought of all the kindness she had encountered, the friendship that was offered immediately and without strings.

He turned his head to give her a suggestive look. "Don't worry, kid, I'll liven things up for you."

"I didn't mean—" There was no point in even trying to explain herself. "I'm not sure you're going to stick around that long," she replied dryly.

"You never can tell. It might not be so bad to be a big frog in a little pond."

His condescension set her teeth on edge, goading Michele into a remark she wouldn't normally have made. "I suppose it's better than being a tadpole in the big city."

"Hey, don't think I couldn't cut it there." An aggrieved expression marred his smooth good looks. "If it hadn't been for all those bleeding-heart liberals, I would have been a partner in my last law firm."

"What does that have to do with it?" Michele asked blankly.

"It's the bloody minority system. The colleges are turning out women lawyers faster than General Motors can make cars. They don't know a damn thing, but the law says you have to hire them." Frank warmed to an old grievance. "They get all the promotions, and the rest of us sit around with our finger in our ear. Well, I don't have to put up with that!"

Michele was beginning to get the picture. After rising to the level of his own incompetence, Frank was stuck in neutral. How long would it be until vanity coupled with ineptitude sent him on to the next town?

He was so completely out of touch with a changing world that Michele almost felt sorry for him. It softened her next remark. "I guess Chicago's loss is Greenfield's gain."

Frank nodded, accepting her compliment as his due. "I

think I'm going to like it here.'' He squeezed her hand. ''You and I are going to shake up this little town, baby.''

Michele was delighted to see the Pennington house ahead.

The party was being held in a large downstairs playroom that was perfect for entertaining. A built-in bar stretched across one corner of the room, with high rattan stools drawn up to it. The couches and chairs had been pushed against the walls, leaving the polished floor clear for dancing to music from the elaborate stereo system.

''What a wonderful room for a party,'' Michele exclaimed to their hostess.

Jane laughed. ''Now that all the roller skates and chemistry sets are stashed away. Usually this place looks like the local rec center.''

''How wonderful for the children to have a place to bring their friends.''

''They do tend to come in droves,'' Jane agreed. ''That bar dispenses more soda pop than scotch.''

''You just said the magic word,'' Frank told her, heading for the bar.

''Well, how do you like him?'' Jane asked eagerly, when they were alone. ''Isn't he handsome?''

Michele's smile didn't quite reach her eyes. ''He reminds me of someone I used to know.'' It didn't answer the question, but Jane didn't seem to notice.

''You two make a stunning couple—you're both so blond and beautiful. I'm expecting big things from tonight.''

''I wish you wouldn't,'' Michele cried.

Jane patted her shoulder. ''Don't worry, I noticed how Frank looked at you. I'm sure he likes you.'' She looked critically at Michele's distressed face. ''You have to have more confidence in yourself.''

"I just don't want you to be disappointed after you went to all this trouble," Michele murmured hopelessly.

"It was a good excuse to have a party anyway," Jane assured her. She glanced toward the door. "Oh good, here are Drake and Marilyn."

Michele was rooted to the spot, even though she had expected it. At least he hadn't brought Shelley. She watched Jane greet the newcomers, noticing Drake's casual arm around his date's shoulders. Marilyn was laughing at something he said, reaching up to tug his ear playfully. Their casual intimacy told its own story.

Michele drew a deep breath, preparing to join her own date. At that moment Drake looked over the room, as though searching for someone. His eyes held hers. A warm tide rose in Michele as they stared at each other. In that one electrifying moment her senses registered everything about him, the shock of black hair that fell over his tanned forehead, his dark, intense face, the breadth of his shoulders under the navy blazer. She jumped when someone put a glass in her hand.

"Boy, are you skittish," Frank remarked.

"I . . . I didn't see you."

"I brought you a drink." He raised the glass to her lips. "You need to loosen up and get lively."

Michele took an obedient sip, although she disliked scotch. "Isn't this a nice party?" The polite words came automatically, without her having to think about them.

"And it's going to get better." Frank led her to the middle of the floor. "Let's dance."

She put her glass down, moving reluctantly into his arms.

"Mm, you feel sensational." He held her closer than she liked.

Michele discovered that the width of Frank's shoulders

was mostly due to the padding in his jacket. In a flash of déjà vu, she remembered clinging to Drake and feeling the hard muscles under her clutching hands. Her fingers unconsciously dug into Frank's coat, seeking to dispel the image.

"The little kitty has claws, huh?" he murmured, his hand sliding down her back.

Michele was reminded of Drake's low, amused voice asking if her claws were retractable. That had been teasing; this was disgusting!

"Bet I can make you purr," Frank continued confidently.

Michele was about to advise him that he would be unfit for combat if he tried it, when she saw Drake and Marilyn dancing next to them.

She lowered her lashes enticingly. "I'm sure you could make a woman do anything."

Drake overheard, as Michele intended. His reaction, however, wasn't the one she desired.

He snorted derisively. "You'll notice she said *a* woman. She didn't necessarily refer to herself." Drake stopped dancing to extend his hand, introducing himself. "I understand you're new here. How do you like Greenfield?"

"Seems like a nice little town," Frank answered patronizingly. "It isn't New York or Chicago, but what is?"

"That's true." Drake was deceptively submissive. "I guess we here in the boonies will just have to make do."

"Shame on both of you." Marilyn wasn't going to accept their disparagement. "More isn't necessarily better. That also includes crime, pollution and overcrowding."

Frank smiled tolerantly. "I'm afraid I've gotten your wife's back up."

"That's very flattering, but Marilyn isn't my wife," Drake informed him.

"Really?" Frank took a more comprehensive look at the pretty brunette.

"It's entirely my loss," Drake continued smoothly.

Marilyn laughed. "If you believe that, you'll believe anything. Drake is a confirmed bachelor."

"Nothing is written in stone, my dear," he murmured.

"That's what keeps all of us going," Marilyn teased. "The challenge."

"He can't afford to be as independent anymore. Now he has competition." Frank's interest had quickened as soon as he discovered Marilyn was unattached.

Michele had taken no part in the conversation, enduring it numbly until she could put distance between herself and Drake. He included her now.

"Surely you wouldn't want to look any farther afield when you have as charming a companion as Michele?" Drake commented.

Frank was reminded of the old adage about a bird in the hand. He put his arm around her. "You're right. Michele and I discovered tonight how much we have in common."

Drake's mocking blue eyes held hers. "Is that true, Michele?"

It took an effort to endure Frank's caressing arm, but Michele stood it. She even managed an adoring look at him. "I couldn't believe it myself."

"You don't know what a victory you've scored," Drake told the other man. "Michele has been very vocal about not wanting to get involved."

"It must be kismet," Frank remarked lightly. "We hit it off right away."

"If you're thinking of settling down together, Marilyn might be able to help you," Drake persisted. "She's in the real-estate business—specializing in vine-covered cottages.''

Michele's outraged expression was balanced by Frank's dismayed one. "We just met tonight, old man," he protested. "Give us a chance.''

"Don't pay any attention to Drake," Marilyn advised. "His sense of humor is a little bizarre at times. I am in the real-estate business though, if you're ever in the market for an apartment or anything," she told Frank.

He smiled weakly. "I'll keep it in mind.''

"What did you think of the house Drake took you through?" Marilyn asked Michele. "Isn't it a dream?''

"It's magnificent," Michele answered sincerely.

"I know I'm cutting my own throat, but I think it's a shame to waste it on him." Marilyn smiled mischievously, echoing Michele's earlier thought. "Don't you agree?''

"I must admit I do." Michele realized that her antipathy toward Marilyn had been unfounded. She was warm and outgoing, an eminently suitable companion for Drake. It was a bittersweet conclusion.

"If I promise not to put mirrors on the ceiling, will that satisfy you ladies?" Drake asked dryly.

Marilyn wrinkled her nose at him. "I know you better than that. You're a wily gent, but you've never been guilty of bad taste. I just want that house to go to a family who would appreciate it. You would only qualify if you filled all those bedrooms with little kids.''

Drake gave her a slow smile. "It isn't beyond the realm of possibility.''

Michele felt a stabbing pain between her breasts. "I believe I'd like another drink," she told Frank.

He accepted the excuse gratefully, leading Michele to the

long bar. "I thought shotgun marriages only took place in the hills. Is that guy related to you?" he asked.

"No, he's my boss," she answered tersely.

"He sure takes an interest in you."

"Not really." Michele knew that wasn't entirely true, but the interest Drake had in her wasn't the beneficial kind. "He just likes to stick pins into people to see how they'll react."

Frank wasn't entirely convinced "Look, Michele, you're a great-looking chick, but—"

"Don't bother to say it," she interrupted. Michele had taken enough from both of them. "Let me put your mind at rest. I don't want to marry you. I don't even want to go out with you again."

"I didn't mean to hurt your feelings," he said awkwardly.

"You didn't. Actually, I'm grateful. You gave me a chance to say what I really mean."

Frank took both her hands, holding on when she would have pulled them away. "Don't be like that, baby. No guy likes to be rushed, but that doesn't mean we can't keep on seeing each other. Let's just let nature take its course."

Michele closed her eyes, counting slowly to ten. It wouldn't do to make a scene. When she opened them, Drake was regarding her with interest.

"Were you praying?" he asked politely.

"How did you guess?" she returned acidly. "It didn't work though, you're still here."

As soon as Drake joined them, Frank dropped Michele's hands. Murmuring something unintelligible, he headed for the other side of the room.

Drake watched his departure with amusement. "Your boyfriend seems remarkably nervous."

"I wonder why?" she asked sarcastically.

He shrugged. "I really did you a favor. You wouldn't want to get tangled up with a guy who has no sense of humor."

Drake's smug assumption that he had successfully broken up her budding romance nettled Michele. She hid it under a serene countenance. "I think it's refreshing to find a man who takes serious things seriously."

Drake's sardonic smile disappeared. "He's a loser, Michele. I've seen too many of his kind. You're well rid of him."

"What makes you think I'm rid of him?" she demanded. "Your juvenile attempt to scare Frank off was unsuccessful."

"You're going to go on seeing him?" He frowned.

"Regularly, I hope," she answered defiantly.

They were standing in the middle of the floor, scowling at each other while dancing couples swirled around them. When someone accidently jostled Michele, Drake's arms closed automatically around her. Michele's taut body attempted to maintain its distance from his, while still giving the semblance of dancing.

He impatiently jerked her closer. "Don't be any more of a little idiot than you already are," he muttered. Rightly guessing her intention to stalk off the floor, he held her firmly.

"Hi, you two," Polly hailed them. She and Tim were late arrivals. "Isn't this a peachy party?"

Michele was forced to let Drake hold her. She tried to manage a smile. "It certainly is." As soon as the other couple moved off she hissed at Drake, "Will you kindly let go of me!"

A muscle bunched at the clean line of his jaw. "I don't

intend to let everyone here know we've had an argument. You're going to dance with me and look as though you're enjoying it.'' When Michele flung her head back, a ghost of a smile warmed his wintry eyes. ''All right then, just dance with me.''

There was nothing else she could do; Michele could see his logic. It would make things awkward at work if everyone knew their disagreement had blossomed into a full-blown feud.

She rested her hand as lightly as possible on Drake's shoulder, but she could still feel the solid bone and muscle underneath—unlike Frank's wadded padding. Her fingers moved in unwilling appreciation of his splendid athlete's frame, unable even now to deny its attraction.

As though he couldn't help himself either, Drake drew her closer, resting his cheek against her soft, scented hair. His arms wrapped her in a warm cocoon. She was enveloped by him, her senses registering the subtle male smell of him, the touch of his hard thighs brushing her own. Drake's hands wandered restlessly over her back, creating ripples of sensation that spread out in widening circles. The sound of his heart merged with hers, making Michele feel she was part of him. In a strangely hypnotic state, she relaxed completely in his embrace.

''I hope you'll remember that Michele is Frank's date tonight, Drake.'' Jane's laughing admonition broke the spell. ''You're dancing awfully close.''

They both looked rather dazed as they drew apart, staring at each other. Then realization swept over Michele, filling the void with blazing anger. Drake would stoop to anything to impose his will! If he couldn't scare Frank off, he'd try seduction on *her!*

''It won't work,'' she stated flatly.

Drake looked at her blankly. "What are you talking about?"

"Was I supposed to compare the two of you and find you more attractive? Well, I don't. You aren't even in Frank's league."

"Thanks for the compliment, but would you like me to prove that your first statement is wrong?" He moved closer, taunting Michele with his knowledge of her vulnerability.

Before he could carry out his threat, she stepped back hastily. "You think everything can be reduced to the level of sex, don't you?" Her lowered voice was nonetheless deadly. "Well, I happen to prefer a man with a little more sensitivity."

"And you think that's Frank?" Drake's raised eyebrows were mockingly incredulous.

"Did I hear my name called?" Frank appeared at Michele's side.

She put her arm around his waist, gazing up with a seductive pout. "I thought you forgot all about me."

He gave her a molten look. "Let's go over in a corner so you can refresh my memory."

Drake shook his head. "That's sensitivity all right."

With an outraged look, Michele took Frank's arm and walked away.

The rest of the evening was pure torture. Drake watched her like a giant cat, making it necessary for Michele to carry out the fiction of being attracted to Frank. He basked in her admiration, his smug assumption of divine right making him even more difficult to stomach. If only the party weren't being given for her, she might have pleaded a headache. Under the circumstances, Michele felt the obligation to stay till the bitter end.

Just as all good things come to a finish, bad ones do too.

Eventually the party wound to a close and they were able to leave.

Michele was very quiet on the way home, feeling she had more than fulfilled her social duties for one night. Frank didn't seem to notice. He carried the whole conversation quite happily.

When they reached her house she prepared to say good-bye at the door, but Frank insisted on coming in.

"I'll just make sure there aren't any intruders lurking about," he said. "A woman living alone can't be too careful."

"I don't live alone and, besides, Carole's here."

He gave her a sharp look. "You said she was going home."

"Well yes, but—" By that time they were inside.

Carole got up from the couch where she had been reading. "Hi, did you have a good time?" She went to turn off the stereo, which was playing softly.

"Leave it on," Frank intercepted her. "It's nice and soothing."

"It was a lovely party." Michele answered Carole's question, exchanging a glance with her.

Frank gazed at his watch. "I had no idea it was so late. You must want to get home, Carole."

"Not necessarily." Carole looked at Michele for guidance. "I never go to sleep early anyway."

Michele knew why the girl was offering to stay, but she was reluctant to keep her up any longer. It was unfortunate that Frank had insisted on coming in, but she could get rid of him. He wasn't the first man whose ardor Michele had cooled.

"Run along, Carole. I'll see you Monday evening." After she had gone, Michele turned to Frank, who was examining some knickknacks on a shelf. "You'd better be going too."

He gave her a smoldering smile. "I never go to sleep early either."

"It isn't early," she informed him crisply.

Her curt tone diluted his self-confidence a tiny bit. "Aren't you going to offer me one for the road?"

"No, I'm not." Michele made no attempt to soften the blunt words.

Frank looked hurt. "That isn't very friendly. What's wrong, Michele?"

In spite of the fact that he was a fairly repulsive human being, her conscience began to hurt. She *had* used him tonight. After hanging on his every utterance at the party, Michele could understand how he would be confused by her abrupt turnabout.

"I'll give you a drink if you really want one," she told him grudgingly.

"That will do for starters." His suggestive smile set her teeth on edge.

"Just so there's no misunderstanding, that's *all* I'm offering," she answered sharply.

"I understand," he said soothingly.

Why did she have the feeling he didn't? Michele was tempted to rescind her offer, but a lifetime of training in courtesy prevented it. What difference did another half hour really make?

After she had mixed them each a drink and they were seated on the couch, Michele tried to make amends. "I regret everything about this evening, Frank. It was a mistake from start to finish."

"I wouldn't say that." He tried unsuccessfully to take her hand.

"If I gave you the wrong impression, I'm sorry."

Her words didn't seem to be registering. Frank's eyes had a hard glitter. "I like a girl who's shy. It makes it more exciting."

"I was telling the truth tonight when I said I didn't want to see you again," Michele said desperately. "You're a very nice fellow, but we have absolutely nothing in common."

Frank took the drink out of her hand, putting it on a table. His arm circled her shoulders. "We have the oldest thing in the world going for us, baby." His free hand cupped her breast as he leaned forward to kiss the side of her neck.

Michele shivered with disgust at the contact of his slack, wet mouth. She tried to pry his fingers away from her breast. "I want you to leave now, Frank."

His hand tightened painfully as his mouth covered hers. "You know that's not what you want."

Michele felt as though she were smothering. While his tongue almost prevented her from breathing, his hands were everywhere on her body, crawling up her thigh under her skirt, sliding inside her neckline to fondle her breasts. He was like an octopus. Every time she dislodged one tentacle, it fastened itself in another place. Finally Michele fought free, jumping to her feet.

"You are the most loathsome man I've ever met," she cried breathlessly. "If you don't get out of my house this minute, I'm going to call the police!"

His passion-swollen face took on an ugly expression. "You can drop the act now, it's starting to wear a little thin. We both know you've been hot to trot all night."

Michele felt almost sick with revulsion. She forced down the nausea. "I meant what I said, Frank. You'd better leave immediately."

When it finally got through to him that she was serious, his eyes narrowed dangerously. "Listen, sister, no little tease is going to play me for a chump. You've been sending out signals all evening; now you're going to come across."

As Michele turned toward the phone he made a grab for her, catching the cowl back of her dress. It ripped to the waist, startling her so that she stopped in her tracks. In that off-guard moment Frank pounced, throwing Michele to the couch and falling heavily on top of her.

She struggled wildly, but he was too strong for her. As she scratched and tried to bite, he pinned her wrists above her head, grinding his body into hers.

"That's right, fight, you little wildcat," he muttered thickly. "I love it."

"Let go of me, you maniac!" Michele twisted wildly, her strength almost gone.

Frank's knee was between her legs, his arousal all too evident. "Okay, baby, play time's over," he grunted.

When the doorbell rang, Michele thought she must be imagining it. It was only wishful thinking that someone would save her. It wasn't until Frank lifted his head, a wary expression replacing the untamed passion in his eyes, that she realized help was actually at hand.

Someone was pounding on the door now. Frank swore violently, indecision evident on his face. Michele seized the moment to wriggle out from under him, racing to the door and throwing it open.

"Michele, I—" Drake took a look at her disheveled state, his face freezing in murderous rage.

She threw herself into his arms, whimpering incoherent little words. He held her close, making reassuring sounds, but his eyes were on the man who was hurriedly straightening his clothing.

"Listen, old man, this was all a mistake," Frank began placatingly.

"And you made it." Drake's voice was a primal growl. "I hope you know I'm going to kill you."

When he tried to disentangle Michele's arms she clung tighter. "Please don't leave me," she begged.

"It's all right, sweetheart." Drake kissed her temple, smoothing her tangled hair. "You're safe now."

Frank seized the moment of diversion to make his escape. Sidling swiftly past them, he made an ignominious dash for the door. Drake's muscles tensed like steel coils, but Michele held him back.

"Let him go," she pleaded. "I just want him out of here."

The frantic squeal of tires told that it was too late anyway. For a moment the primitive fury of a predator deprived of its prey smoldered in Drake's eyes. Then he turned all of his attention to Michele.

"Did he hurt you?" His hand gently raised her chin.

"No, you came along in time. But he . . . it was . . ." She started to tremble uncontrollably.

"Let it all out, sweetheart." Drake lifted her in his arms, carrying her over to a big chair.

It was a long time before Michele could control herself enough to talk about the brutal assault. Then it all came tumbling out.

"I didn't know there were men like that in the world," she whispered. "Not so-called civilized ones."

"It's unfortunate," Drake agreed, stroking her back soothingly.

Anyone else would have said I told you so, but Drake wasn't that kind of person. Michele said it for him. "You tried to warn me but I wouldn't listen. How did you know,

Drake? How did you happen to be here just when I needed you?''

"I thought you might be in for a spot of trouble. I would have come sooner, but I had to take Marilyn home.''

Michele had virtually forgotten about the party. The memory of her churlish behavior toward Drake filled her with remorse. Her long lashes fell as she unconsciously played with a button on his shirt. "I'm sorry,'' she murmured, ''. . . about everything.''

He stared at the shining crown of her head for a long moment before gently sliding her off his lap. Her tiny sound of protest was ignored as he got to his feet.

Drake thrust his hands in his pockets. "Try not to think about it anymore. I guarantee he won't bother you again.'' His granite face reinforced the promise.

She reached up to clutch his arm. "Please let it drop! I couldn't bear it if the story got out.''

Drake's clenched fists tightened the slacks over his rigid thighs. It clearly went against his nature, but her agitation convinced him. Hunching down in front of her, he took both of Michele's cold hands in his.

"He doesn't deserve to get off that easy, but okay, honey, if you say so. Why don't you go to bed now and get some rest.''

As she stared into his strong face, Michele was overcome by a longing more compelling than any she had ever known. She didn't want to be alone. She wanted to lie next to this man, to feel his warmth invading her body. She wanted his arms around her, his mouth covering her own.

After the experience she had just gone through, the slightest contact with a man should have been repugnant. But Michele finally admitted the truth to herself. It wasn't the need to be comforted, or gratitude for what he had done.

She was in love with Drake—totally committed, without hope of ever being free. It was futile to deny it, especially now when she needed him so.

Michele's soft mouth trembled, a hint of tears in her lovely eyes. "Stay with me," she murmured, the pleading words a mere whisper.

Tiny flames turned Drake's eyes brilliant. His hands urged her slender body toward his. Then the flame died as he sat back on his heels. "You don't have to be afraid. Frank won't be back."

Didn't he know what she was asking? She touched his mouth tentatively. "I don't want you to go."

Drake caught his breath. His hand closed around her wrist, lifting her palm to his lips. "You're upset and confused, sweetheart. One man taking advantage of you tonight is enough."

Although the rejection was sugarcoated, it was painfully real. Drake didn't want her. He might even be expected back at Marilyn's after his errand of mercy. When would she learn? This was the second time he had repulsed her.

She stood up, holding her torn dress together in the back. "You're right, of course. I understand."

"No, I'm afraid you don't. I told you I hoped you would want me one day for the right reason—this isn't it."

How could she say her reason was the best one in the world? It wouldn't make any difference anyway. If he cared even a fragment for her, he wouldn't keep making all these conditions.

Michele raised her head proudly. "I'll be fine now, you can leave."

He put his hands on her shoulders, searching her face. "We have to talk about this, but not now. Not while you can't think clearly. Will you have dinner with me tomorrow night, Michele?''

"No!" How could he even suggest it?

"We have to settle this thing between us."

"Don't worry, I won't throw myself at you again," she said bitterly.

A smile lightened his strained expression. "I don't know where I'm getting the strength to turn you down. You're responsible for an awful lot of cold showers."

It didn't help a single bit that he was trying to salve her pride. Michele tried to twist away from him. "Please, Drake, I'm really very tired."

"I know, darling. Get right into bed." He kissed the tip of her nose. "Tomorrow night at seven?"

Why didn't he just leave her alone? Every caress, even the meaningless kiss he had just bestowed, made the gnawing ache inside her more painful. If she didn't have to see him, maybe it would go away. Michele knew that was like wishing grass were purple, but at least it would make life more bearable.

He lifted her chin with a long forefinger. "How about it, honey?"

She gave in with a soft sigh of defeat. Drake always got his way. She could deny him nothing—even a gift he didn't want. There was another reason. She couldn't withstand her own terrible need to be with him, to take whatever crumbs he would give her.

Michele nodded her head in resignation. "Tomorrow night at seven."

Chapter Nine

It was a good thing Michele started getting ready for her date early the next night, because she changed clothes three times before she was satisfied.

Corey was next door at Flora's. Their neighbor had volunteered to give her dinner too, saying she didn't see enough of Corey now that Carole was on the job.

The outfit Michele finally chose was a soft gray wool skirt topped by a gray crepe de chine blouse with full sleeves and a ruffled collar. The snakeskin belt that cinched her slim waist matched her gray pumps. The effect was dressy, yet not too much so.

The doorbell rang as she was applying perfume. Michele almost dropped the bottle. She was a jangling bunch of nerves as she went to answer the door, pausing in front of it to try and compose herself. All she could hear in the quiet house was the deafening sound of her heart beating.

Drake's eyes gleamed with approval when he greeted her. He lifted his dark head, sniffing appreciatively. "Mm, you smell like flowers."

His relaxed behavior should have relieved her tension, but it didn't. Michele couldn't forget last night. "Would . . . would you like to come in?"

"I think we'd better get started if you're ready. I made a reservation at the King's Arms in Brixley." It was a small town about twenty miles away.

When she was strapped in the black leather bucket seat, Michele couldn't think of a single thing to say. Fortunately, Drake carried the conversation. He talked quite unselfconsciously about the party the night before.

It reminded Michele of something she wanted to say to him. "I'm glad I got to know Marilyn better. She seems very warm and friendly." It was a tacit apology.

"Yes, she's a good person."

"Have you known her long?" Michele asked casually.

"Ever since I came to Greenfield. Marilyn found my apartment for me."

"I see." Michele knew her next question showed undue interest, but she couldn't help asking it. "What does Shelley do?"

Drake grinned. "Chases men mostly."

"That isn't a very nice way to talk about one of your girl friends," Michele commented primly.

"She isn't one of my girl friends. You don't honestly think I could spend any time with a little bubble head like that?"

"Well, she said . . . I mean I got the impression . . ."

"You weren't listening very hard. She invited herself to Clarice's the other day; Tim was fit to be tied. That girl is the worst tennis player east of the Rockies."

A lighthearted feeling gripped Michele. "I gather that's a hanging offense."

"Coupled with her other shortcomings. Didn't you

hear her at lunch? I expected Clarice to have a minor seizure.''

"I thought you liked women who knew their place," Michele remarked tartly.

"So did I." He raised a mocking eyebrow. "So why is it that all the women I really admire are the ones who argue with me?"

Michele shrugged. "Maybe you're just combative by nature."

His slow smile warmed her all the way to her toes. "Or perhaps I appreciate a challenge."

Her eyes fell. That could be it—she didn't test his mettle. A man like Drake wouldn't want it to be easy.

As though aware of what she was thinking, he added softly, "And you, my dear, represent Mount Everest."

"That isn't true." Michele's low voice was unsteady.

Drake's free hand captured hers, lacing their fingers together. He faced the issue head on. "I could take you to bed, but it wouldn't win me anything but your body. I want more of you than that, honey."

"That's all there is to give." He must never know that he already had her heart.

Drake shook his head. "Maybe with some women, but not with you. I want your trust and affection. I'm not a high-school boy who pants after a romp in the hay. There has to be some measure of sharing and caring."

"It sounds very much like you're talking about love." She watched him secretly under lowered lashes. "I can't give you that."

Drake hesitated. "Can't, or won't, Michele? Is it because of a sense of disloyalty to Corey's father?"

"That has noth—" Her impulsive words stopped abruptly. Why not let Drake think that? It was an easy solution. "He was my husband," she finished.

"But he's dead and you're alive. He wouldn't want you to make yourself a shrine to his memory."

Michele's mouth twisted in a semblance of a smile. "You didn't know Gary."

Drake turned his head to give her a penetrating look. "I think I'm beginning to."

The restaurant appeared ahead, affording Michele a respite from Drake's too perceptive eyes.

It was furnished, predictably, as an English pub, with concessions to the American desire for comfort. The waitresses wore short costumes and perky little mobcaps. A dart board that was purely for show adorned one wall.

"The decor is a little self-conscious, but the food is good," Drake commented when they were seated in a leather booth.

Michele looked around at the intimate atmosphere created by paneled walls and muted lights. "Is this where you have your secret assignations?" As soon as the words were out she regretted them. "I'm sorry, Drake! I didn't mean to say that."

His eyes were cool. "You might as well, as long as you're thinking it."

One unguarded phrase had made them adversaries again. Although it was her fault, Michele didn't think she could stand another argument with Drake. "I shouldn't have come," she said hopelessly. "It always turns out like this. Perhaps you'd better take me home."

His face softened as he looked at her bent head. "Maybe we can salvage the evening if we work on it together. Let's make a list of the subjects that are taboo. There's my love life, and your love life," he ticked them off on his fingers. "And of course sex in general. What does that leave?"

Michele smiled unwillingly. "How about the weather?"

"What can you say about winter in Illinois? After we estimate how many inches of snow are going to fall, what's left? I think we'd better have an alternate subject."

Michele was beginning to relax and enjoy herself. "I don't suppose you'd like a recipe for brownies?"

"I don't know how to cook, remember?"

"That's just a convenient excuse," she scoffed. "If you can understand a formula, you can figure out a recipe."

"Formulas don't have to be whipped, stirred and beaten."

"Actually, there's a great deal of similarity," she said slowly, "although I never thought of it before. A lot of ingredients go into a product, and they have to be mixed very carefully—like the Chidactron I'm working on."

Drake dropped his bantering tone. "Are you making any progress?"

"The initial tests are very exciting, but I didn't want to send you the results until I checked out the side effects."

"We can't be too careful with a product like this," he agreed approvingly.

She nodded. "You mean because of lawsuits."

"I was thinking more of the potential for human suffering if we marketed anything that wasn't absolutely safe." His dark face was intense. "I can't impress on you enough, Michele, how very thorough we have to be. Nothing must come out of your department that hasn't been painstakingly checked."

"You don't have to tell me that!"

"I tell the same thing to everyone who works at the lab," he stated firmly.

"When I put my approved stamp on a test run, you'll know it's okay to proceed. You needn't be concerned about *my* work," she insisted stubbornly.

Drake refused to give an inch on this point. "It's my job to be concerned about everything that goes on at Blaylock."

The waitress arrived with their drinks, defusing another potential argument. Michele had time to reflect that she and Drake were on the same side. By the time they had given their order, after discussing the merits of the house specialty and the roast beef, the subject was tacitly dropped.

"It's strange that beefsteak-and-kidney pie never really caught on in this country," Michele mused, after the waitress had gone. "We've adopted dishes from so many other places."

"Like pizza," Drake agreed. "That's become almost as American as hamburgers."

"And chop suey," she reminded him.

"That *is* an American invention." He grinned. "The Chinese never heard of it."

"Well, you know what I mean. In Chicago there are all sorts of little ethnic places."

Drake's expression became enigmatic. "Do you miss Chicago?" he asked casually.

"Not the food."

"But you do miss it?" he persisted.

She considered, thinking about the benefits Greenfield offered Corey. Michele didn't have to worry about letting her out of her sight anymore. There was also their little house instead of the cramped apartment. But most of all there was friendship, a warm sense of being part of the community. And there was Drake. That was something he must never know.

Michele concentrated on the drink in front of her. "I miss my sister and her family, naturally. It's lonely not having anyone of your own. I mean family you can count on," she explained carefully.

Drake was silent for a long moment. "Chicago isn't that far away," he said finally. "You could drive up for a visit."

"That's true, but I've been so busy getting settled, I haven't had a chance. I really should take Corey before the weather gets bad. Once winter sets in with a vengeance the roads will be too chancy."

"I guess you'll just have to resign yourself to being stuck here," he commented lightly.

"I didn't mean that it was a hardship," she answered sharply.

Drake's mocking tone belied the watchfulness of his eyes. "Surely you can't be contemplating spending the rest of your life in Greenfield?"

Then Michele understood what motivated his sudden interest. Drake was trying to find out whether she had given herself a time limit. He never gave up, did he? If she had hoped that his attitude might change, Michele knew differently now.

"I don't think that would be nearly as strange as your settling down in such a small town," she replied coldly.

"There are worse places."

"Especially once you take over Blaylock and get to run things your own way," she commented dryly.

He shrugged. "I'm in no hurry. I more or less do that now."

Michele could have reminded him of the areas where he had no control, yet it would have been pointless to look for trouble. "Are you still considering that big house?" she asked instead.

"More than that. I told Marilyn I'm taking it."

"I really can't blame you," Michele admitted. "It's beautiful."

"How would you like to help furnish it?"

She shook her head. "I don't know anything about decorating. You should have a professional."

Drake rejected the idea completely. "I want it to look like a home, not a place where people are afraid to sit down. Decorators haven't discovered that a house is meant for living."

"I know what you mean," Michele said, laughing. "I've been in homes where I felt like taking off my shoes before I walked on the rug."

"Not my place," he asserted.

She gave him a dubious look. "You're going to have to be careful of that white carpeting in your bedroom."

Drake's smile was seductive. "I won't mind if you take off your shoes in there." The rest of his invitation was clearly implied.

Michele ignored it. "You really should give some thought to those throw rugs I mentioned."

"I will if you help me pick them out. There's no telling what I'd wind up with, left to my own devices."

Michele looked at the elegantly tailored man next to her. His tie was a perfect choice for the dark suit that had been custom made for his rangy frame. The accompanying shirt had a discreet white-on-white design, and the gold watch on his wrist was expensive yet restrained.

"I'm sure you have excellent taste," she remarked.

Laughter sparkled in Drake's blue eyes. "Do you realize that's the first compliment you've ever given me?"

"We do tend to throw brickbats rather than bouquets at each other," she admitted ruefully.

"Not so. I compliment you all the time." He took her hand, running his thumb in lazy circles over the pulse in her wrist. "I tell you that you're beautiful, desirable, that your hair is like liquid sunshine. It isn't my fault you don't believe me."

"You never said anything about my hair," she mumbled.

"An oversight that has to be rectified immediately." His long fingers combed slowly through it, stroking the soft skin in back of her ear. "It's like the spun gold crowning an angel on top of a Christmas tree."

Michele had trouble hiding her pleasure. It wasn't the sort of remark she was supposed to take seriously. "I think I like the line about liquid sunshine better," she said consideringly. "It has more of a flow to it, if you'll excuse the pun."

He touched her flushed cheek gently. "Why do compliments embarrass you, Michele?"

She sighed, admitting what was obvious. "I guess because I'm not very good at the repartee that goes on between a man and a woman. It's been too long."

"Much too long," he murmured.

"I can't change," she told him quietly. "That's why this evening was a waste of time. You want a woman who is a combination of Shelley and Marilyn—willing in bed, yet able to carry on an intelligent conversation before and after."

Drake grinned. "So far, you fit the description."

Her cheeks flamed, remembering just how willing she had been on two memorable occasions. Michele stared down at the table, unable to meet his eyes. "No, I'm not good at sexual sparring, and for me it would be only a physical experience. You said there had to be more than that."

"You don't think you could learn to care about me?" His lean face held no emotion.

Bitter anger swept through Michele at the casual question. She was aching with love for this man. It was torture to have him touch her without being able to respond, to sit next to him and be so conscious of that supple body that she wanted to throw her arms around his neck and press her lips to the strong column of his throat. But to Drake it was only a matter of intellectual interest.

"Why should I?" she answered his question bitingly. "You're not planning any lasting attachment to *me!*"

"Would that make a difference?" he asked intently.

"Certainly not!" Michele knew a trap when she saw one. She had a moment of panic. Had Drake guessed that she was in love with him? Was his offhand question a test? Her handling of the situation was crucial. "I don't want any commitments—either permanent or temporary."

Drake smiled easily. "Well, that's a relief. There's nothing worse than having a lady mistake your intentions."

"You've made yours clear all along," she remarked coldly.

He chuckled, his relaxation a marked contrast to her tension. "You can't say you weren't warned then."

"Nor can you," she replied tightly.

He sighed. "It's always fatal when a woman sees through you. I suppose I'll have to give up on you, Michele."

His statement left Michele bereft, although she knew it was an unexpected gift. She might not have been able to withstand Drake if he had intensified his efforts.

"At least now that we understand each other, you can help me with the house. If I rely only on my own judgment, it's bound to be too masculine for . . . uh . . . guests to be comfortable. I need a woman's point of view."

Michele examined her fingernails with great interest. "If you have someone in mind to share it with you, wouldn't it be better to consult her?"

Drake smiled beguilingly. "You're feminine enough for me. I'll trust your decisions."

It wasn't the answer Michele wanted. Why should she fix up the house for his steady stream of girl friends? The opportunity to create something beautiful held an undeniable attraction, however. It would be fun to select things without counting the cost for once.

"What period did you have in mind?" she temporized.

"Does it have to be rigid? Can't we mix things?"

"I prefer it that way," she nodded approvingly. "Even decorators are doing it. It's called eclectic."

"I'm glad it's accepted practice," he remarked dryly. "I have a few good antique pieces that I've picked up through the years. I wouldn't consider parting with them."

"You don't have to. Those are what give a home character. We'll work around them," Michele said earnestly, not realizing she was committing herself.

"Are you sure you know what you're promising? I have a French armoire big enough to hide a body in."

"No problem," she assured him. "That house is built on a grand scale. The difficulty is going to be filling it up."

"I'm rather attached to the piece," he mused. "I wouldn't want it stuck away in some dark corner."

Michele considered the problem. "Does it have shelves or drawers?"

"It has those massive double doors," Drake said helplessly.

"Yes, but what's inside?" she asked impatiently.

"Well, there's a long space on one side, and some shelves on the other."

"That's perfect!" Michele's eyes sparkled. "A friend of mine had a decorator do a really smashing bedroom. They do have good ideas. She built the television set into an armoire with a pull-out swivel shelf so you can watch in bed."

Drake's white teeth gleamed in his tanned face. "Next you'll be suggesting I give green stamps."

"Everyone takes a night off now and then," she told him caustically.

"That's true," he agreed, trying to stifle his laughter. "I've been meaning to slow down."

Michele was too enthusiastic about her idea to be sidetracked by Drake's amusement. "It would be a shame to have to take out too many drawers," she mused. "I'd like to measure the inside of that wardrobe."

"We'll stop by my place after dinner," he offered promptly.

"Oh . . . well, I didn't mean . . ."

Michele stopped in confusion. It was out of the question, but she didn't want to act like a frightened virgin, aghast at the idea of going to a man's apartment—especially after Drake had said he was giving up on her. Things had a way of getting out of hand between them, though.

"You can take a look at the rest of my things at the same time," he was continuing smoothly. "I have a rather nice tansu chest you can find a place for somewhere."

"I haven't said I'd do it yet," she pleaded weakly.

"Of course you will. You're bubbling with ideas already." He ignored her obvious reluctance, treating her agreement as an accomplished fact.

In spite of her nervousness, Michele enjoyed seeing Drake's apartment. It was a tribute to the good taste she knew he possessed. Antique pieces coexisted comfortably with the best of modern, subtly complementing each other.

As she looked around, noticing a Sèvres crystal dog, a Florentine desk set, an antique blunderbuss with a flaring muzzle, Michele's eyebrows rose. "Where did you get all these fabulous things?"

"I've collected them here and there." He took her coat. "Sit down, I'll make some coffee."

"No thanks, I can't stay that long," she answered quickly.

"You just got here," he pointed out. "I'll make instant."

Michele shook her head decisively. "Coffee keeps me up."

"I wouldn't want to be responsible for disturbing your sleep." Her nervousness amused him. "How about a drink? What does that do to you?"

"Not a thing," she replied coolly.

He sighed. "In that case, let's go into the bedroom and get it over with." As her startled eyes flew to his face, he grinned devilishly. "You did want to measure the armoire, didn't you?"

She lifted her chin haughtily. "It's what I'm here for."

Michele's embarrassment subsided as she examined the massive piece of furniture, using the tape measure Drake provided.

"We're in luck!" she exclaimed. "The TV set will fit right on this shelf. You won't lose any drawer space at all."

"That's a relief." He smiled into her animated face. "I was afraid I'd have to store my underwear in the shower."

"Go ahead and laugh. You're going to thank me one of these nights."

Something flickered in the depths of his eyes. "I'm glad you're coming over to my side."

Michele turned away. "The only thing we have to worry about now is whether the wall between the dressing room and the bathroom is wide enough. There wouldn't be any point in putting this thing across the room from the bed," she explained. "You'd have to use binoculars." Her brow furrowed in thought. "I do wish I'd paid more attention when I was there."

"How would you like to go over now and take a look?"

She stared at him blankly. "At this time of night?"

Drake looked at the gold watch on his wrist, nestled among springing black hairs. "It's only a little after ten-thirty."

"But how would we get in, and what would we do after we got there? There's no heat or electricity."

"I still have the key," he patted his pocket. "And we can light a fire in the fireplace and use candles."

"That's crazy!"

"I know." He grinned. "Haven't you ever done anything outrageous?"

"Not since I was nineteen."

Not since she married Gary, Michele might have added. He had been very conscious of his dignity, and as his wife, Michele had to maintain hers. Gradually the urge to do spur-of-the-moment things had left her.

She was unaware of Drake's slight frown as he noticed the faint regret on her face. "Tonight you're going to be nineteen again," he stated decisively.

Her smile was wistful. "I've forgotten how."

"We'll remember together." Drake masked the tenderness in his eyes before it could frighten her off. Taking

Michele's hand, he led her into the dining room. "You get the glasses, I'll get the wood."

"What do we need glasses for?"

"We're going to christen the new house."

She stared at the sparkling Baccarat goblets in the breakfront. "You're not going to smash this beautiful crystal, are you?" she exclaimed in horror.

Drake came out of the kitchen, brandishing a bottle of champagne. "No, I thought we'd put it to better use."

As she watched him bend down in front of the fireplace to put some wood in a canvas carrying sling, Michele started to laugh. "I feel as though it's summer, and I'm going on a weenie roast."

"You see, the years are starting to roll off already," Drake commented approvingly.

It was true. Michele felt as lighthearted as a girl, out on a date with her best boyfriend. She gazed down at the tall, virile man, watching his capable motions. Drake could never be mistaken for a boy, but she was going to pretend along with him that just for tonight they were both nineteen.

The big house was very imposing in the darkness. Drake lit a candle in the alcove by the front entry, giving it to Michele to hold while he unlocked the door.

She glanced over her shoulder doubtfully. "I hope the neighbors don't think we're prowlers and call the police. I'd hate to be jailed for breaking and entering."

"You can't be arrested for going into your own house."

"You don't own it yet," Michele pointed out.

"A mere technicality." He ushered her into the front hall. "I have an oral agreement with Marilyn. Besides, there aren't any neighbors close enough to notice, and no one can see in from the street. If there was a pool, we could go skinny-dipping," he teased.

"Knowing you, you'll build one."

"It's an idea." He chuckled. "Then I could hold indoor-outdoor orgies."

"You grew up awfully fast," she commented dryly. "What happened to being nineteen?"

"That's the best time for an orgy. It's when a man is at his sexual peak."

"That's reassuring," she said demurely. "It means I don't have anything to worry about. You're on a downhill slide."

The shifting light of the candle gave Drake's lean face and narrowed eyes a predatory look. His husky voice reinforced the illusion of a giant cat growling. "You like to live dangerously, don't you?"

She was quiveringly aware of him, of the taut body that was so blatantly masculine. Michele forced down her awakening desire. "Isn't that the kind of repartee teenage girls indulge in?" she asked lightly.

"If they want to get taken to bed," Drake asserted. His hand cupped her cheek, trailing down her neck to slide inside her coat. He caressed her shoulder, the warmth of his palm burning through her thin blouse. "Is that what you want, Michele?"

Her breath seemed to catch in her throat momentarily. Michele swallowed hard. "You're half-right. I want to go to the bed*room*—to measure that wall." She started up the steps, Drake's soft laughter accompanying her.

The single candle did little to illuminate the big room. "I'll start the fire while you light the other candles," Drake said. "That should make it bright enough in here."

When the fire was roaring up the chimney and all the candles were distributed around, the room looked very festive. Michele measured the wall she was concerned about, finding to her delight that it was exactly the right size.

"Everything is working out just perfectly!" she exclaimed.

"Up to a point," Drake remarked dryly. "Shall we have our champagne, now that we have something to celebrate?"

It had warmed up enough for Michele to take off her coat. She tossed it on the floor and sat down in front of the fireplace, glancing around appraisingly. "I've been thinking a lot about this room."

"I was hoping you would," he murmured, handing her a glass.

"If you don't knock off the innuendos I'm going to resign—as your decorator," she added hurriedly.

Drake's smile was mocking. "I knew what you meant." He took off his tie, putting it in the pocket of the jacket he removed before joining Michele on the floor.

"I was thinking that the love seat and those two chairs in your present living room would be perfect here in front of the fireplace," she told him. "You really need more massive pieces downstairs."

"Whatever you say," Drake agreed indifferently.

"It's *your* bedroom. You ought to be taking more interest," she cried indignantly.

"You have my full attention, I can assure you," he remarked lazily, lifting her hand to his lips and kissing each fingertip.

She snatched her hand away. "I've just been wasting my time! The services you require are ones I don't perform."

As she put her glass on the marble hearth, preparing to get up, Drake's arm snaked around her waist. "I don't *require* your services in the way you're implying. Actually, my dear, I think it's the other way around."

"Of all the conceited, arrogant—" Her furious words ended in a gasp as his hand curled around her breast.

"How long has it been since a man made love to you?" His thumb gently circled her taut nipple, sending shock waves through Michele's entire body.

She grabbed for his hand, but the arm around her waist tightened. His other arm encircled her shoulders, cushioning her as he gently guided her backward onto the thick carpet. Drake's body half covered hers, his dark head poised over her. The flames from the fire were reflected in his eyes, turning them molten.

"How much longer can you go on denying you're a woman," he murmured, seeking out the tiny buttons down the front of her blouse, "with normal, healthy needs like everyone else?"

She was powerless to stop him. As each button gave way, Michele's efforts became more feeble, her protests mostly vocal. "That . . . that's the oldest line in the world. I don't need you or any man."

"Not even for this?" He unfastened the last button, revealing the lacy bra underneath. His lips trailed a fiery path across the curve of the breast that swelled over its confinement. "Or this?" His teeth gently worried the hardened tip under the delicate scrap of fabric.

Michele's body arched in a desperate attempt to escape the tantalizing mouth that was generating a need so primitive it frightened her. "All right, I admit it," she moaned. "But you said desire wasn't enough."

"I was wrong." He unclasped her bra, running his fingertips lightly over her breast in an erotic pattern that turned Michele liquid inside.

When his mouth closed around her nipple, rolling it between his ardent lips, her fingernails dug into the thick carpet. "You planned all this," she cried hopelessly.

His head raised and he looked deeply into her eyes. "No, it was inevitable." As his mouth descended to hers, Drake murmured huskily, "You know that, don't you?"

With a sigh of surrender, Michele wrapped her arms around his neck. He was right. Each encounter had brought them inexorably closer to this moment. Michele couldn't deny her aching need any longer—not just for a man, as Drake thought, but for *this* man. Her lips parted in a soft sigh of anticipation.

A low growl of satisfaction sounded deep in his throat as Michele relaxed in his arms. His mouth covered hers, moving from her lips down the pure line of her neck to the small hollow in her throat. Lifting her gently, he slipped off the filmy blouse, then unfastened the clasp at her waist. Kneeling over her, Drake removed her skirt, his hands unbearably sensual as they trailed down her long, silken legs.

Michele crossed one leg over the other as his eyes devoured her body, but he tenderly separated her thighs. "Don't be shy with me, darling. You have the most beautiful body I've ever seen. I want to know every glorious inch of you."

His fingers slid inside the waistband of her pantyhose, slipping them down a fraction to caress the satin skin of her stomach. Bending his head, Drake dipped his tongue in her navel. As she quivered in anticipation, her pantyhose slowly slid down her hips, followed by his avid mouth. He paused at the juncture of her thighs, driving Michele into a frenzy of excitement as liquid fire seemed to consume her.

When her nylons had been removed completely, Drake started the return journey, stroking her ankles and her long, slim legs. He kissed the soft skin of her inner thigh, inching his way up until Michele held out her arms to him, unable to bear the sweet agony any longer.

"Please, Drake, I need you so," she whispered.

"I know, darling." He gathered her in his arms, molding her to his hard body. Parting her lips with his tongue, he began a dizzying exploration, promising unlimited rapture.

Michele's shaking fingers undid his buttons, pulling his shirt aside so she could finally feel his hard chest against her bare breasts. The sensation was so exquisite that she moved sensuously against him, drawing in her breath sharply.

Her fingers flew to his belt buckle, fumbling in their haste. Drake helped her complete the job, shrugging off his shirt before leaving her for a moment to remove the rest of his clothes.

When he returned Michele arched against him, shuddering. Her hands roamed over his beautiful body, restlessly urging him closer.

As he slowly parted her legs, Michele waited with throbbing anticipation for the ultimate embrace. When it came, she was filled with an ecstasy so great that her whole body was consumed by it. Drake's driving force was carrying her ever higher, each wave of joy followed by another more intense.

When she reached the limit of endurance, the molten tide crested, easing the almost unbearable tension and leaving only absolute satisfaction.

A warm feeling of fulfillment accompanied Michele on the downward spiral. She opened her eyes when Drake kissed her tenderly.

"My sweet, passionate Michele." He brushed the damp hair off her forehead. "I knew it would be like this."

"I did too," she whispered softly, tracing the straight line of his nose up to his peaked eyebrows.

He kissed the tip of her finger, curling his hand possessively around her breast. "Then why did you fight me so hard?"

How could she tell him that her worst fears had been realized? That having known the full power of him, she would never be free. Whenever Drake wanted her she would come to him; whatever he did to her she would forgive him. Michele accepted the depth of her love, but Drake must never know it.

She concentrated on twining her fingers in the dark hair on his chest. "I didn't really. You were the one who wanted some kind of commitment. It wasn't until tonight that you admitted it isn't important." He was silent for so long that Michele glanced up, reading nothing in his expression.

"It was all sex between us just now?" he asked unemotionally.

"Of course. You know that as well as I." Michele forced herself to look straight at him.

"I suppose I do." He grinned disarmingly. "I'm just not used to the lady being the one to point it out."

"Do they usually ask you to pledge undying love?" she asked coolly.

"Not necessarily, but it's nice to pretend there's a little feeling involved," he remarked dryly.

"You knew there wasn't when you started this thing tonight."

"Perhaps I thought you'd be so carried away that you would develop some of the softer emotions," he observed mockingly.

"In other words, you'd like me to pretend to be in love with you."

He traced the shape of her ear, leaning forward to nibble on the lobe. "I wouldn't mind." His low voice was husky.

Michele jerked her head away from his seductive mouth. "You can forget that notion! Why should I be the one to pretend?"

Drake's eyes were watchful as he smiled derisively. "You want me to join you in the charade?"

His amusement twisted her heart. "No, of course not! Neither of us should bother with hypocrisy. Why can't we admit that we're physically attracted to each other and go on from there?"

"I suppose that's only sensible. But if you ever feel like whispering abandoned words of love in my ear, please feel free," he said sardonically. "I won't take it personally."

"I'm sure that will never happen," she answered stiffly. "As a matter of fact, I'm beginning to regret what occurred here this evening." She sat up, reaching for her clothes.

He put his arm around her waist, gazing up from a prone position. "You know that isn't true, Michele. Look at me and say it again."

As his hand slowly caressed her thigh, lingering where it joined her body, Michele couldn't. A familiar warmth was spreading its magic. She moved her leg slightly so he could reach his goal.

"No matter why we want each other, the fact remains that we do." His voice had a low throb that echoed inside her.

"Yes." It was a soft sigh of resignation.

His fingertips trailed up her arms and over her rose-tipped breasts. "Do you know how beautiful you are in the firelight? You're like a golden statue sculpted by a genius." He guided her down beside him, twining his legs around hers.

Michele went willingly into his arms, fitting her soft curves to his male angles. She returned his kisses ardently, trembling under the caresses that grew more and more demanding.

When Drake moved her body under his, she welcomed him, matching his urgency with her own. They climbed the tumultuous path to heaven once more, emerging from the fiery inferno into a place of peace.

Drake's head was pillowed on her breast, a look of complete contentment on his strong face. As she gazed at the thick lashes feathering his high cheekbones, Michele felt a rush of tenderness. If only she could tell him how much she loved him. Drake had said he wouldn't take it personally. Did she dare?

Drake's eyes opened. He smiled up at her, reaching out to tangle his fingers in her tousled hair. "Hello, beautiful. Do you feel as wonderful as I do?"

Her soft mouth curved in a smile. "Maybe better."

He levered himself up on an elbow, leaning over her while he stroked her cheek gently. "I don't believe that's possible. For two people who don't love each other, I think we have a fantastic thing going for us."

"You may be right," Michele murmured, concealing the desolate feeling that gripped her. She could never say those magic words to Drake—not even in jest.

Chapter Ten

$\mathcal{M}$ichele scarcely slept at all after Drake brought her home, but this time she welcomed the wakeful night. It gave her a chance to think about him and all the wonders that had occurred. She hugged her body ecstatically, remembering every warm kiss, every erotic caress.

When the alarm rang, reality set in, tempering her euphoria. What would Drake be like at the lab? He had pursued her on former weekends, only to turn into a different person when Monday rolled around. Surely the situation was different now, she argued with herself. Not really, the cold voice of reason pointed out. If anything, he was more apt to revert to type. Drake had accomplished his purpose last night, Michele was forced to acknowledge. After the hunter was sated, he usually lost interest.

She was excessively jumpy in the lab, drawing George's sardonic interest. "What's the matter, too much night life over the weekend?"

She gritted her teeth, picking up the test tube she had dropped. "Nothing like that."

"Wasn't that a good party at Jane's?" Tim asked.

He wasn't being intentionally cruel. Tim was so ingenuous that he honestly thought the reason George wasn't at any of the social functions was because he didn't enjoy them. It was a logical assumption, since George denigrated everything and everybody.

"Very nice," Michele agreed, having almost forgotten about it.

"Your date was a handsome guy," Tim continued. "Are you going to see him again?"

"No!" She attempted to modify her explosive answer. "Actually, he was a bit of a bore."

"Well, hang in there," Tim laughed. "The ladies will undoubtedly dredge up more recruits."

"Maybe the boss lady has her sights set for the boss man," George remarked maliciously.

She looked at him warily. "Where did you get an idea like that?"

George shrugged. "Can you think of better job security?"

Michele was beginning to see the wisdom of Drake's little lecture, although she still considered that he had been unfair. "I already have job security," she answered George. "It's called ability."

The morning passed without a call from Drake, which was a bad sign. He wasn't exactly an importunate lover, impatient to hear his beloved's voice, was he? Well, what did she expect? Michele admonished herself. A hopeless little voice gave the answer.

When lunchtime came she was resigned to the situation. She no longer even wanted to see Drake—quite the opposite in fact. It would be too humiliating to have him treat her with indifference. Drake could turn his emotions on and off because they didn't run any deeper than physical desire. Hers did.

Michele decided to go home for lunch in order to avoid the possibility of running into Drake in the cafeteria. As she was walking to her car, his unmistakable voice stopped her.

"Michele! Where are you running off to?" Drake asked as he caught up with her.

Her breath lodged in her throat as she looked up at his beloved face. "I . . . I thought I'd go home for lunch."

"I'll come with you." Although he didn't touch her, his voice curled around her like a caress.

"No, I . . . I don't think that would be a good idea."

"I'm afraid you're right." His rueful smile and glowing eyes acknowledged the nature of the danger. "Let's go into town for a hamburger instead."

Michele was still slightly miffed. "Are you sure you can spare the time?"

One eyebrow rose as he regarded her questioningly. "What's wrong, honey?"

"You seem very busy this morning," she replied distantly. "I realize you only have time for me in your off hours."

"I wanted to call you, sweetheart, but I've been in a meeting all morning."

"You don't have to explain."

Drake frowned at the disinterest Michele managed to put in her voice. "No, I don't, since your only interest in me is physical."

"That's a rotten thing to say!" she exclaimed.

"Isn't it true?" He waited tautly for her reply.

What could she answer? "That's no reason for making me feel like a . . ." Michele turned away, tears threatening.

He groaned, clasping her shoulders and burying his face

in her neck. "I'm sorry, darling. You bring out the best and the worst in me."

"Drake! People will see us."

"I don't give a damn." He turned her to face him. "I've been thinking about you all morning, remembering last night. Don't spoil it, Michele."

The memory of that night of love stoked the fire that always burned when he was near. Her lashes fluttered down. "I don't think anything could."

His hands tightened. "Let's go home."

Drake bundled her into the passenger seat of her car, taking the keys and sliding into the driver's seat. He drove like a madman, but Michele didn't protest.

When they entered the small house, he lifted her in his arms, carrying her into the bedroom. There was urgency in the mouth that covered hers, the hands that undressed her. Michele helped him remove his clothes with the same impatience, reaching for him hungrily with a knowledge of what was in store.

His caresses aroused her to a pitch of feverish excitement, lingering in all the places he knew to be responsive. Michele cried out her delight as his hands cupped her breasts, his tongue circling each rosy nipple. She kneaded the straining muscles in his back, arching her body against his in a need as old as time.

Drake's possession was fierce yet tender. He built a fire inside her, stoking the flames with every thrust. A final explosion sent her soaring—and then the fire died to a gentle glow.

They lay in each other's arms afterward, satisfied but unwilling to break the bond.

Drake was the first to stir, holding Michele's delicate

face between his palms as he kissed her deeply. "How will I be able to go back to work after this?"

She smiled lazily, curling around him seductively. "I should think you'd be all charged up."

"Are you kidding? I want to sleep for an hour, and then wake up and make love to you again."

Michele's tongue explored the inner contours of his ear. "You *are* an older gentleman."

"You're going to pay for that!" His hand slid up her leg, tantalizing her in a way he knew only too well.

"Drake, no!" she gasped. "It's getting late and we have to get back."

He drew her hips close to his, moving against her with rising interest. "The world won't come to an end if we're late."

It was a temptation she resisted with difficulty. "It wouldn't do for both of us to be late."

"You're right as usual." He sighed. "Would you mind putting some clothes on that delectable body before I lose the little restraint I have left?"

Her hands caressed his muscled chest, trailing down below his waist. "I could say the same thing."

He drew in his breath, reaching out for her, but she slid off the bed. "If there's one thing I can't abide it's a tease," he growled.

"I'd say I fulfilled all my promises," she answered complacently, reaching for her bra.

Drake was beside her in an instant, bending his head to kiss her breast. "I can never get enough of you."

She trembled as he stroked her thighs, melting all her resolve. "Drake, I . . ."

He sighed. "I know, sweetheart, I'll behave."

She didn't want him to behave, but Drake had started to put on his clothes. Michele did the same, trying not to look at the magnificent body that had so recently brought her rapture.

When they parted at the door to the administration building, he touched her cheek lightly. "Tonight?" he murmured.

Michele nodded, lowering her lashes. Not in shyness, but for fear he would see the love shining out of her eyes.

Her life changed so drastically after that weekend that Michele was almost frightened. Could bliss like this last? Or was she being paid back for some obscure sins? Was she being shown what heaven was like so her suffering would be even greater when it was snatched away?

Michele told herself she was being an idiot. Caution had gotten to be too ingrained. It mustn't be allowed to spoil her happiness.

Drake became a permanent fixture in her life and Corey's, delighting them both. The initial rapport between Drake and her daughter had blossomed into a deep affection that was also a source of worry to Michele. Corey treated him like a father, indicating in countless ways that she expected the relationship to continue indefinitely. Would she feel rejected when it didn't?

Those were the specters that surfaced in the middle of the night, but the rest of the time Michele was too euphoric to dwell on them.

The weeks rolled by filled with new experiences. When autumn gave way to winter, Drake taught Corey to ice skate on the frozen pond near their house. All the local children skated there, the smaller ones accompanied by their parents.

Corey was ecstatic at having one of each for the first time that she could remember.

Drake cut a dashing figure in his scarlet jacket and ski pants. Michele's eyes followed him, admiring the graceful, lithe body she had come to know so intimately. The knowledge was a protective shield against the cold, warming her to her toes and curving her generous mouth in a smile.

When Drake joined her at the big bonfire on the edge of the ice, his answering smile held remembrance. "Why does this snow look like white carpeting to me?" he murmured.

Their eyes met and held until Corey clamored to be taken out on the rink again. Drake complied without irritation, leaving Michele with the unspoken promise that her time would come. That was the wonderful thing about their relationship. Far from resenting Corey's intrusions, Drake adapted himself to both of them.

Their nights together continued to be magical. Michele knew she would never get enough of Drake, but she worried sometimes that the novelty would wear off for him. It never happened. Each time was like the first, brimming with excitement. A single exchanged glance could make them both throb with passion.

Michele was no longer shy with him. She welcomed the flames of desire that lit his eyes when they devoured her body. She trembled under his burning caresses, returning them until neither could stand it any longer. Then Drake brought them both to the pinnacle with his taut, driving body.

The whole world became a place of enchantment where each day held a promise. Michele's blissful state was reflected in her face. She had always been lovely, but now she was ravishing.

Polly remarked on it in an oblique way. "I'm so glad you and Drake got together. He was the one I had picked out for you."

They couldn't keep their relationship completely secret because she and Drake had been seen out together, but Michele tried to minimize it. "I'm helping him decorate his house, so he's around quite a bit. That's all there is to it."

Polly refused to be taken in. "I should have known when he said he was buying that big place."

"I don't know what you mean."

"Come on, Michele," her friend cried impatiently. "Drake just *happened* to ask you to help select the furniture? It wasn't because you're the one who has to be satisfied?"

"Where did you get such an idea?" Michele gasped. "There's nothing like that between us. You mustn't spread those stories."

"All right, if you want to keep it a secret," Polly sighed.

To Michele's despair, nothing she could say changed Polly's mind.

Clarice was more subtle, but she had gotten the same impression. Michele found out about it at a going-away luncheon Polly held for the older woman. The Blaylocks were taking a six-week cruise. During the afternoon, Clarice made time for a private word with Michele.

"Drake tells me you're doing smashing things with his house," she remarked.

"I just hope he likes the finished product. After all, he's the one who will be living there," Michele took care to point out.

Clarice's regard was enigmatic. "I'm glad to see he's settling down. I'd begun to despair of that man."

"I imagine owning a home will make him rather settled," Michele replied.

"That and a few other things," Clarice observed dryly.

She could be referring to Drake's added responsibility at the lab, Michele reminded herself. In spite of what Clarice and Polly might think, Michele knew Drake wasn't considering marriage. He had never alluded to it, even after their most passionate lovemaking. And Michele had been careful to continue the fiction that Drake's sole attraction for her was sex.

"Drake has sewn enough wild oats to fill a field," Clarice was continuing. "I think he's ready to get out of the fast lane."

"I doubt if a man like that is ever ready," Michele commented lightly.

Clarice smiled. "They all reach the point eventually. All that's needed are the right . . . circumstances."

She could still be referring to business. "I suppose that's true," Michele answered politely.

Clarice sighed. "I do hope you'll work on it while we're gone."

"I . . . I don't . . ."

"The house," Clarice interposed smoothly. "I hope it will be all furnished by the time we return."

Michele had to laugh—bitterly—when she thought back on that conversation. Clarice and Polly had been so sure, that Michele had begun to hope in spite of herself. But everything began to go subtly wrong after the Blaylocks left, like a beautiful song played in the wrong key.

The first jarring note was a degrading conversation she overheard. Michele was in the hardware store, comparing the merits of several brands of rubber gloves. The high shelves hid the two men on the other side of the aisle from her, but she recognized George's voice. He was in the middle of one of his usual tirades.

"They give you all this garbage about wanting to be treated just like men. That's a laugh!"

Michele sighed. George was off and running on his favorite subject. His next words galvanized her as she realized that he was talking about Drake and herself.

"What man keeps his job by sleeping with the boss? That's the only reason she was made head of the department instead of me." When his companion murmured something unintelligible, George answered angrily, "Of course I know it's true! He gave up all his other little dollies for her. You think a virile guy like Hollister sits around discussing the weather?"

Michele left the store quietly, feeling faintly ill. It was useless to tell herself that George was worthy only of contempt. His nasty words made her feel soiled.

Although she tried to throw off the feeling, it was reflected in her attitude toward Drake that evening. They were in a restaurant having dinner.

"What's wrong, honey?" Concern creased his wide forehead. "Something's been troubling you all evening."

Michele smiled brightly. "You're imagining things." She changed the subject hurriedly. "I stopped by Polly's this morning; she's really blooming. It doesn't seem possible that the baby is due in just seven weeks."

Drake reached over and covered her nervous fingers. "I want to know what's bothering you, sweetheart."

"It's nothing, really," she insisted.

Michele tried to keep up the pretense, but Drake was adamant. After much hesitation she told him the conversation she had overheard, but not that George was the culprit.

Drake reacted furiously, as she had expected. "Tell me who said it and I'll rearrange his face so drastically even his mother won't recognize him."

"No, Drake, it . . . I guess gossip was unavoidable. Everyone knows we've been seeing each other. They're bound to draw conclusions. It's all so ugly though. It isn't as if we were—" Michele stopped in horror. She was doing this all wrong.

"Engaged?" He finished the sentence for her, becoming very still. "Are you saying we should get married?"

"No! Of course not." The last thing she wanted was to scare him away.

Deep lines carved themselves around Drake's mouth. "Then I presume you're suggesting that it would spike the gossip if I saw other women."

The very thought made Michele's heart plummet. Pride prevented her from telling him, though. "It's entirely up to you," she answered coolly.

"Perhaps it's a good idea at that—especially since it wouldn't bother you," he remarked grimly.

"Not at all. Why should it?" She raised her chin, willing back the tears.

"Good, then that's all settled. Would you like to go to a movie?"

"No, I . . . I have a slight headache. If you don't mind, I'd like to go home."

They were like two very courteous strangers. Drake walked her to the door, expressing the hope that her headache would be better. After kissing Michele's cheek, he left. It was that correct peck on the cheek that told her it was all over.

As she reviewed the terrible evening later, lying in a little heap of misery on her bed, Michele began to see things that hadn't been immediately apparent. Drake had been very quick to suggest seeing other women. Had he been waiting for just such an opportunity? Had he tired of her already? She had always known their relationship wouldn't last forever, Michele told herself. It didn't help.

Hope doesn't die a merciful death. As the days passed, Michele kept expecting Drake to come back. Every night she waited for the phone or the doorbell to ring. Neither did. But one day he called her down to his office.

She arrived breathlessly, determined not to reproach Drake for his neglect. Just the thought of seeing him again after almost a week kept Michele's feet from touching the ground.

Drake was sitting behind his desk, his face wearing the expressionless mask she had come to distrust. "Sit down, Michele. I think we have a problem."

"What's that?" she asked warily, her joyful anticipation replaced by apprehension.

"I've just reviewed the tests on the new mouthwash. That's the sloppiest work I've ever encountered."

"I didn't do them," she cried. "I didn't even see the results."

His frown deepened. "It came from your department. You *should* have seen them."

"I assigned that product to George," she said defensively. "He must have turned in his report without showing it to me."

"Is that standard procedure?" Drake asked ominously.

"No, of course not! I've told him repeatedly that I'm to check everything before it's sent in."

"Then why didn't you do it?" Drake continued implacably.

"Because he didn't give them to me." Michele ground her teeth in frustration.

"We're going around in circles," he stated. "Let me put it another way—I don't have time for incompetence. If George disobeyed your express orders, I fail to see how you could put up with it."

"Are you saying you don't believe me?" she asked tautly.

"I'm questioning you on a very basic principle," he replied patiently. "Either you're the head of the department, or you're not."

Michele was surprised at how calm her voice remained. "Are you firing me?"

He sighed. "No, Michele, I'm not. I am merely trying to force you to do your job."

She knew Drake was waiting for her to complain that George had tried to sabotage her at every step. It would give him an opportunity to point out that a good department head could handle her people. She didn't intend to play his game.

Michele squared her slender shoulders, as though ready to take a blow. "I accept full responsibility for the incomplete report, and I can assure you it won't happen again."

There was an expression in Drake's eyes that could almost be described as tenderness. It was gone so quickly that Michele knew she had been mistaken.

"I'll accept that," he replied curtly. When he picked up some papers on his desk, she knew she was being dismissed.

Michele used restraint in the lab, her voice nonetheless deadly as she told George the way it was going to be. She didn't allow any rebuttal, ending the conversation with a flat statement.

"I'm the head of this department, and if you don't recognize that fact, it will result in your dismissal." She walked away without waiting for a reply, closing the door to her office very softly.

The expression on George's face was one of impotent rage, but he didn't attempt to follow her. After a long moment he turned back to his table, the ugly look in his eyes warning that it wasn't over.

Michele didn't know how she got through dinner that night. Fortunately Carole had done the preliminaries, and she didn't seem in any hurry to go home.

"You didn't leave a note, so I made spaghetti sauce just in case. I hope that was all right, Mrs. Carter."

"Yes, it's fine. I'm very grateful to you, Carole."

"If you're going out to dinner with Mr. Hollister, I can stay with Corey."

Michele swept the pale hair off her forehead with a slender hand. "No, I'm going to bed early tonight. I'm exhausted."

"You do look bushed." Carole dismissed that for more interesting topics. "Mr. Hollister is a real hunk."

"Hunk of what?" Corey asked with interest.

Carole grinned at Michele. "I meant he's a living doll."

"That's silly," Corey said, giggling. "How can Uncle Drake be a doll? He's a grown man."

"He is that," Carole murmured appreciatively.

Michele's nerves were at the screaming point. Carole's insistence on talking about Drake, coupled with Corey's use of the word *uncle,* grated on a raw place. It was the universal term employed by children for their mothers' transient lovers. It had offended her when Corey started using it, but she didn't know what to put in its place. *Mr. Hollister* was too formal, and *Drake* too informal. It was all academic now, although Corey didn't know it yet.

During dinner she harked back to the subject. "Uncle Drake hasn't been here in almost a week. I miss him."

"I wish you wouldn't call him that!" Michele rasped.

Corey's eyes widened at the unaccustomed sharpness of her tone. "Why?"

"Because he isn't related to you," Michele ground out. "You have only one uncle, who lives in Chicago."

"Aunt Flora isn't really related to me, but I call her *aunt,*" the little girl pointed out.

"That's different."

"Why?"

"Because I said so!" Michele was reaching the end of her endurance. "Finish your dinner."

Corey stuck out her lower lip mutinously. "I don't want any more."

Michele's heart sank as she looked at the defiant little figure, realizing that she was taking her frustration out on her own daughter. "I'm sorry, honey," she apologized gently. "I didn't mean to snap at you. I just have a rotten headache."

"That's okay." Corey's tense body relaxed at the explanation. With childlike ease she returned to her own concerns. "When is Uncle Drake going to take us skiing? He promised to teach me." Her eyes sparkled with excitement. "None of the other kids know how. I'll be the only one."

Every word was driving a spike deeper into Michele's breast. She had to tell Corey that Drake wouldn't be taking her skiing—or anyplace else—yet she couldn't bear to extinguish the pleasure in that small face.

She finally bargained for time. "We'll talk about it later, dear."

After Corey was in bed Michele took a long, hot bubble bath, hoping it would make her sleepy. It didn't. She was as tightly wound as a steel spring. It was pointless to go to bed; she would only lie there for hours, staring up at the ceiling.

Leaving her hair piled in a mass of careless curls on top of her head, Michele slipped into a pale pink bathrobe. She turned on a lamp in the living room, curling up on the couch with a book she had been wanting to read. The lamp turned her hair to spun gold as Michele bent her head to stare at the printed pages, without absorbing a word.

In spite of every effort, her thoughts reverted to Drake. Why hadn't he fired her today? It was the opportunity he had been waiting for, so why had he veered off? Knowing Drake, there was probably a very Machiavellian reason behind his forbearance. It didn't mean the axe wasn't poised to fall—it only meant the timing wasn't right for some reason. Michele's fingers curled tightly around the book. How long could she continue to play this cat-and-mouse game?

The doorbell rang sharply, shattering the awful quiet. Michele almost jumped out of her slippers. Who could it be at this time of night?

"Who . . . who's there?" she asked tentatively, through the closed door.

"I have to talk to you, Michele." Drake's deep voice made her heart thunder.

Michele's hand went to her tousled hair. "It's late . . . you can't . . . I'll see you tomorrow at work," she stammered.

"I have to see you now. Open the door."

The quiet determination in his voice told her that Drake

wasn't going to accept a refusal. Disjointed thoughts raced through Michele's mind. Was he going to tell her not to come in to the lab tomorrow? Did he intend to fire her on the spot? Maybe then he could tell everyone she just quit without notice. Michele's hands were shaking as she opened the door. She stared at him warily.

Drake's coat collar was turned up against the biting wind that had powdered his dark hair with snowflakes. There were harsh lines in his face, making him look older. A blast of frigid air accompanied him inside.

Michele shivered, nervously tightening the belt around her slim waist.

Drake looked at her for a long moment. There was some kind of powerful, suppressed emotion behind the eyes that traveled over her delicate face. "Did I waken you?" he asked finally.

"No, I was reading." She turned her back, unable to look at this dark, intent man any longer. In spite of everything, she still loved him so much it was agonizing. "All right, get it over with. You don't have to lead up to it," she said tautly. "Just speak your little piece and go."

He moved closer. "Why do you think I'm here, Michele?"

She whirled around to face him angrily. "We both know that, so stop playing with me."

He clasped her shoulders. "Do we both know I've gone through hell without you this week?" he murmured huskily.

"That's really rotten!" she cried. "Can't you just fire me without pretending you hate to do it?"

"Fire you?" He looked at her incredulously. "Didn't you hear what I said?" Drake folded her in his arms convulsively, holding her so tightly that she felt bruised by his hard, taut body. His hands moved restlessly over her back, tangling in her bright hair so that it spilled out of the confining ribbon to cascade around her shoulders in a shining curtain. "It doesn't matter anymore why we need each other. The important thing is that we do!"

Michele's legs began to tremble so much that she could hardly stand. Drake had come back to her! It was a miracle she was afraid to believe in.

"You were the one who decided we shouldn't see each other anymore," she said tentatively.

"I was a fool," he groaned. "We fulfill each other, sweetheart. You can't deny that I bring you pleasure. Let me keep on doing that."

When his mouth closed over hers, all conscious thought ceased. Michele felt herself sinking into a warm, dark oasis of joy. Drake's image was printed inside her closed eyelids, his body making itself known to her. His drugging kisses kept her captive, seducing her will.

"You missed me, didn't you, darling?" He parted her robe, cupping his hand around her breast and gently worrying the nipple between his fingers.

"I . . ." The sensation was so exquisite it took Michele's breath away.

"Admit it," he teased, tracing the sensitive inner curve of her ear with the tip of his tongue. "You need me."

If he only knew how much! The sensual side of her wanted to accept this unbelievable gift without reservation, but another side of Michele resented him. Drake had put her through torture, only to turn up at his own convenience, expecting her to welcome him back without question. She gathered the tattered remains of her pride, steeling herself not to respond to his caresses.

"I don't *need* anyone," she stated, trying to pull her robe together.

He untied her belt in one swift movement. His hands slid lingeringly over her warm, bare skin to curve around her hips, drawing her lower body against his. When he moved against her, Michele drew in her breath, digging her fingernails into his shoulders.

"All right, you don't need me. But try to deny you want me."

"I didn't have other men waiting in the wings," she said defensively.

Drake mussed her hair lovingly. "That's one thing I didn't have to worry about."

It was true, but she resented his casual air of possession. "You took out other women, didn't you?"

He shrugged them off. "You told me to."

The knowledge that he actually had, hurt Michele deeply. "Then I have to assume they didn't perform as well as I."

Drake's fingers tangled in her hair, pulling her head back so he could glare at her. "Don't ever say a thing like that!"

"Well, it's true, isn't it?" A malicious devil drove her on. "Why else would you be here? The other day in your office you weren't exactly enamored of me."

He drew back slowly, looking down at her with a slight frown. "What happens at the office has nothing to do with our personal lives. I thought we agreed on that."

"I don't remember any agreement."

"It was implicit," he returned steadily.

Sudden anger swept Michele. Like all men, he wanted the best of both worlds. "I see. I'm supposed to be sweetly compliant in both places."

Drake's mouth thinned dangerously. "We both know you're only compliant when you're forced to be, or when you want something."

"I've never wanted anything from you!" she flared.

"Haven't you, Michele?" His mocking eyes went over the widened neck of her robe, making her scramble to close it. "You've made yourself quite clear on that point."

"Are you saying that *I* was about to take advantage of *you* tonight?"

"Don't worry about it—I'd have been happy to be of service," Drake said derisively. He stopped at the door. "Oh, by the way, I have a message for you. Simon called from Acapulco, and Clarice got on the line. She said to tell you she expects a good progress report on that matter you both discussed—whatever that means." The door closed after him.

Michele stared at it, unable to believe what had just happened. One moment she was walking among the stars, and the next moment an evil cloud had extinguished their light. The pain in her chest was almost unbearable. When it subsided to a dull ache, her mind started to function again.

Why had Drake come here tonight after almost a week of silence? Michele knew better than to believe it was because he couldn't live without her. If she hadn't precipitated an argument they would have made love. Like all men he would have accepted the bonus, but that wasn't his primary purpose. Then what was it?

She paced the floor, looking for a solution. Finally it occurred to her! His last words were unwittingly revealing. Drake thought she was involved in something with Clarice, who wouldn't take it well if he banished Michele to oblivion in her absence. Since he was still unavoidably stuck with her, Drake must have decided it would be wise to reestablish his hold over her. And who knew better than he how to do it?

The only thing that made her feel a tiny speck better was the fact that she hadn't succumbed. Did Drake know how close she had come? Michele made a solemn vow to herself, willing away the misery it brought. From this moment on, she would never allow Drake Hollister to touch her again!

Chapter Eleven

There were circles under Michele's eyes the next morning, attesting to another sleepless night. Drake probably slept like an infant, she reflected bitterly, getting out her equipment.

George was even more sullen than usual, but that was to be expected after yesterday's go-around. Tim was the only one who could be counted on. He was a continuing delight, always cheerful, with a good word to say for everyone.

"How's Polly?" Michele asked him. "She looked like a chubby little cherub last time I saw her."

Tim's open countenance clouded momentarily. "Her back has been giving her trouble lately, poor kid."

"It's an occupational hazard," Michele consoled him, "more than compensated for by that little package the stork gift wraps."

"I guess you're right." Tim grinned. "Although I'm not the one who has to lug Junior around."

Michele returned his smile. "That's the one problem we haven't solved yet."

George regarded them sourly. "If the children's hour is over, can we have a little quiet around here? I'm trying to concentrate."

Michele gave Tim an eloquent glance, stifling all the responses she could have made.

Quiet prevailed for a couple of hours. They were all immersed in their separate work when the phone rang. Tim was closest to it so he answered as Michele stiffened defensively. She had been expecting some reprisal from Drake all morning. It was just like him to draw out the suspense, she reflected angrily.

The call wasn't from Drake, however. Tim's face blanched as he listened.

"Okay, honey, don't panic," he said soothingly. "I'll be home in a few minutes."

"What's wrong, Tim?" Michele asked fearfully.

"It's Polly. She's going into labor. I have to get her to the hospital right away."

"But it's . . ." Michele swallowed her next words—*it's too soon*. Arranging her face in a reassuring expression she said, "Don't worry, Tim, everything will be fine."

There were deep lines in his boyish face. "The baby isn't due for six weeks yet."

"Premature births are no problem nowadays," Michele said with a calmness she didn't feel.

"It's Polly I'm worried about," Tim cried.

"She's going to be just fine. You go to her and I'll meet you at the hospital." Michele ran into her office, stripping off her lab coat on the way.

Tim grabbed his coat out of the closet and headed for the door, pausing for a moment when he got there. "I don't know when I'll be back, George. The tests on that cough syrup I'm working on are due today. They're all completed except for a final check. Will you do it for me?'' He finished struggling into his coat and raced out the door without waiting for an answer.

Michele followed close behind him, calling over her shoulder, ''Take any calls. I'll be back as soon as I can.''

George stared after her, his thin mouth curling in a sneer. ''Yes, Your Royal Highness,'' he said to the empty room.

Sauntering over to Tim's table, he flicked the pages on it scornfully. ''All of a sudden I'm his best friend when *he* wants something,'' George muttered. ''And how about that broad? 'Take any calls,' '' he mimicked bitterly. ''What do they think I am, the office boy around here?''

Resentment etched harsh lines in his face. Why should he check someone else's work? That was the high-and-mighty trollop's job. Hadn't she chewed him out because he'd skipped one little procedure? It's a wonder she'd even trust him to check Tim's work. As preoccupied as Tim had been lately, there could very well be some errors.

George became very still. An unaccustomed look of pleasurable excitement suddenly spread over his narrow face. He walked into Michele's office with calm deliberation, opening the top drawer of her desk and rummaging around until he found the rubber stamp he was looking for. After stamping the report he had brought with him, George scribbled Michele's initials. As an afterthought, he carefully smudged his writing, so it was legible but indistinct.

''There, two birds with one stone,'' he muttered, dropping the report in the Out basket. A glance at the clock told him the morning pickup would be in fifteen minutes.

It was a long day for both Tim and Michele. She got to the hospital in time to see Polly being wheeled off to the delivery room, a determined smile on her white face. Tim managed to appear cheerful for his wife, but he broke down in the waiting room.

"She wants this baby so much—we both do. But Polly's the one I'm worried about." He buried his face in his hands. "I couldn't live if anything happened to her."

"I'm sure she isn't in any danger, Tim."

It's doubtful that he even heard Michele's reassuring words. Restlessly, he paced the length of the room. "It's almost scary to build your whole life around one person, but you know what I mean, Michele."

She looked startled until she realized that Tim was talking about her defunct marriage. He didn't know that Drake was the only man who had ever been that important to her—and Drake couldn't care less. If anything happened to her, if she had an accident or something, he probably wouldn't even send flowers.

Michele threw off her dark thoughts. This was no time to dwell on her personal miseries. Tim was the one who needed bolstering.

She brought up endless cups of coffee when Tim refused to leave the waiting room long enough to go down to the cafeteria. Michele also brought a sandwich that he ignored. There wasn't anything else she could do for him. Time passed with the same speed as an ocean being emptied with an eyedropper.

After what seemed like an eternity, a cheerful doctor appeared to tell them that Polly had experienced false labor pains. She was back in her room, and they could see her.

"That's wonderful news!" Michele threw her arms around Tim. "The longer Junior can put off his grand entrance, the better."

After giving Tim some time alone with his wife, Michele visited for a few minutes.

"Is it all right if I don't come in tomorrow?" Tim asked. "I'd sort of like to hang around here and keep Polly company."

"I think that's a good idea." Michele gave them both an impish grin. "As a matter of fact, you ought to change places with Polly—you've been pacing the floor while she's just been lying here getting a lot of attention."

After stopping to order flowers for Polly at the florist shop on the main floor, Michele headed for home. It was almost five-thirty, so there was no point in going back to work. Michele felt a stab of guilt because she had not phoned the lab all afternoon, but she stifled it. There was nothing that couldn't wait—including Drake.

She wasn't surprised at his urgent summons the next morning. It promised to be one of those days. Drake's voice had dripped icicles, and George's smugness bordered on insolence. She started for the executive offices with a sense of fatalism.

Drake was in a state of controlled fury. He didn't bother with any preliminary niceties. "Do you ever listen to anything I say, Ms. Carter?" There were white lines around his grim mouth.

"Every word, Mr. Hollister," she assured him calmly, although her own anger was beginning to rise. If he had something to say, why didn't he come out with it instead of treating her like a fourth grader in the principal's office?

"Then I take it you don't believe I mean any of it," he remarked sarcastically.

Michele's nails dug into her clenched palms as she remembered all his whispered words of endearment. "I think there are times when that's true," she agreed tautly.

Drake's hands splayed out on the desk top, supporting his weight as he leaned toward her. "That's been your problem all along. Unfortunately it's now my problem."

"I don't see how," she answered coldly.

"Let me enlighten you, since we're obviously not talking about the same thing. Do you recall my telling you that everything that comes out of your department must be painstakingly checked?"

"It *is!*"

"Including the mouthwash?" he asked bitingly.

"That's not fair! Nothing like that has happened since. I've checked every single one of George's reports before I sent them in."

"George is not your only responsibility."

"You were the one who told me to whip him into line," she cried in outrage.

"Which you were so busy doing that you neglected your own work—and Tim's."

"What are you talking about?" Michele was momentarily startled out of her anger.

Drake waved a piece of paper at her, crumpling it in his fist. "Do you realize that if Product Control hadn't caught the error in this cough syrup formula, little children could have taken it and been seriously harmed?"

Tim had been working on the cough syrup. Michele thought rapidly. "Tim has been under a strain lately. It isn't like him to make a mistake." There was a muted plea in her voice.

"All the more reason why you should have checked it more carefully. My God, Michele, don't you know what could have happened to your own reputation? You wouldn't have been able to get a job mixing sodas!"

"I didn't know he was through with it yet. I never saw the results." Michele was thoroughly confused. Tim wouldn't have sent it in without her approval.

Drake smoothed out the crumpled paper. "This is your stamp, isn't it? Okay to Proceed. M.C."

"Yes, but—" She studied the smudged initials. "I didn't sign this. I never saw it before."

Drake hesitated, staring into her impassioned face. "I'm afraid I'll have to suspend you while the matter is being investigated," he said heavily. "It's standard procedure in a case involving an error of this magnitude. You'll receive your salary, of course."

"You know what you can do with your money! This is just an excuse to get rid of me! Why don't you admit it? I can prove—" The heated words died under the weight of hopelessness that enveloped her.

Tim would back her up, but what good would it do? Drake had evidence to show Clarice—a damning piece of paper with initials smudged just enough so that no one could be sure they weren't her own. It would justify her dismissal.

"You can prove you didn't sign this, Michele?" Drake was asking urgently.

How clever he was. Even a handwriting expert couldn't do that. "I'm not on trial!" she flared, thrusting out her small chin pugnaciously. "Go ahead and investigate! Was that supposed to scare me into quitting? Well, it won't work. I'm not going to make it easy for you!"

Drake's eyes were on her slender figure as she marched stiffly out the door. His soft words were almost smothered in a sigh. "You never have," he murmured.

Michele's plans were formulated on the drive home. She had to get out of Greenfield for a while, away from Drake.

This latest trick of his was contemptible—striking at her through her work! No matter what he thought of her personally, Drake should have recognized her professional integrity by now. Michele was grateful that no one was home. She slammed doors and drawers, venting her hurt and outrage.

By the time Corey got home from school their bags were packed, Fluffy was at Flora's and Michele had managed to compose herself.

"Guess what, honey?" she said brightly. "We're going to Chicago to visit Aunt Fran."

Corey wasn't as delighted as she expected. "How about school? I'm hallway monitor this week."

"I imagine they'll get along without you for a few days," Michele assured her.

In the car, Corey's conversation was all about Greenfield rather than the coming reunion with her cousins. Michele's heart sank as she realized how acclimated the child had become. How would she ever be able to explain why they had to move?

Michele's misery deepened as Corey persisted in including Drake in her chatter. He figured prominently in a good many of her daughter's plans. Fortunately, the highway took most of Michele's attention. In addition to the road's being narrow due to the snow banked on both sides, it was treacherously slippery in spots. She eyed the sky apprehensively. If only the storm held off until they got to Fran's. The weather report said this was going to be a big one.

"Whatever possessed you to drive up in this kind of weather?" Michele's sister asked when they finally reached her house after long hours.

"That's a fine greeting!" Michele's comment was only half-joking. She badly needed stroking, not criticism.

"Well, of course I'm thrilled to see you." The sisters hugged fondly. "It's been a positive age! You couldn't have come at a better time either. Jerry's away on a business trip and I was lonely. I would have worried myself silly, though, if I'd known you were on the road."

"That's why I didn't tell you," Michele said lightly.

After the children were in bed their mothers settled down for a good old-fashioned gabfest. Letters and brief phone conversations just weren't the same thing.

"How is your boyfriend?" Fran asked expectantly.

Michele had mentioned Drake during the happy, hopeful days of their relationship. Now she was sorry. "He isn't a boyfriend," she disclaimed casually. "Just a fellow I used to go out with."

"You don't see him anymore?" Her sister was clearly disappointed.

"No." Michele changed the subject. "How are the boys doing in school?"

"Fine," Fran replied absently. "I hope you were serious about having them for a visit this summer. They're looking forward to it."

"Oh. Well . . . the thing is, I might not be there. I'm thinking of moving back to Chicago."

"You're joking! After all those glowing reports about the joys of small-town living—the wonderful people, the clean air."

Michele tried to laugh. "Maybe my lungs just aren't used to it."

Fran was silent for a long moment. "What happened to the dream, Michele?"

It would be too glib to say it turned into a nightmare—but that described it. Michele bent her head, examining her

fingernails with great care. "Dreams are for children."
Drake was right. Wishing for things didn't make them
happen.

"Is it a man—that Drake Hollister?"

"You know how I feel about men." Michele tried to
sound careless.

"Yes, and that's why I know this one is special."

"If you call all-out war between two people special, then
I suppose you're correct," Michele remarked coolly.

Fran leaned toward her earnestly. "Conflicts can be
resolved if you work them out together. Don't run away
from him, sis. You have so much to give. Stop being afraid
of love."

Michele's laughter had a touch of hysteria. "Your
conclusions, unfortunately, are faulty. Drake Hollister
discarded me like yesterday's newspaper." Her smile was
bitterly self-mocking. "After he had read it thoroughly."

"Oh, my dear, I'm so sorry," Fran whispered.

Michele squared her slender shoulders. "Don't be, I'll
survive."

The next day she was almost lighthearted. There was one
good thing about reaching the bottom of the barrel, Michele
reflected—it left nowhere to go but up. That was before she
knew what was in store for her.

She and Fran spent a lazy afternoon enjoying each other's
company. By tacit agreement Drake's name wasn't mentioned, so the day passed pleasantly.

Taking advantage of the fact that it wasn't snowing yet,
they took the three children out for an early dinner, and to a
movie afterward. It was an unexpected treat on a week-
night. When they came out of the theater, the storm had hit
full force. Driving home was already difficult.

"Oh boy, maybe we'll be snowed in and I won't be able to go to school tomorrow," Mike crowed, dropping his coat by the front door.

"Don't count on it," his mother warned. She switched on the television, saying to Michele, "We'd better listen to the weather report, though."

While the children got ready for bed, Fran and Michele watched the news. In the middle of a dull segment on local politics, the anchorman suddenly interrupted the report.

"This bulletin just in. Word has just reached WCGO that there has been an explosion at the Blaylock Chemical Company in Greenfield. One man is dead and several are seriously injured. We'll have more details for you as soon as they're available."

Michele was frozen in her chair, the awful words ringing in her ears: One man is dead. It couldn't be Drake!

"Oh, Michele, I'm so sorry," Fran exclaimed. "I hope none of your friends are involved."

Michele's shaking lips had trouble forming the words. "I have to go to him."

"Darling, you can't! Not in this weather."

"I have to." Michele held herself together very carefully, as though she were made of glass that might shatter into a million pieces.

"There's no reason to believe Drake was one of those men. We'll telephone and find out." Fran was already dialing. After a frustrating few minutes she replaced the receiver reluctantly. "The phones are temporarily out of order, but they're working on them. We'll get through, honey, don't worry."

Michele was already putting on her coat. "Take care of Corey for me."

"You'll never make it!" Fran was wringing her hands.

"Yes, I will." Determination shone in Michele's eyes.

Getting to the outskirts of the city was difficult, with cars inching along all around, but once she was on the open road it was worse. Without streetlights and other cars to guide her, she was alone in a smothering white cocoon.

Michele stifled the impulse to step down on the accelerator, knowing it would be fatal. She had to keep her head and drive slowly, although every instinct urged speed. She *had* to get to Drake—to see him again even if it was for the last time. The panic that thought induced made it difficult to breathe.

Hours passed as Michele fought the elements, searching sometimes by instinct for the narrow path between the snowbanks. Her eyes burned from staring out at the swirling snowflakes, and her hands gripped the wheel so tightly that her fingers were numb.

She hadn't turned on the radio, not wanting to be distracted, but suddenly the need for human contact was overwhelming. Static greeted her, broken by snatches of music now and then, and disconnected phrases. Suddenly a few words came through loud and clear: "Blaylock Chemical Company."

Michele turned the volume up, straining to hear. The sound crackled in and out maddeningly. "Not known if . . . badly injured . . ." And then the words that struck terror to her heart. "Drake Hollister . . ."

Michele's foot pressed convulsively on the gas pedal, sending the car into a spin. There was a sickening crunch as something scraped the undercarriage before the car came to a stop with its nose in a snowbank.

Panic gripped Michele for the first time. Not for herself.

It was the fear that she might not reach Drake. She started the stalled engine frantically, gasping with relief when it roared to life.

Backing cautiously onto the road, she began the deadly trek once more, accompanied now by an ominous metallic sound. The exhaust pipe must have been damaged. When unpleasant fumes started to seep into the car, Michele was forced to open the window. As her body slowly chilled, she remembered her confident words to Fran. Maybe she wasn't going to make it after all, she thought with despair. The glow of lights in the distance produced a surge of hope, parting Michele's numbed lips in a sigh of thanksgiving.

Fran was almost crying on the phone. "Thank God I got through to you! Is Michele all right? Did she get there?"

Drake gripped the receiver tightly, the carved grooves around his mouth deepening. "What are you talking about? She's in Chicago with you, isn't she? That's what her neighbor told me."

"No, we heard about the explosion on the news. Michele was sure you were one of the men who were injured. She insisted on going to you. I couldn't stop her," Fran said helplessly.

The fierce joy that blazed in Drake's eyes was replaced by consternation. "How long ago did she leave?"

"It's hours!" Fran wailed. "She'll freeze to death if she's stuck out there in the storm!"

Drake's face was bleak. "I'm going after her." He slammed the phone down, turning to a nurse at the hospital admitting desk. "Have my car brought around immediately. I'm just going upstairs for my coat.'' He took the stairs two at a time, scorning the slower elevator.

Michele was so stiff with cold she could barely walk to the desk Drake had just left. It seemed like a miracle that she had made it. Now she prayed for a greater miracle.

"Drake Hollister," she whispered through stiff lips. "Is he . . ."

"He isn't seeing anyone," the nurse said primly. "This has been a terrible night for the poor man."

He was alive! Michele felt suddenly lightheaded. She sagged against the desk. "I just want to take one look at him."

Before the nurse could refuse permission, there was a sharp exclamation.

"Michele!" Drake stared at her with disbelief.

Her head suddenly started to spin as she stared back. The shock must have been getting to her. Michele could almost swear that Drake was standing ten feet away, uninjured. She shook her head, trying to retain a grip on sanity. She mustn't crack up now—not this close to her goal!

Drake's arms were very real, crushing her against the hard body she knew so well. He murmured her name over and over, tangling his fingers in her damp hair and feathering her face with kisses.

"You crazy, wonderful little idiot," he groaned. "How could you drive all that way in this storm?"

"You're not hurt?" she whispered wonderingly. "I heard on the radio . . . they mentioned your name . . ."

"I issued a statement on the condition of the men." He held her at arm's length so he could regard her searchingly. "Are *you* all right?"

She nodded wordlessly, touching his face with icy fingers.

"You're freezing!" he exclaimed, rubbing her hands vigorously.

"Tell me how it happened, Drake." That was more important.

"First I'm going to get you home before you catch pneumonia," he announced, bundling her outside and into his waiting car.

But he drove to his house instead of hers. Michele barely took her eyes off his face, neither knowing nor caring where they were going. It was enough just to be with him; questions could wait.

When he led her up the curving staircase, however, Michele came out of her trance. "Why are we going upstairs?"

"I'm getting you into a hot shower. You're chilled to the bone."

As he guided her into the big master bedroom, a pleased look spread over her face. "The furniture came!"

The large four-poster bed looked just as she had imagined it would, stately yet graceful. The glass-topped chests were a good choice too, and also the small Persian rugs on each side of the bed. Their glowing jewel tones were even more vivid against the white carpeting.

"Oh, Drake, the room looks beautiful! Are you happy with it?"

"Very happy." His arm tightened for a moment around her shoulders before he led her to the marble bathroom. "Stay in there until you're pink," he ordered.

The hot water felt wonderful. Michele stood under it for a long time, thawing out gradually. When she finally got out, her delicate skin was the color Drake had insisted upon.

He had brought in one of his pajama tops. The white silk jacket reached almost to her knees, but Michele was conscious of the fact that her body was provocatively revealed beneath it. Why had Drake taken away her clothes? Michele sat down on a padded stool, facing a decision.

Now that her delirious joy had subsided to devout gratitude that Drake was unharmed, she had to face the fact that nothing else had changed. If she accepted the small slice of heaven he was obviously prepared to offer her tonight, leaving him would be that much harder tomorrow. How often could she give him up? With a wrenching sigh, Michele decided to be sensible.

Drake was poking at the fire when she came out of the bathroom. His eyes traveled appreciatively over her. "Would you like to curl up over here by the fire for a few minutes or get right into bed?"

The pink in her cheeks deepened. He wasn't even being subtle about it. "I just came out for my clothes," she said distinctly.

"You're staying here tonight," he answered calmly.

No, nothing had changed. He still expected to have it all. Michele frowned. "I'm very happy that you're safe, Drake, but I didn't come back here to sleep with you."

He lifted her chin in his palm, stroking the soft hair off her temple. "Why did you come back, Michele?"

She blinked her long lashes, trying not to notice the dark curling hair that peeped through his open shirt, or the subtle male scent of him. "I . . . well, naturally I was concerned. We've been . . . in the past we were friends."

He was massaging her tense neck muscles now. "You risked your life for a former friend?"

She pulled away from him, wrapping her arms around herself as she stared into the fire. "That's a very apt way of putting it. And now I'd like my clothes please. Your assumption that I would automatically fall into your bed is not only erroneous, it's insulting."

"It wasn't meant to be. I didn't expect to share it with you." When that startled her, Drake smiled. "There's no lack of bedrooms in this house. I brought you here because you were cold, and your place would take too long to heat up."

Under Michele's embarrassment was an irrational hurt. Drake didn't even desire her anymore. "I'm sorry I leaped to conclusions," she said stiffly.

Drake chuckled. "You weren't entirely wrong. I'd like very much to share your bed, but not under the old arrangements."

What was he up to now? Then it dawned on her! If she would resign like a nice tame kitten, Drake would make it very pleasurable for her. Otherwise, it was cutoff time at the bachelor pad.

Her slim body shook with fury. "You are the most egotistical, conniving man I've ever met! If you think for one minute you can manipulate me any longer, you're crazier than any man has a right to be. I wouldn't—" His mouth effectively stopped her heated words.

He swung her into his arms, holding her struggling body against his as he sat down on the love seat in front of the fire. Patiently forcing her lips apart, he probed her mouth with great satisfaction. Michele's angry cries of protest became muted as Drake's warmth invaded her body. She touched the strong column of his neck tentatively, reaching up to run her fingers through his thick hair.

His hand caressed her breast, sliding sensuously over the thin silk covering it. But as a wild hunger awakened deep inside Michele, he drew back, gently urging her head onto his solid shoulder.

"I think it's time we had a little talk." He looked down at her tenderly. "I'm through sleeping with a woman who doesn't trust me."

Her lashes feathered her flushed cheeks. It was easier when she didn't have to look at him. "You're a fine one to talk—after what you accused me of."

"That's part of what we have to talk about. I had no choice, sweetheart, the proof was right there before me. When I asked you to clear yourself, you refused."

She struggled to get out of his arms, but he wouldn't allow it. "You wouldn't have believed me anyway," she muttered. "You've been praying all along that I'd make a mistake serious enough to get me fired." She warmed to an old grievance. "I wouldn't be surprised if you egged George on to be a thorn in my side."

Drake gave an impatient exclamation. "I was trying to get you to stand up to him! I always knew George was a pain, but I couldn't let his personality influence me as long as he was competent at his job. When Tim told me what he'd done, I fired him on the spot."

Michele stared at him wide-eyed. "Because of me?"

"No, darling. Because he did something dangerous and irresponsible. No matter what my personal feelings for you are, I've always made you pull your own weight at the lab. To treat you any other way would have been patronizing."

She gazed at him doubtfully. "You'll have to admit you didn't want to hire me in the first place."

Drake nodded. "I'd had some negative business experiences with women, but you had another strike against you." When Michele looked puzzled he laughed. "You were so beautiful I was afraid I'd fall in love with you."

She renewed her efforts to get free, subsiding when he wouldn't let her. "Well, that was one thing you didn't have to worry about."

"That's true," he answered calmly. "I never wanted a woman to own me completely, but I've discovered it's wonderful."

Michele was afraid she was reading her own desire into his words. "I . . . I don't know what you mean."

"I love you, sweetheart. I've loved you since that first morning when I walked into your breakfast room and caught you in my arms." He kissed the corner of her mouth. "You don't know what misery you've caused me."

"Be—because you didn't want to love me?" She was having trouble believing him.

"Never that." He grinned mischievously. "Because you said you only wanted my body. After a declaration like that, how could I tell you I loved you?"

Michele blushed a bright, rosy red. She couldn't look at him. "How do you know it isn't still true?"

Drake chuckled. "I like to think I'm good, honey, but I'm not that good. You came back to me for something a lot more powerful than just sex."

, Michele realized that the time for dissembling was over. She smoothed the lock of dark hair off his forehead with a shaking hand. "When I thought you were dead, a part of me died too. I found out then how little pride is worth."

"We both had an overabundance of it," Drake agreed.

He looked at her appraisingly. "Do you think our children will inherit the trait?"

Michele's heart almost stopped. "Are . . . are you asking me to marry you?"

Merriment brimmed in his eyes. "I think it's only fair to the kids." The laughter died as he touched her cheek with reverent fingers. "I love you so much, Michele. You will marry me, won't you?"

She threw her arms around his neck, straining close to him. "Oh, Drake, of course I will!"

His mouth closed fiercely over hers, his arms tightening as though he would never let her go. "Don't ever leave me again, darling. I need you so."

It had always been the other way around. Michele framed his face in her palms, searching his face entreatingly. "Do you really, Drake?"

His eyes glowed with sudden intensity. Lifting her in his arms, he carried her over to the bed. As he stretched out beside her, he murmured, "I'm about to show you just one of the ways."

She trembled with anticipation as he slowly unbuttoned her sleep coat, knowing the rapture this man could bring. The almost pagan worship in his eyes made her feel languorously wanton. His smoldering gaze lingered on her breasts, the flat plane of her stomach, the juncture of her thighs.

"Your body is absolute perfection." His voice was husky. "I want to make love to you night and day for the rest of my life."

When his hands started a slow journey down her body, Michele gave a wordless little sigh of satisfaction. His fingertips were tantalizing, teasing her nipples until they were erect with desire, exploring all the erotic areas he knew so intimately. His lips visited all the places of enchantment, adding fuel to the fire that burned hotter with every caress.

Michele arched her body with delight, tangling her fingers in his hair as she cried out his name. Drake was building a storm inside her as only he knew how to do, his caresses driving her to the brink of ecstasy.

"This is how much I need you, my love," he groaned. His hard body covered hers, conveying his urgency.

"I need you too, Drake," she whispered, pulling his shirt out of his slacks so she could run her hands over his warm, muscled back.

His eyes were brilliant as he framed her face in his palms. "You've never said that to me before."

Michele's hands slid inside his waistband, exploring his body with a lingering appreciation that made him draw in his breath sharply. "You don't know how often I wanted to," she sighed. "I love you so much, Drake."

With a fierce cry of exultation he clasped her in his arms, feathering her face with kisses before parting her willing lips with his tongue. His foray was deep and sensuous, staking a male claim that left Michele aching for more. Her fingers tore at his shirt, needing to feel his warm skin without any barriers.

Drake felt the same need. He left her for just a moment, returning to clasp her quivering body against his own. She moved her legs to welcome him.

Their lovemaking was completely abandoned, their hunger for each other so urgent that they surged through wave upon wave of excitement. A distant goal beckoned, driving them on until they reached the peak; then they plunged into a throbbing sea of peace.

They were content to lie wordlessly in each other's arms afterward. Drake was the first to stir. His hand caressed Michele's breast with continuing satisfaction. "Want to know a secret?" he murmured.

She kissed the hollow in his throat. "I didn't know you were keeping any from me."

"Just one. I didn't think I was going to like this four-poster bed, but it's very comfortable now that you're in it."

"I planned it that way," she said complacently.

"You little devil!" Drake fitted her body more closely to his. "I wouldn't be at all surprised."

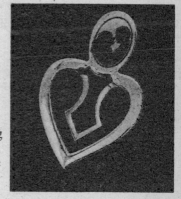

Silhouette Special Edition

MORE ROMANCE FOR
A SPECIAL WAY TO RELAX

$2.25 each

79 ☐ Hastings	105 ☐ Sinclair	131 ☐ Lee	157 ☐ Taylor
80 ☐ Douglass	106 ☐ John	132 ☐ Dailey	158 ☐ Charles
81 ☐ Thornton	107 ☐ Ross	133 ☐ Douglass	159 ☐ Camp
82 ☐ McKenna	108 ☐ Stephens	134 ☐ Ripy	160 ☐ Wisdom
83 ☐ Major	109 ☐ Beckman	135 ☐ Seger	161 ☐ Stanford
84 ☐ Stephens	110 ☐ Browning	136 ☐ Scott	162 ☐ Roberts
85 ☐ Beckman	111 ☐ Thorne	137 ☐ Parker	163 ☐ Halston
86 ☐ Halston	112 ☐ Belmont	138 ☐ Thornton	164 ☐ Ripy
87 ☐ Dixon	113 ☐ Camp	139 ☐ Halston	165 ☐ Lee
88 ☐ Saxon	114 ☐ Ripy	140 ☐ Sinclair	166 ☐ John
89 ☐ Meriwether	115 ☐ Halston	141 ☐ Saxon	167 ☐ Hurley
90 ☐ Justin	116 ☐ Roberts	142 ☐ Bergen	168 ☐ Thornton
91 ☐ Stanford	117 ☐ Converse	143 ☐ Bright	169 ☐ Beckman
92 ☐ Hamilton	118 ☐ Jackson	144 ☐ Meriwether	170 ☐ Paige
93 ☐ Lacey	119 ☐ Langan	145 ☐ Wallace	171 ☐ Gray
94 ☐ Barrie	120 ☐ Dixon	146 ☐ Thornton	172 ☐ Hamilton
95 ☐ Doyle	121 ☐ Shaw	147 ☐ Dalton	173 ☐ Belmont
96 ☐ Baxter	122 ☐ Walker	148 ☐ Gordon	174 ☐ Dixon
97 ☐ Shaw	123 ☐ Douglass	149 ☐ Claire	175 ☐ Roberts
98 ☐ Hurley	124 ☐ Mikels	150 ☐ Dailey	176 ☐ Walker
99 ☐ Dixon	125 ☐ Cates	151 ☐ Shaw	177 ☐ Howard
100 ☐ Roberts	126 ☐ Wildman	152 ☐ Adams	178 ☐ Bishop
101 ☐ Bergen	127 ☐ Taylor	153 ☐ Sinclair	179 ☐ Meriwether
102 ☐ Wallace	128 ☐ Macomber	154 ☐ Malek	180 ☐ Jackson
103 ☐ Taylor	129 ☐ Rowe	155 ☐ Lacey	181 ☐ Browning
104 ☐ Wallace	130 ☐ Carr	156 ☐ Hastings	182 ☐ Thornton

Silhouette Special Edition

$2.25 each

183 ☐ Sinclair	190 ☐ Wisdom	197 ☐ Lind	204 ☐ Eagle
184 ☐ Daniels	191 ☐ Hardy	198 ☐ Bishop	205 ☐ Browning
185 ☐ Gordon	192 ☐ Taylor	199 ☐ Roberts	206 ☐ Hamilton
186 ☐ Scott	193 ☐ John	200 ☐ Milan	207 ☐ Roszel
187 ☐ Stanford	194 ☐ Jackson	201 ☐ Dalton	208 ☐ Sinclair
188 ☐ Lacey	195 ☐ Griffin	202 ☐ Thornton	209 ☐ Ripy
189 ☐ Ripy	196 ☐ Cates	203 ☐ Parker	210 ☐ Stanford

Silhouette Special Edition

Coming Next Month

A COMMON HERITAGE
by Carole Halston

•

NASHVILLE BLUES
by Patti Beckman

•

FETTERS OF THE PAST
by Laurey Bright

•

PERFECT HARMONY
by Fran Bergen

•

PIRATE'S GOLD
by Lisa Jackson

•

YOUR CHEATING HEART
by Pamela Foxe